W9-BVQ-962

Praise for the Giulia Driscoll Mystery Series

SECOND TO NUN (#2)

"Giulia is a sympathetic, well-drawn character who has built a full life for herself after she leaving the convent, but appealing touches of the former nun remain."

– Booklist

"Driscoll's second solo turn as a sleuth (after *Nun Too Soon*) offers a fun and fast read with a lot of appeal."

– Library Journal

"Former nun and current private eye Giulia Driscoll tackles ghosts with the same wit and wisdom she uses to tackle crooks. Great fun."

– Terrie Farley Moran,
Agatha Award-Winning Author of the Read 'Em and Eat Mysteries

"Loweecey's characters are colorful without being caricatures, and once again we're lucky that Giulia Driscoll left the convent behind. She solves the crime with a happy mix of online savvy, humor and intelligence."

– Sheila Connolly,
New York Times Bestselling Author of *An Early Wake*

"Loweecey is herself a former nun, and she brings to Giulia all of this inner conflict, residual guilt, and disillusionment...and how can you not love an author who quotes from the movies *Airplane* and *Young Frankenstein*? Giulia's recent marriage adds a delightful dash of romance, but the real appeal of this series is her genuine likability and fiery independent streak that could never be hidden behind a veil."

– Kings River Life Magazine

"Loweecey has once again crafted a delightful, sassy, smart tale that will send the hair on the back of your head skyward and keep your eyes glued to the page. I loved it!"

– Jessie Chandler,
Author of the Award-Winning Shay O'Hanlon Caper Series

NUN TOO SOON (#1)

"Exciting and suspenseful."

– *Publishers Weekly*

"For those who have not yet read these incredible mysteries written by an actual ex-nun, you're missing out...Brilliant, funny, a great whodunit; this is one writer who readers should definitely make a 'habit' of."

– *Suspense Magazine*

"With tight procedural plotting, more flavoured coffee than you could shake a pastry at, and an ensemble cast who'll steal your heart away, *Nun Too Soon* is a winner. I'm delighted that Giulia– and Alice!–left the convent for a life of crime."

– Catriona McPherson,
Agatha Award-Winning Author of the Dandy Gilver Mystery Series

"You'll love Giulia Driscoll! She's one of a kind—quirky, unpredictable and appealing. With an entertaining cast of characters, a clever premise and Loweecey's unique perspective— this compelling not-quite-cozy is a winner."

– Hank Phillippi Ryan,
Mary Higgins Clark Award-Winning Author of *Truth Be Told*

"Grab your rosary beads and hang on for a fun ride with charming characters, amusing banter, and a heat-packing former nun."

– Barb Goffman,
Macavity Award-Winning Author

Nun But The Brave

The Giulia Driscoll Mystery Series
by Alice Loweecey

<u>Novels</u>

NUN TOO SOON (#1)
SECOND TO NUN (#2)
NUN BUT THE BRAVE (#3)
THE CLOCK STRIKES NUN (#4)
(May 2017)

<u>Short Stories</u>

CHANGING HABITS
(prequel to NUN TOO SOON)

Nun But The Brave

A GIULIA DRISCOLL MYSTERY

Alice Loweecey

HENERY PRESS

NUN BUT THE BRAVE
A Giulia Driscoll Mystery
Part of the Henery Press Mystery Collection

First Edition | July 2016

Henery Press
www.henerypress.com

Trade Paperback ISBN-13: 978-1-63511-049-4
Digital epub ISBN-13: 978-1-63511-050-0
Kindle ISBN-13: 978-1-63511-051-7
Hardcover Paperback ISBN-13: 978-1-63511-052-4

Printed in the United States of America

To my ever patient and always supportive husband Phil.

ACKNOWLEDGMENTS

Huge thank-yous go out to: Rachel Jackson, my indefatigable and eagle-eyed editor. Caleb Joshua Malcolm, wildcrafter extraordinaire, without whom Giulia's cover would have been blown in about half a page. Foinah Jameson, crafter of gorgeous drinking horns and epic costumes: You plant wild images in my literary head. Barbara Early, whose conversation during all our drives to book events clarified essential plot points. She is also the Finder of Awesome Local Restaurants where Giulia sometimes eats. And my fellow Hens, whose support and encouragement is invaluable.

One

Giulia Driscoll led a sobbing grandmother to Driscoll Investigations' entrance door.

"My whole family will say a novena to Saint Anthony in gratitude for how quickly you found my granddaughter."

Giulia handed her another tissue. "Thank you."

"My son says he's not Catholic anymore, but I'll threaten him with no more of my canned ginger pears. He'll do anything for those."

She honked into the tissue and kissed Giulia's cheeks. Giulia waited for the sound of the downstairs door squeaking shut before she closed the frosted glass door.

"I don't know what she doused herself with, but my room needs a whole can of Febreze."

Giulia's all-natural, earth mother assistant Sidney wrinkled her nose. "White Shoulders. When I was a kid, I swore my great-aunt took baths in it."

"My grandfather used Old Spice. A lot of it." Zane, Giulia's tow-haired bodybuilder admin, got his "genius at work" expression. "I should create a statistical analysis correlating the age of older adults with fragrance saturation levels."

Giulia returned to her own office and brought out a red flash drive. "But you really want to use your MIT brain on this research."

The door opened and a tall woman in jeans and a stained brown t-shirt stumbled over the threshold.

"I miss my kids," she slurred. "I can't live without my kids." She staggered forward and fell onto Giulia. "You have to get me back to my kids."

The last word dribbled out of her mouth as her entire weight slumped onto Giulia's shoulders.

Giulia clasped her hands around the unconscious woman's back. "Zane, help?"

He scrambled out from behind his desk and eased the woman onto the floor. "Dead weight is not a cliché."

Sidney squatted next to the woman's head. "She overdid something herbal and smoky." She waved her hand in front of her nose.

Giulia opened the woman's eyes. "Her eyes are dilated. How's her pulse?"

Zane placed three fingers on the scrawny throat at the carotid artery. "Too fast."

Giulia picked up the phone on Zane's desk and called 911. "We have an unconscious adult at Driscoll Investigations." She gave the address and the few details she possessed and hung up. "They'll be here in five minutes."

She knelt next to Sidney and felt the unconscious woman's forehead with the back of her hand.

"Do you know her?" Sidney said.

"She's my sister-in-law."

Two

"Her name is Anne Falcone," Giulia said to the EMTs six minutes later.

"Any idea what she's on?" The ponytailed EMT strapped a blood pressure cuff around Anne's flaccid arm.

"Not a clue. She opened the door, fell on top of me, and passed out."

The bald EMT said, "Bloodshot eyes; pupils big as dinner plates."

"BP one fifty over ninety-nine." She loosened the cuff and put it away.

Giulia stayed out of their way. "Will she be all right?"

"It's possible." The EMT's ponytail swung back and forth as she clipped an oxygen meter on Anne Falcone's left index finger. "Depends on how long she's been taking whatever she's taking, her overall health, her mental state, whether what she's on has been cut with something she's allergic to. Lots of factors."

Anne gasped, sat up like her spine was on springs, and vomited all over her baggy jeans.

A voice said from the doorway, "Excuse me. I have a ten-thirty appointment."

Everyone not vomiting looked up.

The youngish woman's tri-color hair managed not to clash with her fluorescent orange peasant blouse, her brown pencil skirt or her strappy gladiator sandals.

A beat, and Sidney ran into the bathroom for paper towels. The patient collapsed onto the floor again. Ponytail EMT swept her index finger through Anne's slack mouth to clear the remaining vomit. Giulia stepped over the tableau on the floor, hand out.

"Good morning, Ms. Philbey. I'm Giulia Driscoll. As you can see, we had an unexpected visitor. If you wouldn't mind waiting in my office for a few minutes?" She escorted the new client into her private space and closed the door.

The bald EMT extended the collapsible frame on the gurney. "At least her throat's open. That means it's not an allergic reaction. Probably a simple OD. She'll need detox and maybe rehab. You said she came here for help, so she's got a good start."

The stench of whatever used to be in Anne's stomach sent Giulia into the bathroom again for the Febreze. "I know you only trick the nose into thinking the smell is gone," she apostrophized the spray can, "but please trick us." She knew her humor wasn't appropriate for the situation, but she needed something to distract herself from the sight of her sister-in-law in what looked like the penultimate stage of meth addiction.

Ponytail EMT strapped Anne's ankles, hips, and shoulders to the gurney. Sidney finished cleaning the splatters on the floor. Zane disappeared into the bathroom. New retching sounds followed.

The bald EMT said to Giulia, "We're heading to Vandermark's ER. Are you riding along?"

"No." There was no way she could explain her bizarre family situation in less than twenty minutes. Besides, she had a client waiting. "I'll call my brother. He'll meet you there." She hoped.

"Sounds good."

They maneuvered the gurney down the narrow stairs with only a few clanks and bangs. Giulia opened her office door and said to the client, "One more minute, please," before closing it again.

She took out her cell, but returned it to her pocket without unlocking it. At Sidney's quizzical expression, Giulia said, "I don't want my brother to have my new cell number," and picked up Zane's desk phone.

Her brother's phone number came back to her after a moment of mental archaeology. If he hadn't changed it, this should be an interesting conversation.

He answered on the fourth ring.

"Salvatore, it's Giulia. Don't hang up. Anne came into my office a few minutes ago. She's very ill. We called for an ambulance and she's on her way to Vandermark Memorial."

A click and a dial tone.

Giulia glared at the receiver, justified in her choice of an office phone to make the call. Most certainly she didn't need a rerun of her first year out of the convent, when her brother called her every Sunday after Tridentine Mass. Something about Latin inspired him to damn her to Hell in the best Jonathan Edwards tradition. Even this minimal contact roused several Italian and Irish curses in her head, but she refused to let any of them touch her tongue. A few deep breaths later she replaced the phone in its cradle.

Sidney said, "It's not nice of me, but when she draped herself over you, you both looked exactly like Elsa and Anna in the climactic scene from *Frozen*." She poked her phone. "I'll show you."

"*Don't* play that song," Giulia and Zane said together.

The tinkling opening bars of "Let it Go" played from the phone's speaker before Sidney hit Stop.

"That earworm will be stuck in my head all day," Giulia said.

"At least it made you smile."

"When did you become so devious?"

Without waiting for an answer, Giulia walked into her office. The client put her smart phone into her small cross-body bag and slapped a printout on Giulia's desk.

"Are you as good as your reviews?"

Giulia must have missed the memo about today being "startle the PI day." She picked up the paper, used to clients who tried to throw her off-stride as a test of sorts.

This test started with a screencap of Driscoll Investigations' reviews on Yelp. All anonymous, but she knew exactly who'd written each of the fourteen excerpts squeezed onto the paper:

"Saved my life."

"Restored my family."

"Repaired my reputation."

"Found my daughter."

Five more of the latter, substituting "biological mother/father/twin/sister/brother."

"Compassionate yet tenacious."

"A bulldog in human form."

Giulia remembered the "bulldog" case well. DI had more than earned its fee that month.

If prison officials would ever let an inmate post to Yelp, she wondered what The Silk Tie Killer's review would do to her overall rating.

She raised her eyes. "We strive to bring all our cases to a satisfactory conclusion."

Ms. Philbey's light brown eyebrows expressed an unflattering opinion of Giulia's answer. "Come on. That was bland. These reviews were written about someone daring with guts."

Giulia set the paper on her desk. "How can Driscoll Investigations help you, Ms. Philbey?"

A minuscule one-shoulder shrug. "I'm here and you have the best reviews of the local detective agencies, so what the hell." She unzipped her narrow purse and set a four-by-six photo on top of the printout. "This is my twin sister, Joanne. Before you ask, yes, we're identical."

The photo showed two women lit from beneath by the candles on an elaborate birthday cake. On the left, the client's brown hair was streaked with only blonde highlights and her skintight tie-dyed shirt was austere compared to today's outfit. Green glitter eye shadow and peacock feather earrings overpowered her hazel eyes and thin lips.

Her twin's baggy gray sweater didn't hide the difference in their figures. She carried at least fifty pounds more than her sister. Where the twin at Giulia's desk combated the bland on multiple levels, her sister either didn't care or had given in to it. Her light brown hair fell straight to her shoulders, free of embellishment. She wore little makeup and no jewelry. Her shoulders slumped, but her smile was genuine.

"Joanne made that cake for our twenty-fifth birthday, two years ago."

"Where can I sign up to take lessons from her?" Giulia said.

The bottom layer of the cake was decorated to look like the redwood base of an above-ground pool. The top layer framed pool-blue frosting with two marzipan figures on it. On the "water," a girl in a bikini lounged on a float made of gummy worms. On the "redwood" deck, another figure in shorts and a shirt played with a cat.

"I'm not joking," Giulia said. "Your sister is talented."

"She's also been missing for three months."

Three

Giulia flipped to a fresh page on her current legal pad.

Diane Philbey sat up. "Now I'm happier. Do you always pull a quick-change act when you get down to business?"

Giulia said, "Where does your sister live?"

Diane's thin lips quirked. "Thank you for assuming she's still alive."

"Since you're here, I presume, if you'll forgive blunt speaking, the police haven't found her body."

"Don't." She trampled Giulia's final word. "Everyone's telling me to 'accept reality.' Her friends, the people at the nursing home where she works, even the police. Guess my sister isn't important enough for them to spend more than three weeks on. She's an adult, they said. Sometimes adults choose to start a new life, they said. Then they asked me if we'd had any differences recently." Diane faced northwest and flipped off the world. "Everybody's Jo's friend. She's not like me. I'll shoot my mouth off when I think it's called for. Drives my boss nuts."

Giulia wrote faster than she thought possible rather than put the brakes to this revealing gush of information.

"Jo never drives anyone nuts," Diane continued. "Even her ex-boyfriends hang out with her after they split up. She dated this one singer. Man, he was six feet of walking ego. Even though she dumped him, he sent her flowers for her last birthday." She swallowed. "Not her last-last, because she's not dead. I meant her—our—most recent birthday."

She sprang out of Giulia's client chair and leaned out the window. "A Tarot Reading shop and a pizza place. Get your future told first in case you're supposed to die right after you eat that pizza. Best last meal choice ever, right?" She turned around and sat on the windowsill. "I'm not scattered like this when things are normal. I've been bottling up my escalating freak-out about Jo, and I have to keep moving or I'll break something. Jo got into Tarot once. She dragged me to this Halloween setup with a guy in a wizard cape. He told me I'd been separated at birth from a long-lost male twin. I suggested he keep his day job."

"Does your sister often find new hobbies and hope you'll join her in them?"

"Nah, not so much. She's into cooking and hunting and cats and guys with mondo shlongs. Who isn't? Into mondo shlongs, I mean. The Tarot thing happened when her boyfriend from Le Cordon Bleu school dumped her on their graduation night. She got over it when she got over him." Diane walked over to the framed watercolor on the wall facing Giulia's chair. "Not bad. At least it looks like what it's supposed to be, a garden with lots of flowers. I dumped a mondo shlong because he only liked radical modern art." She massaged her temples. "I'm getting distracted again." She turned on Giulia. "You're like the missing person whisperer. You've got to find Jo. All those reviews have to mean something. I wouldn't have come here if I wasn't impressed by them." She wiped her eyes with her ring fingers. "I swore I'd keep my act together. Did I smear my mascara?"

She pulled a tissue from the box Giulia held out to her. "I haven't said any of this out loud to anybody except our older brother since April." She opened the tissue and made an approving face at its lack of black mascara streaks. "What was I saying?"

"You were telling me how well people liked your sister."

"Oh. Right. So you see what I mean when I told the detective in Penn Hills to get her head out of her butt. Jo didn't have a fight with an ex. She isn't involved in dangerous activities. She bakes fancy cakes as a side job. I mean, seriously, what's dangerous about that except packing on the pounds?" Diane leaned both arms on Giulia's desk. "And she didn't up and decide to walk away from everything and everyone, no matter where her cats went."

"Cats?" Giulia kept her voice at the same encouraging yet neutral level.

"Yeah, her super-friendly rescue cats, and I mean super-friendly. Weirdo beasts think they're lap dogs. I like cats who don't give a crap if you're in the house or not. Hers are huge, like fifteen or twenty pounds. When they flop on your lap, you know it. The orange one is missing an ear and the gray one's got seven toes on its front paws."

"The cats are missing too?"

"Yeah. Good thing, I suppose, since when I got her landlord to open her apartment, I was sure we'd get a noseful of rotting cat carcasses." A deep breath. "My brother doesn't approve of gallows humor, but I've got to cope somehow."

Giulia's imagination gifted her with a detailed multi-sensory image of a closed apartment perfumed by deceased cat.

"Her place was in perfect order, like always. She's the OCD twin. I'm the wild twin. The police said the neatness of her apartment was a classic sign of someone trying to drop off the grid on purpose." She slammed the balled-up tissue into the wastebasket. "They are wrong, wrong, wrong, and I want you to prove it."

Giulia set down her pen. "This kind of investigation can take time. Here are our rates." She took a half-sheet of paper from her center drawer and slid it across the desk.

Diane studied it. "I expected worse. I've got some savings, but do you take plastic? My credit card gives me cash back."

"Certainly." Giulia buzzed Zane. "Please bring in a standard down-payment invoice for Ms. Philbey."

After the payment finished processing, Giulia flipped to a fresh page on her legal pad and asked Diane several specific questions about police involvement so far, sifting through Diane's rancor for essential information. "Today is Monday. I'll spend the next two days gathering information and traveling. I should be back here Thursday. Expect a preliminary report Friday morning."

Diane typed it into her phone. "Finally something concrete. I've been a pig on ice for weeks."

"If we have an unanticipated breakthrough, of course we'll call."

Diane dropped her phone into her purse. "If you succeed in four days where the police failed in three months, you'll have earned another gushing review. But only if you bring my sister to the PT clinic where I work so I can kick her butt."

Giulia tried a tentative smile. "Why there?"

"So I can begin the physical therapy she'll need after I pound some sense into her."

Four

After showing her new client out, Giulia called her former temp, now personal assistant to Captain James Reilly of Cottonwood Precinct Nine.

"Jane? It's Giulia."

"Oh my God, how did you know I was going to call you? Are you in league with the psychic across the street now?" Jane Pierce's sometimes bitter voice rivaled Sidney's in excitement. "My ex got caught padding hydrocodone prescriptions and selling the extras. He lost his medical license and his fancy house and his fancy fiancée dumped him. Schadenfreude is my new favorite word."

Giulia loved hearing happy Jane. Her smile got wider as Jane took a catch breath and barreled on.

"Suddenly my mother is thrilled I took nothing in the divorce except health insurance. Even better, I dropped the jailbird's insurance last week for our insurance here, so I'm free, free, free. I hope his next move is really stupid and he gets dragged in here while I'm at work. Payback, sucker." Another quick breath. "Oh wait. You called on business, I bet."

The smile evident in her voice, Giulia said, "Yes, but your story was worth the wait. I could use Jimmy's influence. Would you ask him to give a heads-up to a Detective Okorie over in Penn Hills?" She spelled the name. "I'll need access to the missing persons reports and cold case info for Joanne Philbey. Hopefully he can smooth the way for me."

"Just a sec." The sound of Jane's hand over the receiver turned the call into the equivalent of putting a seashell to the ear. Giulia heard male and female voices like the teacher voice buzz in all the *Peanuts* cartoons. Then the seashell got tossed back into the ocean. "He's calling right now."

"He's a gem and so are you."

"Anytime. I'll keep you updated on my ex the ex-doctor." Jane's laugh dripped with gloating as she hung up.

Giulia opened her door in time to catch Sidney yawn like a bear about to hibernate.

"Jessamine's first tooth is coming in," she said. "The poor thing is too miserable to sleep, which means mama and daddy don't sleep either."

"Tell Jessamine she has to push that tooth out now, because you and Zane are in charge for the next two days."

Sidney and Zane, one after the other, rattled off their existing caseloads. Giulia gave them two thumbs up.

"I've trained you well. I'm headed to Penn Hills, which is just far enough away for it to be a waste of time and energy for me to drive back and forth at rush hours while I interview every name I extract from the police reports. I could run back here in case of emergency, but I don't expect to. Unless," she said to Zane, "you think the deadbeat dad will Hulk out on you."

Zane's formidable chest expanded. "I haven't told you about last night. I followed him to his usual bar and picked a fight on purpose."

"What?"

"No worries, Ms. D. I learned how to choreograph a fight in karate back when I was ten. Did you ever see that old John Wayne movie *The Quiet Man*?" When Giulia nodded, he continued, "We played it out like the climactic fight between Wayne and Victor McLaglen, but I didn't throw him through the front door. Afterwards, we drank to seal our new bond of friendship and respect. He invited me to his house on Wednesday for his weekly poker game. The police will be making a scripted appearance."

Giulia fist-bumped him. "I knew you'd be good at undercover work."

Shouts and screeching tires came from the street. All three of them ran to the window.

Ken Kanning, the face of *The Scoop*, Cottonwood's wannabe-*TMZ* show, lay flat on the sidewalk outside Lady Rowan's Tarot Shoppe. As shorter Giulia switched places with taller Zane to see better, Jasper Fortin, Lady Rowan's nephew and apprentice, chased *The Scoop*'s cameraman out of the shop with raised fists. The cameraman dived into the open door of their white creeper van while Kanning butt-walked off the sidewalk into the street. A taxi swerved into the opposite lane, horn blaring.

"He's talking into his mike while beating an ignominious retreat, isn't he?" Zane said.

"I would expect nothing less," Giulia said.

The cameraman's arm reached out the passenger door and yanked Kanning into the van. A second later, the van pulled into traffic without signaling. More cars honked and swerved out of its way. Jasper returned to the Shoppe. From the way the purple awning shuddered, Giulia figured he'd slammed the door with a wee bit of excessive force.

"I guarantee Kanning's defenestration was well deserved," she said.

"Ms. D...." Zane said.

"I know. Jasper tossed him out of the door, not the window. But it's such a lovely word."

Five

At seven o'clock that night, Giulia and her husband Frank ate barbecue chicken on their patio.

"Wife time and home-cooked food before another all-night stakeout," Frank said. "Life is good."

Giulia kissed him after he licked a dab of sauce from the corner of his mouth. "I keep thinking I should go to the hospital to check on Anne."

Frank sucked more sauce off his fingers. "Your brother's slammed the door in your face how many times since you jumped the wall?"

"That doesn't matter if their kids need help." Giulia downed half her lemonade. "I put too much hot pepper in this batch of sauce. Weird. I didn't change my recipe."

"Tastes the same to me. Look. You've got clients. Your brother can take care of his own family."

"It's what she said, 'Get me back to my kids.' I think she may have left him."

"Any sane person would have left your brother years ago."

Giulia set down her plate. "No argument from me, and you're right. I have a client who's sending me to Penn Hills for the next two days. I'm crashing at the Quality Inn to use my time with the most efficiency."

Frank whooped. "Pizza and beer for dinner."

"As long as you remember to water the vegetables. See all

those huge green tomatoes? If you forget to soak them every night, they'll crack." She stepped off the patio over to the raised bed and cupped an unripe tomato in one hand. "Neglect this beauty now and there'll be less sauce for your spaghetti in January."

Frank made the *malocchio* at her. Even as she laughed at his inept attempt at the Italian evil eye, she still pointed her index finger and pinky at him in the traditional *corna* to ward it off.

He said with wounded dignity, "I would never do anything to jeopardize your sauce. You hear that, plants? Cooperate and I won't let the neighbor's hyperactive terriers into the yard."

Giulia facepalmed. "Haven't you heard the research about talking softly to plants to make them grow bigger and stronger and more succulent?"

"Driscolls don't pamper their plants. How else will we win the war? It's us against genetically modified food."

"Have you been talking to Sidney?"

Giulia turned on the hose and began watering the peppers in the far corner.

"No, to my brother Ben. His middle child, the future entrepreneur, came home from some agricultural summer camp aflame with purpose. Big corporations are poisoning our ground water and killing off the monarch butterfly population and they must be stopped. I remembered an important appointment when he started on the honeybee die-off."

"Do not introduce him to Sidney. They'll be arrested for sabotage, and who'll take care of the office while I'm away?" She turned the water onto the tomatoes. "Speaking of, Jimmy paved the way for me to talk to the police in that precinct."

Frank stuffed a giant forkful of potato salad into his mouth and said around it, "My boss still worships you even with Jane at his side." He swallowed. "Maybe it distracted him for a few minutes from the two teenagers we found dead."

"What?"

"Three days apart. One in the park, the other behind a convenience store dumpster. Both OD'd on something, but initial tox reports aren't coming up with the usual suspects. We're waiting on more in-depth results."

Giulia turned off the water. "What if there's a connection between Anne and those kids?"

His fork in the last of the potato salad, Frank said, "How and why?"

"Drugs are as out of character for Anne as leaving her family was. The EMTs this morning seemed to think the same thing you just said about the teenagers, that Anne appeared to be on something out of the ordinary."

Frank held out his hand for the hose. Giulia gave it to him and he watered the cucumbers without leaving his lawn chair. "VanHorne started in narcotics. I'll see what he thinks. Anything to stop him talking about his nephew's Pop Warner football games all night."

Giulia watched Frank's watering technique with approval. "You'll be that dad one day."

"God forbid. Soccer all the way." He reached out his free hand and patted her still-flat stomach. "Did I ask you how you felt about naming him Zlatan?"

Six

The next morning, Giulia entered the Penn Hills police station wearing the top half of her hated navy blue interview suit, but khakis and flats on the bottom. Not even the Second Coming could force her into pantyhose on a dripping humid July day.

Well, maybe the Second Coming.

The Penn Hills and Cottonwood police stations shared fashionista receptionists and garbled shouts from the depths of the holding cells. Penn Hills' linoleum needed replacing, however, and those hospital-green painted walls—ugh.

Detective Okorie came out herself to greet Giulia. "Good morning, Ms. Driscoll. Your friend Captain Reilly could charm the scales off a snake. Come on back to my desk."

Giulia followed the detective, admiring her warm gray suit, her rich black hair with a subtle blonde streak in her wraparound braids, and her elegant walk. Giulia didn't waste time envying all those things. She knew she'd never be elegant and had long ago learned to like her short hourglass figure and wild curly hair.

The detectives' group office was a mirror image of Cottonwood's as well. Six desks so close they might as well be on top of each other. Older, clunkier computer screens obscured by coffee mugs and stacks of file folders. More scuffed linoleum flooring beneath well-used rolling chairs.

The shouting from the depths increased in volume. "Don't mind the trio in the holding cells," the detective said. "They're at the mutual recrimination stage of their latest arrest."

Giulia gave her a genuine smile, not one of the numbered ones reserved for various levels of annoying interactions. "I'm used to it. My husband's a detective back in Cottonwood."

"Oh, good. I have an empty desk for you and a pile of reports for your reading pleasure."

Her desk and Giulia's temporary one snugged into the corner nearest the lobby door. A crooked stack of manila folders perched in the center of the empty desk.

Giulia sat in an armless chair and took a legal pad and pen out of her messenger bag. "This is very kind of you. What am I looking at?"

The detective lifted the top folder. "The initial missing persons report." She ran her fingers down the rest of the stack. "Compiled interviews of friends, family, and coworkers. My reports from three weeks of investigation."

Giulia opened the first folder and saw a copy of a copy of a copy of a fill-in-the-boxes form. Firm, broad handwriting overflowed most of the little boxes.

"Would you like a coffee?"

"Thank you, no," Giulia said. "I'm good."

"Smart choice," Detective Okorie said. "Our coffee is punishment for our failure to find rich, eligible spouses to entrap." Her desk phone rang. "Poke me if you need anything."

Giulia blocked out the ambient noise of multiple conversations, suspect intake drama, and still more shouts from the holding cells.

Milo Chapers, Human Resources director of Sunset Shores, had made the phone call on April tenth to initiate the missing persons report. An ID card photo of Joanne Philbey was paper-clipped to the report, in which she looked much the same as in the twenty-fifth birthday picture.

Details about Joanne filled the rows of narrow boxes: Height, weight, eye color, hair color, skin color. Tattoos, none. Drat. So much for an easy way to identify Joanne if she'd gone the "make a new life" route.

Home phone, work phone, cell. A note next to the home and cell phone numbers read, "Cell goes to voicemail; home phone rings without ans. mach. picking up."

Giulia wrote down everything. Chapers' story filled the bottom half of the report. His version mirrored Diane's, but in dry officialese.

"Ms. Philbey last showed up for her usual shift on April second. She has always been punctual and conscientious. We telephoned her several times over the course of the next three days. When we received no answer, we contacted her landlord. He and I entered her apartment on April fifth. The apartment was neat and organized. There was no sign that Ms. Philbey had been in the apartment recently. At this point, I made the decision to contact the police, as Ms. Philbey's nearest relative lives out of town and I didn't wish to alarm her."

He didn't call her sister. Good Heavens. Giulia would have to exert extreme control when she interviewed Mr. Pole Up His Butt.

Okorie hung up from a second phone call and rolled her chair next to Giulia's. "I'm not surprised the family hired you. We see a lot of desperation. Not all PIs are as polite as you, though."

Giulia finished a sentence. "It would be short-sighted of me not to be polite when you're doing me a favor. Should I ask about the PIs with whom you're comparing me?"

"Oh, you should. We got an imitation Mike Hammer last year. Dressed and acted the part, especially treating us like the enemy. For some reason he couldn't fathom, he got little cooperation from us. Better than him was the Archie Goodwin: 1940s suit, imitated the walk from the old TV show, everything." She called across the room, "Hey, Martinson, remember that Archie Goodwin type a year ago Christmas?"

Martinson nodded his shaved head. "He brought out the Nero Wolfe addict in me. I kept feeding him lines from the books, and he'd lose his place in the files trying not to respond."

"He sure looked good in the suit, though."

"Not my type."

"More for me." Okorie turned to Giulia again. "Anyway, I could have told the Penn Hills version of Archie Goodwin not to waste his time. He'd been hired to find a thirty-five-year-old sales manager. She'd ditched her phone in the Steel Museum and the security camera footage was the last anyone saw of her. We questioned her last two boyfriends, but they had no reason to kill her and the few other leads fizzled out." She picked up a homemade Missing Person flyer from one of Giulia's folders. "We have dozens of these in our cold case files. It's tough on the families, but sometimes people want to disappear."

Fatalistic attitudes brought out all Giulia's stubbornness. She couldn't squander the goodwill here, but she had to make some kind of reply.

BANG.

The gunshot came from the entrance. Shouts filled the hall. Detective Okorie ran for the door and Giulia dived behind the desk. Without her own gun she'd be a liability.

Another bang.

A female voice in the hall shouted, "You give me Cal or I'll shoot this Barbie doll bitch."

Detective Okorie's voice: "I can bring Cal to you."

"Then get him out here now, bitch!"

"Wouldn't it be better if we went to a quiet room where you and Cal can talk?"

Harsh laughter. "Hell, no. Do you think I'm stupid? You drag his scrawny ass out here so we can go home."

A scuffle, more shouts, and one final gunshot. The bullet came through the wall above Giulia's head and shattered the glass in a framed photo of the governor of Pennsylvania.

Two detectives wrestled a massive woman with a meth-riddled face and matted blonde hair into the office. She cursed them, their mothers, and their manly parts as she kicked desks and chairs on her way to the holding cells.

A female detective came in next, following the trajectory of the third bullet.

Giulia pointed. "It hit the governor's picture."

"I see it. Thanks." She took photographs of the wrecked photo and frame, the glass on the floor, and the hole the bullet made in the wall.

The receptionist came in with a tall detective who resembled Idris Elba. When he spoke, he ruined Giulia's hope that his voice matched Elba's as well. Real life could be so disappointing.

"You're sure you're all right, Cassidy?"

The receptionist fluttered her blue-tinted eyelashes at him. "Really, I am. That crazy meth-head ripped my sleeve, but nothing else. She was shaking like an earthquake when she grabbed me."

"Then let's get your statement so we can keep her in a cell next to the love of her life." He unlocked his computer.

Cassidy adjusted her torn shirt. "I am going to get so much mileage out of this."

Detective Okorie returned to her desk.

"You have the knack for negotiation," Giulia said.

Okorie straightened her jacket. "The drugs helped. Cal's true love took an extra hit or two for courage. I know the signs." She looked Giulia over. "You're okay, yes?"

"The last bullet missed the top of my head by several inches. I didn't expect my day to imitate a Snoopy novel." When Okorie looked puzzled, Giulia quoted Charles Schulz: "It was a dark and stormy night. Suddenly a shot rang out."

"The maid screamed," Okorie said.

"A door slammed," Detective "Idris Elba" said from one desk over.

All three of them finished together: "Suddenly a pirate ship appeared on the horizon."

"Huh?" the receptionist said.

Everyone bent their heads over their work.

Seven

Joanne's apartment house was as nondescript as her choice of clothes. Four floors of brown brick face over cinder block. Giulia knew the drill. The brick face added anywhere from twenty to forty dollars to the rent. She walked around to the back of the building. Minimal balconies wide enough for two plastic chairs and little else. Hanging window baskets on several. Limp American flag bunting on a few. The stairwell would smell of cabbage or garlic or onions.

She opened the central door, nodded at the mailman filling the narrow mail slots, and continued through the inner door. Onions. Santa ought to tuck a tiara with "Sleuthing Queen" in multicolored rhinestones in the top of her stocking this Christmas.

A middle-aged man with a salt-and-pepper goatee and wearing a two-piece plaid suit stood next to the elevator, giving orders into a Bluetooth headset.

"I paid you to fix the leaks in the ceilings...Don't give me that. I'm standing in a puddle on the first floor, you hack...That's better. I'll meet you here tomorrow morning at seven sharp." He touched the headset and held out his hand to Giulia. "Ms. Driscoll? Ron Jankowicz."

Giulia returned his firm handshake. "Thank you for meeting me."

"Not at all. Glad to see some progress in the search for 3B. She was the ideal tenant." He pressed the Up button and ushered Giulia into the elevator before him. "I'd rather have three buildings full of tenants like her than win Powerball."

Giulia gave him an arch look.

"I mean it. I like to work. I hate deadbeats and people who sneak rabbits into my apartments. Those long-eared demon rodents chew through the wires and eat the wallpaper. Then the tenants give me grief about losing their security deposit."

A subdued ding and the doors opened. The flat indoor-outdoor carpet on this floor matched the orange paisley carpet on the first floor. The off-white walls needed painting and this floor smelled like someone's trash should've been emptied last week.

It was still better than Giulia's first two post-convent apartments.

"I understand Ms. Philbey's sister is paying the rent until her sister returns."

"No skin off my back," the landlord said. "She pays on time, she can keep the apartment as long as she wants. So, you're a private eye. I don't see many women in that profession." He took out a pass key. "You carry a Glock, right? I love old-fashioned guns. Got a collection. A tenant pulled a knife on me once. I shoved my .45 in his face and he pissed himself." He brayed rather than laughed. "The apartment is exactly the way 3B left it. I knew the cops would want it intact." He opened the door. "Thank God she took her cats with her."

Giulia followed him into generic apartment A with generic floor plan B. A lingering musty smell reached her nose combined with a faint odor of cat. A square entrance with a coat closet on the right and an open living room on the left. Ahead, a narrow hallway with one door on the left and another at the end. To the right, a square dining area with a round table and two chairs. Off of that, a galley kitchen. The closed living room curtains created twilight at noon. Jankowicz flipped two light switches.

Now Giulia could see Joanne had fought against generic for her living space. The apartment reflected the creativity she poured into her fancy cakes. The walls in every room were painted a different color. Lemon in the kitchen. Raspberry in the dining nook.

"Girly in here, isn't it?" Jankowicz said. "I'm a plain white wall guy myself. White or paneling, like my grandparents taught me. But if my tenants want to paint, I let 'em paint. Happy tenants renew their leases." He touched his ear. "Jankowicz...Again? Tell her if she can afford to hit the casino three nights a week, she can damn well pay her rent on time." He said to Giulia, "I'll be checking the hundred different things I need to inspect. Call me when you're done." He issued instructions to his minion on the other end of the phone call as he walked away.

Giulia closed the door and stood in the entrance way, getting a feel for the place. The standard beige carpet sank into deserved obscurity beneath the hydrangea-patterned sofa and chair in the living room. Those walls were periwinkle and matched the flowers in the upholstery.

She walked down the candy apple red hallway. The left-hand door opened into a bathroom with kiwi walls and matching shower curtain. In the last room, three creamsicle walls offset the single vanilla wall in the entire apartment.

Giulia would've killed for a creamsicle right then. Instead, she opened the window's matching striped curtains and started in on the nightstand drawer.

Two romance novels, a composition notebook, and a mechanical pencil. Giulia flipped through the notebook: Sketches for fancy cake decorations. She set it on the bed to take with her. You never know.

Next, the closet. Five pairs of khakis and five polo shirts, the latter with a Sunset Shores logo on the single pocket. Two pairs of sensible sneakers with arch support and a few ghosts of food stains on them. On the far left, a black wool winter coat, black fur-lined boots, and a beige raincoat. On the shelf above, sweaters in white and tan and gray.

The dresser yielded much of the same. Gray t-shirts with "Crazy Cat Lady," "Bakers Make It Rise," and "Bambi: He's What's For Dinner." If Joanne wasn't dead, she'd either bought specific clothes for her new life or she'd joined a nudist colony.

Onto the bathroom. Toiletries. Makeup. Interesting that she'd left makeup behind. Giulia hadn't worn it during her ten years in the convent, naturally, but now she seldom left the house without putting on a face.

The kitchen gave Giulia an inferiority complex. The best quality pots, pans, and utensils. Cookbooks several pay grades above her own skills, and Giulia was an accomplished cook.

Fridge, freezer, and pantry, all empty. Cleaning supplies under the sink. Shoved behind them into the back corner, one cat dish for "Wilton" and one for "Springsteen."

So the cats died? Both at once, conveniently in time for Joanne to disappear? Giulia wasn't buying it. She opened the memo feature on her phone and made a note to check the local SPCA online archives. Joanne's cats were distinctive enough to make a search a notch above hopeless.

She opened the living room curtains on a bare balcony. Next, she turned on the TV looking for the channels Joanne had marked as favorites, but only the four broadcast stations came in. Duh. The cable would've been shut off with no one here to pay for it. So much for that line of inquiry.

To the bookshelf. Every Adam Sandler DVD on the top shelf plus all the parody horror movie franchises. Below them, a boatload of romances in all the modern genres: paranormal, erotica, fantasy, historical, suspense, contemporary. Between them, framed photographs of the twins at high school graduation, on their twenty-first birthday, Joanne in camouflage holding the antlers of an eight-point buck, Joanne at Diane's college graduation and vice-versa. On the bottom shelf, Stephen King hardcovers and the complete works of Jane Austen.

Giulia finally found Joanne's personal papers inside the ottoman. One of those square plastic document boxes was stuffed with hanging folders docketing Joanne's recent life: bills, tax returns, receipts, a few extra photos.

"Come to Giulia, you beautiful organized life story." She worked the box out of its tight inner space.

Twelve "meows" sounded from the cat clock on the dining

nook wall. Giulia didn't look down on Joanne for her choice of kitsch, since Giulia's favorite Christmas clock played snippets of different carols every hour.

Hotel check-in time at last. Also time to eat. Little Zlatan apparently wanted a turkey club.

Eight

When Giulia opened the door of her room at the Comfort Inn, her first thought was: "I need a bigger desk." Her second: "Maybe I should be happy the only available room had a king-sized bed."

The bed could accommodate her, Frank, Frank's gaming PC, and all her research for this case. Of course, if she brought Frank into this huge bed, they'd get no paying work done at all.

She unpacked her few clothes and inspected the coffee supplies. No, she would not be squandering her two cup per day pregnancy ration of coffee in here. The local shop she'd passed on the way from Joanne's apartment would be her first stop tomorrow morning.

A bite of the turkey club reinforced her belief that local shops created the tastiest food. She opened a 7-Up since caffeine was now reserved for coffee only and lucked into the last twenty minutes of *Godzilla 2000* on the cable TV. The only Godzilla movie with the underlying message, "Smoking will get you stomped."

She set the contents of the file box on the bed and pulled out one folder after another. Joanne had left her an unexpected gift: A pocket calendar. As Godzilla's closing music played in the background, Giulia read about birthday cake commissions, the start of hunting season, reminders to check sales prices at mega-outdoor stores, and a whole series of notes about someone named Marjorie.

"Make vet appt. for Marjorie." "Make more Jo's Special for M." On every Sunday: "M – 1 pm."

Giulia opened the back of the calendar. Diane's name at the top had an old address scratched out and the address and phone number she'd given Giulia written beneath it. Below that, "Marjorie's new cell."

Giulia dialed the number.

Marjorie's vintage 1950s teal ranch house was under siege by plastic pink flamingos. Their siege engines looked suspiciously like multi-level cat scratching posts.

Giulia liked Marjorie already. She waved at the wrinkled face peeking through the lacy window curtains.

The face disappeared and several locks snapped and rattled at the door. The door opened with one chain lock still attached.

"Please show me some identification."

Marjorie's voice was what Giulia's father used to call a whiskey tenor: low and gravelly.

Giulia held up her PI license. Marjorie squinted at it before closing the door. The chain slid free. Three cats streaked past Giulia when the door opened.

"I'm Marjorie Briggs. Old women living alone can't be too careful. Everyone thinks we're ripe for the latest scam. Come in. You're not allergic to cats, are you?"

"I'm not. Thank you for seeing me on such short notice."

If Giulia had been allergic, Marjorie would be calling 911 any second. Even with the windows open, the house smelled of litter boxes, canned cat food, and flowery air freshener. The carpet pile showed the reverse-nap streaks of recent vacuuming, but cat hair of every possible length and shade clung to the baseboards and the bottoms of chairs.

"Come on into the living room. Can I get you something to drink? I'm so glad you're trying to find Joanne. The cats miss her."

Giulia sat in an armchair upholstered in yellow fabric plus cat hair. A trip to the Dollar Store for a lint roller was in her near future. The chair Marjorie sat in had the same upholstery scheme.

"Ms. Briggs, I found your phone number in Joanne's pocket calendar."

"Just Marjorie, please. Ms. Briggs is my older sister, the banker. I remember that calendar. Joanne lived by it. She said calendars on those smart phones couldn't be trusted."

Marjorie answered Giulia's next leading question before she asked it: "If Joanne left behind that calendar, she may be dead after all." Marjorie's wrinkles scrunched together and tears appeared in her eyes.

Giulia cut them off. "Not necessarily. There's also the chance Joanne wanted to start a new life."

"Horse puckey."

Giulia smiled. "Why?"

"Joanne had everything a girl could want if she wasn't out hunting for a husband. She had two good jobs and lots of friends. She had boyfriends too. She used to tell me all about them when she came here for the ferals."

"Ferals?"

"Stray cats. Wild cats. Any cat too skittish to want to be queen of a household." A calico strutted into the room and sat at Marjorie's feet. She reached down to scratch its head. "I'm the crazy feral cat lady. Joanne used to make cat food from the discarded vegetables and meats at the nursing home. She'd bring two big buckets of her own creations every Sunday and we'd feed the cats together."

A short-haired tuxedo cat jumped out of nowhere into Giulia's lap. Its gold eyes scrutinized her before its paws kneaded her thighs and it settled into her lap, purring.

Marjorie pointed. "Groucho likes you. Now we'll see if Tallulah approves."

Giulia looked around. A long-haired white cat strolled into the room followed by a gray with mismatched eyes and a tabby with a fox tail. The tabby didn't acknowledge Giulia's presence. The gray sniffed her shoes and moved on. The white cat inspected the occupant of Giulia's lap, sprang onto the arm of the chair, and swatted the tuxedo cat with one long paw. With a huff, Groucho moved to Giulia's left leg and Tallulah took possession of Giulia's right.

Marjorie settled back against a yellow and white checkered cushion. "That's all settled. When Groucho and Tallulah approve, I know you're a trustworthy person. They sat on Joanne's legs like that every week. Now how can I help you find her?" She stopped petting a one-eared orange cat. "I've been worried she might have been kidnapped, but the police haven't said anything about a ransom note."

Giulia had considered and discarded the kidnapping idea yesterday. Also, she didn't want Marjorie panicking and clamming up. "It's extremely unlikely. Joanne's been missing since early April, yet her family received no ransom demand."

"True. Joanne wasn't rich. You don't work two jobs if you don't have to. Did you ever see one of her cakes?"

"Yes, I've seen pictures." Giulia steered the conversation into a useful direction. "Can you tell me if Joanne seemed different the last few Sundays before she disappeared?"

"That nice young detective asked me the same question, but I'm sure the police don't share their information with private investigators."

"They sometimes don't." Not too much of a lie.

Marjorie jerked her head toward the TV. "I've seen a lot of private eye movies. They do like to rub the police's fur the wrong way. Right, Lucille?" She dragged her palm backwards along the cat's spine and the cat arched and hissed. "Joanne had self-esteem issues. I've seen the doctors on *Ellen* and *Oprah* talk about self-esteem, and Joanne was like one of their patients they bring out as an example. She said she was too fat and she dressed like she was trying to fade into the wallpaper. But here's the thing." She picked up the meowing cat and deposited it on the carpet. "Lucille, you won't starve while I talk to the private eye." An all-black cat immediately took Lucille's place. Marjorie began stroking it as she talked. "Even though Joanne put herself down and dressed herself frumpy, she was savvy enough to build her fancy cake business and to be angling for a promotion at work."

Giulia stroked both her thigh-busting felines as her legs went numb. "Perhaps she felt unattractive only in personal relationships?"

Marjorie rolled her faded brown eyes. "Men. Give me cats any day. Joanne had her troubles with men, sure. Some thought she'd be easy—you know—because she weighed a few pounds more than Hollywood says she should. One of her boyfriends dumped her right before Christmas."

"So he wouldn't have to buy her a present."

"Bingo." Marjorie nuzzled the black cat's nose. "You'd never dump me unless I couldn't work the can opener anymore, right, Rudolph?" Rudolph twisted himself upside down and presented his belly. Marjorie obliged with more petting. "When the gutless wonder tossed Joanne away, she got real mopey for about a month. One Sunday at the end of January she told me she'd given in and registered on some dating sites."

"More than one?"

Giulia didn't know whether to rejoice or cringe at the research in her future.

"She said sites, plural. But that's not the point." Marjorie leaned forward. "In the middle of February, she came here all excited. She wouldn't say who the man was, but she dropped little teasers like 'Dating sites weren't always the refuge of the hopeless.' She started to dress differently too."

Marjorie stopped talking to comb Rudolph's fur, and Giulia said, "In what ways did Joanne dress differently?"

"Right, we're up to February. She started to wear hunting clothes when she came to visit. She used to wear t-shirts and shorts or sweaters and jeans. Regular casual clothes, you know. After a few more weeks she started to act differently. Joanne was always sweet and friendly. When the middle of March hit, she got all secretive and superior."

Giulia would have given a week's allotment of coffee to record this on her phone. She kept her attention on Marjorie like she was wearing mental blinders. "That doesn't sound good."

"I know. I used to wonder if she'd knock on my door one Sunday with a new greeting. See, she'd always announce 'Crazy Cat Lady in training,' and I'd say, 'Enter and be instructed, acolyte,' and we'd both laugh. But those last few Sundays she dropped the greeting altogether. She gave me the cat food like it was a chore." Marjorie's wrinkles drooped. "I miss who she used to be."

Nine

The Nunmobile made it two entire blocks before Giulia made a hard right into a mall parking lot. Phantom flea itches and four different colors of cat hair covered her body and clothes. She parked and yanked up the legs of her khakis and pulled out the waistband. No bites. Now to convince her body of their absence.

She hadn't wanted to spook Marjorie by creating a voice memo while parked in front of her house, so she fell back on her old teaching trick of mnemonics. As soon as she established her flea-free state, she whipped out her phone and repeated every word Marjorie had said to her.

Ten minutes and thirty-seven seconds later, she hit Save and opened Google Maps for the nearest purveyor of lint rollers.

After her successful acquisition of the Holy Grail of wardrobe rescues, she found a *Remington Steele* rerun on the hotel room TV and allowed herself a twenty-minute break.

Her cell phone rang and Sidney's picture filled the small screen.

"Oh, good; you're not driving. The new client called. She forgot to give you her sister's social media accounts."

Giulia smacked herself in the forehead. "Can I claim baby brain this early on?"

Sidney laughed. "You can milk baby brain as soon as the pregnancy test stick shows two pink lines. Do you have a pen and paper?"

Giulia pulled the hotel notepad and pen toward her. "Go ahead."

Sidney spelled out the usernames and passwords to Joanne Philbey's Facebook, Twitter, and Instagram accounts.

"Thanks. May you return home to a shiny new tooth in Jessamine's mouth."

Sidney whimpered. "I need sleep so bad."

Energized by the prospect of learning about Joanne in her own words, Giulia turned off the TV before Laura and Remington caught the killer.

But first, her notes from the police files. She spread them out on the king-sized bed and booted her laptop. The Wi-Fi connection fetched a small mountain of emails, but she dealt with them so efficiently it smacked of ruthlessness.

Her handwriting was a true casualty of her police station visit. She'd had to cover so much information in minimal time, not counting the time lost to the angry girlfriend with gun interlude. Her notes looked like a hungover chicken had tried to write to her dictation. She regretted not giving in to her impulse to take surreptitious pictures of the documents with her phone.

Talk about squandering goodwill. She was definitely not that stupid.

Half an hour later, she finished transcribing Marjorie's interview. Frank would be wrapping up at the precinct and preparing for another night on stakeout. Sidney would be hoping to find that first tiny white bump in Jessamine's mouth when she got home, the herald of several hours of unbroken sleep.

What would Joanne be doing at three o'clock on a Tuesday afternoon if she was home? Breakfast shift at Sunset Shores meant no late-night partying.

Giulia logged on to Joanne's Facebook page.

Enough cat memes to rival I Can Has Cheezburger. Pictures of her own cats, Wilton and Springsteen, plus pictures of Marjorie's herd. Giulia scrolled past eleven cat albums until she found one of hunting trips.

Joanne in camouflage with a hunting rifle. Another with the same eight-point buck in the framed photo on her bookshelf. With a group in various shades of camouflage around a bonfire toasting each other with bottles of beer.

Her About page gave Giulia one piece of information she didn't already have: A link to "Cakes by Joanne." Clicking on it brought up a separate website whose main page ought to have one of those yellow triangle pop-up warnings for dieters. The longer Giulia looked, the more pounds she added to her thighs.

Giulia read through the comments. The most recent one had been posted on April third. She returned to Joanne's Facebook page. Her last status update had been on March thirtieth.

"Tired of shopping. Does that make me less of a girly-girl?"

A winking emoji followed, with several friends adding laughing cat stickers and comments like "You're only a girly-girl if you hunt deer in Jimmy Choos" and "Does buying ammo count as retail therapy?"

Then nothing. Friends posted variations of "Happy Birthday! Don't bake your own cake!" but Joanne never responded. On April sixth, the same friends who had joked about shopping posted "Where did you run off to?" and "Are we still on for bar-hopping tonight?"

A week after that, the posts were no longer casual. "Has anyone heard from Joanne?" "Did anyone call that nursing home where she works?"

Giulia opened a second tab for Joanne's Twitter feed and a third for her Instagram. Joanne hadn't been as prolific on Twitter as on Facebook, and her Instagram account was eighty percent cakes and twenty percent cats.

No boyfriend pictures on any of the three. Yet Diane and Marjorie specifically mentioned Joanne's boyfriends, plural.

Back to Facebook. Sixty days after Joanne's last post, one of her friends tagged her in a hunting photo and posted, "May 30. Joanne's been missing two months today. When was the last time anyone saw her with Louis Larabee?" That name was also a tag.

A few replies, all pointing fingers at Louis Larabee. Six hours later, their target replied with a picture of Elmer Fudd flipping the bird. The veiled accusations escalated. Larabee answered in words rather than memes, calling them whores and vultures. After two hours of back and forth, he yelled at them: "DROP DEAD. I'M OUT OF HERE."

Joanne's friends kept taunting and accusing him, but when he didn't reply, the friend who started the thread posted:

"There once was a hunter named Louie
Who snuggled with cows that said 'Moo-ey.'
He liked number nine
Also four was just fine
Oh, what a nice night for a view-y."

No further replies. Giulia's finger hovered over the touch pad to go back to Twitter. She reread the limerick. Read it a third time.

Clicked on the friend's name to get to her home page.

Interests: shopping, the *New York Times* Crossword Puzzle, WWII, Cryptography. All right. What was this angry friend who liked word games really saying? Giulia unpacked it line by line.

Line one she ignored. She already knew the ex-boyfriend's first and last names.

Line two: Snuggle. Cows. Was Larabee a farmer? No, a hunter. People don't hunt cows. What did snuggle mean, then? Hug? Pet? Sleep with? Only if he was too poor to afford his own house and secretly lived in someone's barn.

Snuggle also meant to cuddle. When people snuggled, they...hugged. Spooned. Sat or lay next to each other. Next to.

Larabee lived next to a farm? Possibly.

Line three: Numeral nine.

Line four: Numeral four.

Ninety-four [something] Street.

Cows lived on farms. Giulia opened a new tab and pulled up Google Street View. A search for Farm Street, Avenue, Boulevard, and Lane yielded a lot of nothing. She tried actual farms, but none had an address near ninety-four anything.

Cows say moo. Good Heavens, she was already thinking like a See 'n Say.

Okay, cows who say moo, where are you hiding Louis Larabee?

Barn Street, Avenue, Boulevard, Lane—zilch.

Field Street, Avenue, Boulevard, Lane—the same.

Meadow Street, Avenue, Boulevard...Lane.

One more notch on the sleuthing tiara.

Ten

At three thirty, Giulia parked the Nunmobile in front of the smallest house she'd ever seen. Address: 94 Meadow Lane. Neighbor on the right: A ranch house surrounded by alternating red and white azaleas. Neighbor on the left which was also the corner: A working dairy farm whose address was listed on the cross street.

The house was smaller than small. A Tiny House, that was it. She'd read about them online. This box with windows on a postage-stamp plot of land couldn't be more than three hundred square feet. Instead of a sidewalk to the door, a dirt path bisected a lawn of dandelions and clover. More vegetables and weeds surrounded the sides of the house. She could even see a short way around the back from where she stood.

She banged the deer-head shaped knocker.

"Who's there?"

A mixed martial arts type appeared in the space between houses. Giulia walked toward him. Because he wore only a tight black t-shirt and camouflage pants, she got an eyeful of his arm tattoos and well defined torso. A scar split his left eyebrow; Giulia guessed from a bullet graze. His dark hair was cut in a military-style buzz.

"Good afternoon. I'm with Driscoll Investigations and we're looking into the disappearance of Joanne Philbey. May I have a few minutes of your time?"

"You sound like a door-to-door Bible-thumper." He knocked

dirt from the trowel he was holding. "You can talk to me while I weed." He glanced at his watch. "I don't have to leave for work until four thirty."

Giulia followed him into a regimented vegetable garden. A row of broccoli, a row of cauliflower, rows of beans and peas, tomatoes in cages, eggplant, corn, and carrots.

He knelt next to the first row of beans. "I like my privacy. How did you track me down?"

"I'm afraid you've been doxxed," she said.

"I've been what?" He tossed crabgrass into a compost bin.

"In this case, it means your home address is out on the web. I found it on Facebook."

The trowel stopped moving. He cursed. "I haven't been on that troll pit in months."

"You may want to log in and report it. It's part of a discussion on the two-month anniversary of Joanne's last post. The person who doxxed you disguised it in a piece of poetry."

He indulged in unflattering comments about the women in that particular thread. The weeds got the worst of it. When he wound down, he refocused on Giulia. "Guess I should be glad you were the one to figure it out and not some random stalker. Fine. What do you want to know?"

Giulia opened her mouth, and he cut her off before the first syllable. "Wait a minute. First I bet you want my side of that argument. The one on Facebook."

"As a start, yes."

"You got something to write on? This one has a long history."

"Of course." She brought out her iPad. Holding it in her left hand and typing with her right wasn't ideal, but it was better than having to remember everything for a voice memo later. But first, setting the potentially hostile interviewee at his ease.

"This is what's called a Tiny House, isn't it?"

"Yeah. You interested in the movement?"

"The movement?"

"Smaller footprint. More in tune with nature instead of

subduing it. Off the grid." He gestured with his thumb at the Penelec meter on the side of the house. "I'm stuck with city power while I live here, but it won't last forever."

Sidney might once have fallen in with this movement, but not now that she and Olivier had Jessamine. Giulia couldn't picture two adults and a baby in this minimalist house.

"What about storing clothes and all these vegetables canned for the winter?" She wondered if he was a reader and did a quick calculation of the house's square footage. She and Frank would have to build furniture out of their book collection to fit them all in.

"I dug out a space underneath. It's small, like the house. Has enough room for canned-good shelves and storage bins." He moved onto the grass invading the next row of beans.

Giulia seized the point of connection. "My grandmother's house had a fruit cellar. If I could add to my own house, one of those would be first on the list."

"Yeah, my canning skills are limited, but I supplement them with the right girlfriends." He tossed more inedible growth into the compost bin. "So the whole Facebook thing. Josie and I dated for a while but split up. I'm not going into details. It's my business, not yours. The problem was all her friends who hated hunting decided to hate me too."

He spoke slower than Marjorie and Diane and she kept up with ease, even one-handed. "I've seen pictures of Joanne on hunting trips."

"Trips? Are you kidding? Josie worked two jobs, and I've been at my current place less than a year. A bunch of us like to get together for a weekend out in the woods around here. Josie and I would render the kill and we'd all share the meat."

Giulia's stomach shuddered at the mental movie of gutting, skinning, and carving up a deer. "So the hunters weren't the ones making veiled threats on Facebook."

"Not a chance. When you share death with people you get real tight. Josie's shallow college friends are the ones who had it in for me." He stood and stretched, giving Giulia a better view of his tatted muscles. "I didn't know Josie was missing until her sister posted on Josie's Facebook page."

"What did you think happened to her?"

A shrug.

"Dunno, but if I had to guess, she got carjacked or mugged and the mugger hid her body. Josie was in okay shape, but she never took self-defense seriously."

Giulia cast a lure. "Joanne was somewhat overweight in the pictures I've seen."

"You're looking at old pictures. Josie dropped some flab last spring. Made her a better hunter." He took a step forward. "Are those—" He appeared to rethink his choice of words. "What are those friends of Josie's on Facebook accusing me of?"

Giulia stopped typing and brought up the Facebook conversation. As he read, Larabee's tanned face darkened and his jaw clenched.

"Stupid bint couldn't even manage the classic limerick rhyme. If I knew where she lived, I'd do a hell of a lot more than post bad poetry on the Net."

Giulia put a few microns more distance between them. He saw and backed off.

"Okay. Coming clean because it's no secret anyway. I've got a record. Hung out with a bad crowd in high school. Drugs, you know? I stole money from my mother and cold-cocked my father when he tried to stop me. He called the cops and my gang threw me under the bus. I ended up with six months in juvie plus three years' probation. Try finding a job after that. I joined the Marines, but they were too much like juvie for my stomach. No freedom and too many higher-ups ordering me around. Now I work second shift at one of those big shipping warehouses. When you have muscles, people will hire you no matter what."

Giulia typed it all up.

"A female police detective showed up here a couple of months ago," he continued. "She wore authority like Dracula's cape. We didn't get along." A short laugh. "She looked real disappointed when I told her I hadn't seen Josie in weeks and we were still friends after our breakup."

His watch beeped. "I have to leave for work. Here's why I think Josie was offed by a stranger: Nobody argued with Josie. I mean, not ever. The only disagreements we had were over gun versus bow hunting and those were more like professional debates. Josie gave a crap about people. She listened to you when you talked. She didn't give you half an ear while she thought up what she was going to say next." He knocked more dirt off the trowel and walked between the houses to the front garden. Giulia pretended she didn't recognize his power game, saved her document, and followed him.

"Before you get any ideas, remember what I said: Our breakup was mutual. Our work schedules didn't match, and I like a woman who's more assertive in bed." He glanced at a teenager walking two poodles and texting at the same time. "Who's paying you? Her sister? Tell her if she wants to do something useful, she should set up a cooking scholarship in Josie's name. She would've liked that."

Eleven

At eight thirty Wednesday morning, the Nunmobile entered Sunset Shores' circular driveway. Diane had described Sunset Shores as a huge complex of buildings. Apparently Diane indulged in the occasional understatement.

Sunset Shores was a miniature city. A four-story apartment building faced the street. Along the left and right sides of the driveway, rows of single-story condos. As she drove farther around the circle, a smaller building came into view. Its manicured gardens with wide flagged paths were enclosed by a tall wrought-iron fence. The driveway curved in front of the fence and branched into ten handicapped parking spots. Giulia continued past those to another branch behind the back of the main apartment building with forty empty parking spots.

The double entrance doors slid open on their own. Frosty air enveloped her. Talk about winter in the middle of summer. The air-conditioning here would keep polar bears comfortable. A few steps farther into the lobby and her nose inhaled a complex mix of bacon, coffee, flowery air freshener, and disinfectant. The sand-colored wallpaper complemented the carpet design of primary shapes in maroon, navy, and mustard.

The clatter of silverware and buzz of multiple conversations came from a huge dining room on her right. On her left, she noted a craft boutique and four unisex bathrooms. Facing her, a receptionist more than twice Giulia's age sat at a kidney-shaped desk crocheting a baby blanket.

"Good morning," Giulia said. "I'd like to speak with Milo Chapers, please."

The receptionist set down her crochet project. "May I have your name?"

"Giulia Driscoll."

"One moment. I'll see if he's in his office." She picked up the phone, but instead of speaking into it waved it at a thin, balding man coming out of the dining room. "Mr. Chapers, you have a visitor."

He squinted at Giulia. "Can it wait? We're near the end of the breakfast rush." He vanished through a swinging door down the hall.

The receptionist changed a brief frown in his direction into a smile at Giulia. "You can have a seat in the visitor's lounge." She pointed to a doorway next to the craft storefront.

Giulia made it halfway there when a plump old woman blocked her way with a metal cane.

"Mary Ellen, why aren't you in school?" She scowled at Giulia's...clothes? hair? makeup?

After a moment's hesitation, Giulia said, "We have today off."

The cane thumped a dark blue circle on the rug. "Schools mollycoddle you kids these days. You need more homework, not more days off." She pulled a lace-edged handkerchief from her sleeve and snorted into it. "Back in my day, Sister Mary Catherine beat the catechism into us with a wooden pointer." She stared at Giulia over the handkerchief. "Did Sister Immaculata put you in detention again?"

A middle-aged woman in a nurse's uniform hurried up to them. "Hortense, it's quilting time. We have to get your puppy quilt supplies from your room."

The old woman huffed. "Nag, nag, nag."

The nurse put a knobby hand on Hortense's arm, but the cane came up and the nurse backed off a step.

"Leave me alone. I'm not feeble yet." She reversed the cane and banged it on a crimson carpet triangle.

The nurse made an apologetic face at Giulia, who smiled.

A moment later, Hortense hooked her cane around the nurse's elbow. "Who are you? Why are you here?"

"I'm going with you to find your quilting basket."

"What are you waiting for, then?" She tugged the nurse closer with the cane. "Help me balance. Do your job."

"Ms. Driscoll?" Milo Chapers took the nurse's place as she led her charge away. "What can I do for you?" He had the harried air of a middle manager saddled with an inexperienced staff.

Giulia didn't need Lady Rowan the psychic to tell her this man needed minions. "Is there an office where we can talk for a few minutes?"

"What's this all—" He glanced around at two wizened ladies a foot away comparing knitting patterns and a man looking at the daily activities sheet while adjusting his hearing aid. "Let's use my office."

He led Giulia past the swinging door and opened the door after it. A bronze nameplate at eye level read "Food Services."

At least two managers shared the small office. On the right-hand wall hung several photos of a man and woman with a baby and a Scottie dog: in front of a Christmas tree, on a beach, at Halloween. On the left-hand wall two photos of Milo with an older man and woman: at a birthday party and crossing the finish line in a bicycle race. The top of the desk couldn't be seen under in-out files, an outdated computer, and stacks of paper in various colors.

Giulia sat on the edge of a doctor's waiting room type chair and explained her purpose at Sunset Shores. Chapers changed his hassled expression for an annoyed one.

"At first I was worried Ms. Philbey had met with foul play or an accident of some kind. But when her landlord and I entered her apartment, it appeared more like the living space of someone who had left for an extended vacation rather than of someone who expected to return home at any time. Do you see what I mean?"

Giulia's impression of him from his police statement had been correct. The man might have been born with a pole up his butt.

She played a disingenuous card. "What exactly did the apartment look like?"

"Every surface had been scrubbed clean. The refrigerator was empty. There was no open mail or an unfinished book on a table or even a newspaper in the recycle bin." His narrow chest swelled.

Giulia typed in her iPad as cover. Indignant Chapers looked way too much like the famous *National Geographic* photo of the angry bluebird. She said, "You assumed she simply walked away from her life here?"

The bluebird's feathers ruffled. "It was perfectly obvious to me. Her landlord disagreed, but he was likely thinking about the rent. The police agreed with my conclusion. I said as much to Ms. Philbey's sister when she came here."

This hallway of an office would have been too small for such a confrontation. Giulia had to resort to the note-writing smokescreen again.

A pager on Chapers' hip went off. He frowned at the message on its small screen.

"I'm afraid I have to truncate this interview. If you'll come with me, I'll introduce you to our morning chef. He was much more intimate with Joanne than I was." His pale face flamed scarlet. "I mean, that is, I—"

Giulia tucked her iPad in her messenger bag and stood. "I understand. Thank you." She watched the back of his pulsing red neck as they passed through the swinging door.

Interesting.

Twelve

Head morning chef Edward "just Eddie, please" Marstan looked like a young Colin Firth but without the charisma. Or the voice. An irregular pattern of bacon grease dots marred his uniform, but beneath it lurked the body of a weightlifter. He slumped in the wicker chair opposite Giulia as they sat in the gazebo on the lawn in front of the condos.

"I don't get out here often enough. Joanie liked to come here on break to breathe air that didn't smell like fry grease."

Giulia knew a disappointed lover when she saw one. They always wanted to talk. She wrote a header on a new document in her iPad and counted to herself: Five...four...three...two...

"Joanie and I were equals here. Before she disappeared, I mean. Last month the head chef won two hundred grand in Powerball and quit. If Joanie had been here, the promotion would have been hers, no question. Angie would've tried to stab her in the back, but Angie is a hack. Joanie could make this food service glop taste like real food. I'm not up to her level, but I'm working on it."

Two women using walkers moved past the gazebo, talking in high-pitched voices about the women in the latest episode of *The Bachelor*. Eddie waited for them to cross the parking lot to the other row of condos.

"I'm glad Joanie's sister hired you. She got all in Chapers' face when she came here. Did you know he didn't call her for a whole week after Joanie stopped showing up? The cops guilted him into telling her. We could hear her in his office even through two closed doors. His hairline receded half an inch out of fear. We compared impressions of it after she left."

A skeletal woman opened the back door of the main building. She lit a cigarette and indulged in a long, slow inhale and exhale. Then she dragged two bulging trash bags over to a dumpster concealed behind a privacy fence. After a plastic lid slammed, she walked closer to the gazebo and said, "Marstan, the boss says he needs the canned good reorder list ASAP."

"Will do, Angie." In a low voice to Giulia, he said, "If she'd eat something besides kale smoothies and boiled quinoa, she might learn the difference between savory and over-spiced. She'll never be more than an assistant until she stops being afraid of food."

Giulia picked up the tangent and ran with it. "Judging from her specialty cakes, Joanne appreciated food."

Eddie frowned at Giulia as though she harbored an ulterior motive. "Just because Joanie didn't starve herself—"

Giulia stopped him. "No. That's not what I meant at all."

Eddie relaxed. "Good. I'm sick to death of everyone assuming Joanie was fat and unloved because she didn't wear a size zero. Joanie was—is—a great person. She listened—listens—when you talk. She even helps out this crazy cat lady from her church. She can hunt with a rifle and a bow and arrow and gut a deer. But she can get all girly-girled up when she wants. For Sunset's Christmas party she put on sparkle nails and everything. She's got it all."

Giulia typed: Joanne either had no idea Eddie worshiped her or he had made an overture and she turned him down.

He took an antique pocket watch out of the shirt pocket beneath his uniform. "I can give you another twelve minutes before the ten o'clock group meeting."

Giulia leaned forward. "What do all her coworkers think happened?"

"It was like this: About three months before she disappeared, Joanie started to change. She dropped a bunch of weight and got all 'I know something you don't know.' It got under some people's skin. When the cops showed, the tall, hot one got some of us to talk, but the Alzheimer's patients freaked out her minion. He couldn't even look them in the eye." He sat straighter. "Sorry. Derail. After the cops left, Chapers couldn't stop the gossip." He took out his cell phone and showed Giulia a screenshot. "They started an office pool, like when someone's pregnant and everybody puts in a buck to guess the time and date of birth."

Giulia took a picture of the screenshot and read:

"Pregnant."

"Won the lottery." Someone had written next to that, "Lightning never strikes twice."

"Secret reality TV show contestant."

"Spy called out to a covert rescue mission."

"Eloped." Three different names followed; Eddie's wasn't one.

She handed back his phone. "It that all?"

He shook his head. "We make decent money here, but Joanie started to hit the casinos. She never did before. Chapers went with her a couple of times. They never let on whether they won or lost. Sometimes Joanie would play poker with some of the more with-it residents. I got the feeling she let them win." He stood. "One more thing. Joanie changed the way she dressed too. She used to wear plain pants and tan or black shirts. I used to tell her she'd look good in red or yellow, but she only altered her pattern for the summer picnic and the Christmas party. When all her other changes happened, she started to wear camouflage and Army-Navy surplus stuff. I asked her about it, but she switched on her new attitude and wouldn't answer me."

Giulia walked back to the parking lot with him. "The police are convinced Joanne vanished voluntarily."

"No!" Eddie glanced up at the windows and lowered his voice. "Chapers said that too, and so did the police who came here. The rest of the staff gave up on Joanie. Never mind all the times she listened to them and helped them out with some trouble or other. I don't know why everyone's pretending she doesn't matter. She got in an accident and is in a coma in a hospital in the sticks somewhere. Has to be." He put a hand on the doorknob and said in an even lower voice, "When you find Joanie, tell her she matters to me."

Thirteen

After Giulia spoke with the other breakfast staff, she learned the big pool money was on Joanne either having an unknown boyfriend's secret love child or eloping with a billionaire who'd met her while visiting one of the residents. Third in line was a James Bond scenario from the nursing students, who were thrilled to talk to a real-life private eye.

"Ms. Philbey was really quiet," a pale blonde with polka dot fingernails said.

A redhead with classic green eyes and freckles said, "You know what they say about quiet ones."

"It had to be a cover," from a brunette several inches taller than everyone in the group, including Giulia.

"Right, because she was a good cook." A second blonde, this one with a voice squeaky enough to dub Alvin the Chipmunk. "She had the perfect cover story."

The pale blonde: "We heard she liked to go hunting, so she knew how to shoot."

The tall brunette: "So she wasn't kidnapped because she could defend herself."

The squeaky blonde: "See? The perfect secret agent."

The redhead: "It's so cool."

All four crowded closer to Giulia.

"We liked her a lot, but please don't tell anybody," the brunette said.

"We're only supposed to interact with the nursing staff and the patients," the redhead said, "but Ms. Philbey used to sneak fresh doughnuts to us."

"She was such a great cook," the chipmunk blonde said.

"We miss her." The pale blonde pouted. "The new morning chef is a real workaholic. He never does anything for us. The assistant cook is a real—"

The redhead elbowed her.

"Shut it, moron."

When the Nunmobile passed the "Welcome to Cottonwood" sign two hours later, Giulia's first stop was her favorite food truck for a barbecue hoagie. Her second was home. She opened the windows, poured a humongous lemonade, and set up her laptop at the kitchen table to transfer all her notes. King-sized beds were lovely to sleep in, but real work was best performed on a not-so-comfortable work surface.

Conclusion #1: Marjorie the Cat Lady is a source of information, not a suspect.

Conclusion #2: Ex-boyfriend Louis Larabee was too helpful.

Conclusion #3: Would Larabee say anything to keep from going back to jail?

Conclusion #4: Any woman who dates Larabee should have up-to-date self-defense skills. His façade cracked much too fast.

Conclusion #5: Milo Chapers has issues. No. Has multiple issues. Possibly debts or a gambling problem.

Question #1: Had Chapers slept with Joanne? Had Joanne turned him down?

Question #2: Had Joanne been pregnant when she disappeared? With whose baby?

Giulia reread the last sentence. She hit Enter and typed a subhead.

If Joanne was pregnant by:

1. Larabee: Did he try to convince her to have an abortion? Did

she run away to keep the baby? Did she regret not using protection in a risky relationship?

2. Chapers: What were Sunset's rules about employee fraternization, especially with a higher-up? Did he envision losing his job? Ditto all the above Larabee questions re: Abortion, running, lack of protection.

3. Marstan: What if his puppy-eyed unrequited love act was cover for an unexpected pregnancy, an escalating argument, and a rash action in a moment of anger?

She finished the lemonade. What a sordid mind she'd acquired as a PI. Back in the convent, she'd been much too trusting.

The pregnancy angle might be a leap. Still, it wasn't a question she should ask Diane. Not knowing everything about her twin sister already had her on edge.

She turned on the TV to let the ideas percolate.

"...story will chill the souls of every Scooper parent."

Giulia groaned at Ken Kanning's eager face on her screen. She pressed the on-screen channel guide as Kanning's sincere voice chewed the scenery.

"Two beautiful young girls found dead! One in the park and the other by a dumpster! Sensitive Scoopers beware: What follows is a graphic description of young lives cut short much too soon."

Giulia gave the screen back to *The Scoop*. It filled with side by side shots. On the left, the town park on a summer day: children played, people jogged and walked their dogs, the sun shone. On the right, an asphalt parking lot: cigarette butts in potholes, crumpled fast food wrappers, a stained dumpster; no sun shone when this film had been taken.

"We can't show you the abused bodies of these poor girls," Kanning's voice said. "Their filthy clothes barely cover their blotched, puffy skin. Their faces are swollen almost past recognition. A rash on the skin of the younger girl looks like someone smeared her with maroon paint."

As he spoke, the camera closed in on the dumpster. A rat gnawed something next to it. On the left side, the active townspeople moved past the screen to the sounds of conversation and children laughing.

Kanning's face leaped out at Giulia. "These young women had their whole lives before them and squandered it all on drugs. Their ravaged bodies were found three days apart. Were they connected? Did they stop to take one more hit of the filth they were addicted to? Were they trying to reach their homes?"

The screen cut away from Kanning's expensive dental work to a stock photo of families mourning at a grave. His voice ranted against government bureaucracy, against the sluggishness of the police investigation, against the evils of pushers who cut their drugs with unknown substances.

"The bodies of both young women showed signs of a long and arduous walk. Both appear to have been sexually violated a short time before their tragic deaths. Did they escape from a pimp? Were they being held against their will by a man? By many men?" His rant escalated, this time against drugs and the lengths addicts will go to for the next hit.

Giulia plucked three juicy bits out of today's *Scoop* hash. The girls took drugs, the drugs weren't the usual suspects, and they hadn't only run away from home; they'd returned from someplace much too far to walk.

She hit the mute button and called Vandermark Memorial Hospital. Seven minutes later, she hung up without learning anything. Sisters-in-law weren't on the allowed list for access to patient information. She might have to call her brother again, and she couldn't even fortify herself with wine beforehand.

She put a hand on her stomach. "Little Zlatan, you're not helping."

Next Giulia called Jimmy to thank him for his help with the Penn Hills police department. After that she called Diane to ask about any other relatives who might have information about Joanne. This second call could also be titled, "How to find out if the twin sister might have been pregnant without aggravating the client."

Diane's voice switched from hopeful to huffy. "I'm her identical twin. You don't need to talk to anyone else. We know everything about each other."

Giulia decided to nickname this case the "Wait for it" case. Here she sat, doing exactly that rather than say the obvious into the phone.

Three...two...one...

"Okay, I get it," Diane said. "I guess I don't know everything about Jo since her dickweed manager had to tell me she was missing. Sorry I bit your head off. You could call our older brother, Nick. He lives in Philadelphia."

Giulia wrote the phone number on a napkin, reassured Diane on the progress of the preliminary investigation, and called the twins' brother.

"Diane hired a private eye? She's been fighting with me over that for two months. Said as the twin it was her decision and went ballistic when I talked to one here, so I let it slide. I want peace in my family. What can I do to help?"

Nick's voice resembled Diane's, but an octave lower. It had the same sharp edges, the same briskness with a hint of humor lurking beneath.

"I would like anything you can tell me about conversations you and Joanne might have had in the months before she disappeared. I'm completing my preliminary research."

A pause. "That's too much for four in the afternoon. I work overnights at Children's. I'm a pharmacist."

Giulia mentally reorganized her evening. "What time is good tomorrow? I'll work around your schedule."

"That's real nice of you. You mind Skype? I like to see people when I'm talking to them. I'm on the phone constantly at work."

"Not at all." Giulia's butt did a happy dance in her chair. She agreed with Nick: Nothing beat face-to-face contact.

"Great. I get home around quarter to eight in the morning. Is that too early for you?"

"Quarter to eight works for me. I'll call you at ten of."

Giulia entered the call and his Skype information into her phone and added an alarm, just in case. Then she saved all her work and went up to the bedroom to wake Frank in time for dinner—and other things—before his stakeout.

Fourteen

Four forty-five a.m.

Giulia eased open the nightstand drawer and took out her Glock and its loaded clip. A mid-July morning at quarter to way too early was bright enough for her to see without the risk of fumbling and making a noise. The uninvited intruder downstairs who had tripped on the furniture didn't know Giulia was about to ruin their entire day.

She inserted the clip and walked barefoot to the head of the stairs. The round in the chamber should be plenty, but she knew better than to take that risk. Now the stealthy sounds came from the kitchen. Someone had failed Housebreaking 101. People didn't keep an emergency stash of money in the flour bin or freezer anymore. She descended the stairs quickly and quietly and stopped at the dividing archway between the living room and kitchen. The refrigerator door was open.

Perfect. She stepped into the kitchen and placed herself behind the open door, ready to shoot.

The door closed. Giulia's eleven-year-old niece saw the gun, screamed, and dropped the fork in her hand. A cold meatball exploded on the floor, sauce splattering in a sunburst around it.

Giulia lowered the gun. "Cecilia? What are you doing here?"

"Holy crap, Aunt Giulia! You're badass." The gangly pre-teen pushed wisps of hair away from her eyes. "I guess wussy Sister Regina is really gone, huh? Can I see your gun?"

"No." She set it on top of the refrigerator with one hand and snagged the paper towels from the counter with the other. "Clean up your mess, please."

"Okay." Cecilia got on hands and knees and wiped the linoleum.

Giulia stood over her, arms crossed. "Why did you break into my house at five o'clock in the morning?"

The cleaning paused. "My dad's a dick."

"This is not news."

A pair of startled brown eyes glanced up at Giulia, then Cecilia gave her attention to finishing with the mess. She brought a wad of paper towels and the flattened meatball to the sink.

"The garbage can is underneath."

Disappointment filled Cecilia's face as the towels and meat hit the bottom of the trash bag.

Giulia opened the refrigerator. "Since you're hungry, what would you like to eat? Eggs? Bacon? Oatmeal? Peach pie?"

Cecilia's eyes pleaded along with her voice. "Spaghetti?"

Giulia sighed. "Fine. Macaroni is in the pantry." She pointed. While Cecilia found the box, Giulia filled a small pot with water and a pinch of salt. She sent Cecilia back to the refrigerator for the sauce pot. Conversation consisted of directions to hold the pot while Giulia ladled out a serving of sauce and another meatball. While the sauce heated in the microwave, she pulled out a chair at the kitchen table. "Sit."

Cecilia began talking as though the chair possessed an On button. "Mom's in seventy-two-hour lockdown at the hospital because she OD'd, but mom never did drugs ever, ever, ever. You know mom's all about growing our own food and not using processed stuff. I used to trade my friends her homemade cookies for their Twinkies. Mom even made her own makeup before dad took it away from her."

Giulia stirred the spaghetti in the boiling water. "What?"

Another torrent of words. "Dad's been getting worse and worse for months. He drags us to Latin Mass and we have to study church history with him every night. He won't let Carlo play video games, and he won't let Pasquale go to school dances or anything because, ooh, he might kiss a girl. Dad would go ballistic if he knew about Pasquale's condom stash."

Giulia strained the spaghetti and said in a careful voice, "Didn't Pasquale turn fourteen last January?"

"Yeah."

Giulia mixed the spaghetti into the bowl of sauce while thinking of several medieval punishments for her younger brother. "At least he's smart enough to use condoms."

Cecilia's jaw dropped in the best theatrical way at yet another instance of how much cooler Aunt Giulia was than Sister Mary Regina Coelis. Then her momentum returned. "He won't let anyone not Catholic come over to the house, and he won't let us play any radio stations except EWTN."

Giulia set the bowl and a glass of water in front of her niece, who shoveled in spaghetti and kept right on talking. "He made mom quit her gym membership and her book club and threw out all our novels and CDs. He won't let mom go anywhere but church and grocery shopping. He said she could keep her part-time job, but only because she helps out in the church office." She paused long enough to drink some water. "He measured all my dresses and all mom's and had us make the hems longer. Mom started sneaking out of the house at night sometimes. I saw her twice, but no way was I going to rat her out to dad." She lowered the meatball before taking a bite and whispered, "Honestly, Aunt Giulia, I was afraid he'd hit her if he found out. After we got home from fireworks on the Fourth of July, she snuck out and didn't come back."

In the same calm voice, Giulia said, "What did your father do when your mother didn't come home?"

"Besides turn the house into Saint Pius the Tenth prison? Nothing. He made us keep the same routine and told us not to talk about it." She bit off half the meatball. "This is good."

"Thank you." Giulia kept her body language calm too. "Did you say Saint Pius the Tenth?"

Cecilia took her dishes to the sink. "Yeah. Bo-ring." She rinsed everything and put it in the dishwasher.

Giulia looked at the clock. "Where are you supposed to be at this hour, besides asleep in bed?"

Her niece scrunched up her face. "Babysitting the bratty twins next door, but not 'til six thirty. It's my summer job."

"It's already ten of six. Wait a minute. How did you get here?"

"I biked. It's not even ten miles from our house to yours. No biggie." She dried her hands. "Uncle Frank must sleep great if all our noise didn't wake him up. See, I know his name even though I haven't met him."

"He's on overnight stakeout. How do you plan to get back home?"

"Stakeout like on TV? You guys are so cool." She turned a sweet, winning smile on Giulia. "You'll give me a ride back, please Aunt Giulia? If I'm late to my job, dad will find out and the shit will hit the fan."

Giulia indulged in another sigh. "Scatological interjections are most effective when used sparingly."

"Huh?"

"Stop swearing so much. I'll be dressed in five minutes, then we'll open the garage and hook up the bike rack to my car."

As they secured the bright yellow bicycle to the back of the Nunmobile, Giulia said, "How did you break into my house?"

Cecilia froze for only a moment. Then with another charming smile, she said, "Your super-narrow cellar window has a loose lock. The one on the other side of the vegetable garden, I mean. Those turning locks are super easy to wiggle free." She tugged on the final strap even though Giulia had tightened it a moment earlier. "I would've knocked, really and truly, if I couldn't get in on my own. I wasn't going to break a window or anything."

"Thank God for a solid moral foundation." Giulia caught Cecilia's blush. "What?"

Cecilia twisted her unpainted fingernails. "I got really piss— um, angry at dad last week. He sent me to the grocery store for milk, and I met up with two of my friends he won't let me talk to anymore."

When the pause reached three seconds, Giulia said, "What did you steal?"

Cecilia flinched. In a tiny voice, she said, "A Milky Way Midnight."

"Get in." They buckled their seat belts. "What penance did you get when you went to confession?"

More silence. Giulia turned in her seat. Cecilia appeared to be fascinated with the thread count of her capris.

"Cecilia Falcone."

She dragged her head upright and cringed.

Giulia gave her niece the Stern Teacher Stare. "You will confess the theft this Saturday."

In the same tiny voice, she said, "Yes, Aunt Giulia."

"The priest will probably tell you to donate the amount of the candy bar to charity. Expect a lecture." A new thought intruded. "You're still going to your old church, not a Society of Saint Pius the Tenth one, right?"

Cecilia un-hunched. "Dad can't drag us to his super-special church. It's only for super-special men." She made a gagging face. "The second I turn eighteen, I'm becoming an atheist and never going back to dad's house as long as I live."

Giulia let that slide. She might have thought the same if she were in her niece's position.

"Which way to your dad's house?"

Cecilia gave directions in a subdued voice. Giulia parked around the nearest corner to keep the Nunmobile out of sight. They unstrapped the bicycle and Cecilia put down the kickstand.

"You'll find out what happened to my mom, won't you? You're a detective."

"I'll do my best."

Cecilia squeezed Giulia tight and said into her ribcage, "You're awesome." Her eyes shone a little too bright when she released her. "I'll try to be super good and not call you or anything. Dad still lectures us about you sometimes. He's a total jerk. Bye!" She pedaled out of sight.

Giulia didn't need mnemonics tricks to remember how Cecilia's story strengthened the connection between two teenagers dead from unknown drugs and her sister-in-law collapsing at her feet from a reaction to an unknown drug.

Good Heavens, next she'd be calling Ken Kanning for help.

She turned on the radio. Not on her worst day.

Fifteen

Giulia drove home, showered, dressed for work and hit the coffee shop below Driscoll Investigations for coffee deserving the name. The office was all hers at quarter to seven in the morning. Hers and Joanne Philbey's file folder of bills.

Ammunition. Arrows. Cast-iron baking pans. Three sizes of mortars and pestles. Outdoor winter gear. A Kevlar vest. Heavy-duty gardening tools. Heirloom seeds.

Giulia unwrapped her turkey-kale-bacon sandwich. It had seemed so appetizing when she stood at the Common Grounds counter. Now she wanted a BLT and Swedish Fish gummies.

"Little Zlatan, we have to discuss your meal pairings. Now hush and enjoy this healthy breakfast."

She reread the last set of purchases. Joanne's third-floor apartment had no pots for plants anywhere inside or outside on the balcony.

More bills. Nine hundred dollars for a water purifier. She opened a search window and typed in the address of the company, then followed that link back to a Doomsday Prepper site.

Fifteen minutes later, she remembered her breakfast sandwich cooling at her left elbow. She bookmarked the site, needing more time to process the mindset. Next she spread out all the bills from last March through this March. Patterns emerged right away.

A regular donation to a radio preacher stopped in December. A dating site payment—no, two sites—no, three. Marjorie had been right. Joanne's March MasterCard bill showed pro-rated refunds from all of them. Cable TV payments stopped in February. Fandango movie ticket purchases stopped then too.

She looked up the phone number attached to a charge from an unpronounceable string of letters. It turned out to be an Etsy shop of crafts made out of deer antlers. Buttons. Coat hangers. Beads. Lamp stands. Toilet paper holders.

Her phone chimed. Quarter to eight. She opened Skype and called Diane and Joanne's older brother. After three rings, the face of a tired man who looked nothing like either of the twins filled the screen.

"Morning. Thanks for calling on time." Nick's voice, though weary, still had definite echoes of Diane's.

"I won't keep you long." Giulia recapped her research so far, including a toned-down version of the office rumor pool.

His face showed sardonic amusement at first, then disgust, then frustration.

"What a bunch of old maid gossips. They spend their time inventing B-movie plots instead of figuring out a way to help."

Giulia fed the frustration. "I wondered why no one thought she might be pregnant."

It worked. "I'll tell you why. Jo carried an extra forty or fifty pounds on her and people automatically think no man is going to look twice at a fat girl." His thick eyebrows met and overshadowed his brown eyes. "Jo had her share of relationships. She always called me when things started to sour. She'd vent about the guy's ego or how he screwed around on her and I'd tell her to look for a guy with more in his head than his pants. Lather, rinse, repeat." His eyebrows reversed themselves. "What was the question?"

Giulia kept her voice neutral. She was getting a lot of practice at that this week. "Why do you think none of Joanne's coworkers thought she might have been pregnant?"

"Oh, yeah. Because they're superficial asshats. Jo could've been pregnant, I suppose, but she's smart. She uses protection."

"Condoms break."

"And the pill isn't infallible." He pointed to himself. "Pharmacist." His wry smile was exactly like Diane's. "Look. Jo was—is—everyone's friend. She always has an ear for everyone to talk into and a shoulder to lean on. She had no reason whatsoever to vanish. The police are wrong. They weren't happy when I disagreed with their theory, but I care about Jo, not their hurt feelings. You find my sister. If Di runs into money trouble, call me."

After the call ended, Giulia tapped her pen on a blank legal page as she stared out the window. Rush-hour traffic noise penetrated the closed glass. The room was heating up like the witch's oven in "Hansel and Gretel," but her brain registered the stuffy air and dismissed it.

The pen tapped. The Thursday morning trash pickup truck rumbled past. Her screensaver blinked on with Godzilla's iconic roar. Giulia started, stood, and opened the window as Sidney opened the outer door.

"Hey, you're back. The most wonderful thing happened yesterday! Jessamine's tooth finally came in. We slept for seven whole hours. It would've been eight if the alpacas hadn't started a fight. Rudolph and Blitzen both want to mate with Snowflake." She opened the window on her side of the office. "I haven't appreciated sleep this much since the week before Jessamine was born."

Giulia leaned against her own doorframe. "I'm taking notes for future reference."

Sidney unwrapped a whole wheat bagel and the distinctive aroma of alpaca cheese filled the room. Giulia's stomach flip-flopped. Funny. She never used to mind alpaca cheese.

"Forget notes," Sidney said. "Stock up on sleep."

Giulia returned to her desk and stared at the random blue dots she'd made on the yellow paper. Everyone liked Joanne because of what she did: listened, helped, cooked, taught. No one seemed to consider what Joanne needed. All her friends and coworkers seemed to take without giving back.

The outer door opened. Zane struck a He-Man pose. "I am invincible!"

Sixteen

Giulia joined Sidney in the main office. "The deadbeat dad sting worked?"

Zane paced the length of the narrow wood floor. "Textbook, Ms. D. Eight of us showed up to play poker. Jack and beer flowed. Ridiculous amounts of money changed hands. When I won a big pot, which may or may not have had something to do with counting cards, I offered to buy pizza. I called the cops who were waiting to pounce, then I told the guys thirty minutes to food. At minute twenty-eight, I went to the bathroom. At minute thirty-one, the doorbell rang. I yelled through the bathroom door to our deadbeat dad to take the money out of my winnings. One of his buddies let loose a nasty laugh and somebody must have elbowed him, because he got quiet too fast. Next thing I heard was a whole lot of yelling and cursing. The card table got knocked over. A couple of quarters rolled under the bathroom door. The rest of the poker gang ran out the back and I came back into the living room. The guys had taken some of the money and our handcuffed deadbeat dad was getting his rights read to him. I took my winnings, of which I knew the exact amount. The cops dragged him away and I returned home to sleep the sleep of the conqueror." He finally stopped for breath in front of Giulia. "Ms. D., I love my job."

Sidney applauded. Giulia sketched an actor's bow. "Zane, that was epic. Now go write it up so his wife and four children get every cent he owes them."

She went back to her desk and called Diane for the make, model, and license plate of Joanne's car.

"It's missing too," Diane said. "At least the cops in Penn Hills still haven't found it."

"One more thing. Did Joanne ever talk to you about Doomsday Preppers?"

Diane said after a moment, "I forgot about that. Her first long-term guy after college was a major Prepper. He got Jo hooked on it for a while. When they split, she still talked about going off grid sometimes. You know, if she could save enough money or hit it big enough at the casino to get herself set up. She tried to talk me into going in on it with her, but I have no patience with that end of the world stuff." The sound of car horns cut her off. "Quit shoving mascara on your eyelashes at rush hour, idiot! Sorry, Ms. Driscoll. Nobody knows how to drive anymore. So, yeah, doomsdayers. If the bombs drop, I'm driving to Ground Zero. No reason to hang around without indoor plumbing and limeades from Sonic, that's what I say." More horns, but Diane kept on topic. "The last time Joanne got dumped, she swore she was going to find a decent guy if she had to register on every dating site around."

"By any chance, would you have her logins?"

"Nope. She kept parts of her sex life to herself. I'm pulling into my work parking lot now. Give me a few minutes and I'll send you every username I know she rotated through. Can't help you with passwords, though."

When Diane hung up, Giulia called Frank. "Oh, good, I didn't wake you. Could you log in to your database and check on an abandoned car? My client's sister said the police never located it." She gave him the license plate number.

Frank's tired voice said, "I love your unexpected romantic requests. Just a sec."

She heard him typing and the chime of a finished search. "It's in one of the Pittsburgh impound lots. Found three weeks ago behind a grade school."

"Rats."

Frank laughed. "Such language."

She made a face at the phone. "Thank you and go to bed."

"Yes, ma'am."

The email from Diane arrived as she growled at the phone, "Don't call me ma'am."

Without preamble, it listed seven similar usernames and a corresponding list of dating sites with the largest TV advertising presence.

Giulia wilted. Not for the first time, she wished cloning technology existed, because this case needed two or three Giulias. But wait...She pulled the stacks of Joanne's bills toward her. Right. She knew which three sites to search. Not so intimidating after all. She closed the email for now and continued with her planned research.

This time from the box of Joanne's papers Giulia took every single receipt and sorted them based on information from Chef Eddie and Cat Lady Marjorie. In a short time, she had a definite trail. Army-Navy stores. The water purifier. Camping gear that didn't require batteries or electricity. In addition to the heirloom seeds, disease-resistant wheat and barley. A book on substituting honey for sugar in recipes. Another on the spiritual connection of twins. A third about surgically separated conjoined twins.

She stood and straightened her back. Nine thirty. Time for tea. Since little Zlatan was forcing her to curb her caffeine intake, she'd been driven to herbal tea. So far every flavor was a penance, albeit a much different penance than the ones she'd received after confession in her convent days. Perspective was everything now that she didn't have to scrub the convent kitchen with a toothbrush because she'd neglected one of the many sets of daily prayers.

She sipped the next flavor in her sampler: mango ginger.

Not worth taking a second sip. Her whole body longed for another tall French roast with cinnamon syrup.

Sidney and Zane were both typing when she took the cup to the bathroom sink to dump its contents.

"Which tea failed today?" Sidney said.

"Mango ginger." Giulia came to the bathroom door, drying the cup. "This child owes me so much coffee."

Zane laughed. "My sister said the same thing for both her pregnancies, but for her it was cheeseburgers."

Giulia swallowed. The thought of lovely chargrilled red meat wasn't so lovely at this hour of the morning. "May I hijack both of you for a few minutes?"

"I'm almost finished with the deadbeat dad report," Zane said. "Do you want me to stop?"

"No. That comes first. Sidney, could you look up news stories involving twins? Go back a year from February and grab everything. I'm not sure exactly what I'm looking for."

Giulia dived into the Doomsday Prepper site. Once past the first flabbergasted moments, she studied the site like a lesson. The model standing next to the gigantic water filtration tank like it was a game show prize made her giggle. She screencapped one of the lists of dried and canned foods to hoard. She and Frank hadn't gotten around to stocking their cellar in case of a crazy winter storm.

She couldn't decide which page was the most extreme. How to survive a volcano, with the first piece of advice: "Move away." Tactical discussion points, with a link to "tactical bacon" which was an actual product available for purchase on Amazon. She appreciated the sales trick of the glamorous model posing in tactical bug out wear.

But then there was the Tactical Scarf tutorial. Bug out bags— knapsacks or duffel bags with essential supplies for when the bombs drop and you have to get to your bunker in a hurry. First aid, energy food, water purifier tablets...the list could apply to an extended hike in an area without cell phone reception. Conscientious Preppers made a bug out bag for their dog too, though none of the bags offered for purchase were intended for yappy little dogs.

Next, the advice to buy several hundred sandbags to keep both water and bullets out. An article explaining why not to dress the whole family in camouflage when you live in the 'burbs: If your family looks like the only prepared family on the block, your neighbors will reenact the Electromagnetic Pulse version of "The Monsters Are Due on Maple Street." Apparently EMP and limited nuclear war were duking it out for the most likely way humanity would destroy itself.

When she clicked the "Unique Survival Tools" page, she knew she had a clear winner.

"Trivia, guys: Do you know the four ways tampons can be used as a survival tool for the zombie apocalypse?"

Silence. Even the typing stopped. Then Zane's voice with a hitch in it: "Is this a test?"

Sidney said, "Stop a bloody nose."

Giulia said, "Really? How? Oh, wait."

"One of Olivier's brothers referees high school soccer. In one girls' game two of the players clocked heads and they both got bloody noses. Their coaches each took a tampon from their first-aid kits and the girls stuck them up the bleeding nostril."

Zane's voice got very small. "I feel the need for a mental health day."

Still at her desk, Giulia said, "You knew the risks when you took a job in an office with two women."

Typing resumed. Giulia checked her notes and the connection fell into place. When Joanne started to change in February and on through March, the advice on the Prepper site about how to survive the coming doom matched it all. Acquire self-sufficiency, sharpen your hunting and cooking skills, join a tight-knit community, and be part of a chosen group.

"It's a cult." Giulia blew out a breath. She knew cults. "This isn't good."

Zane knocked on the doorframe. "Report finished and ready for your stamp of approval. Please tell me you need help with something other than feminine hygiene quizzes."

Seventeen

Giulia squashed the temptation to list the four tampon survival tricks she'd read a few pages earlier. "I need your expertise. I have a hunch about a local Doomsday Prepper group, but there's no footprint on the web. I don't have anything else to go on."

Zane rubbed his hands together. "Simon says: Hack!"

"What?"

"*Underdog*, Ms. D. The old cartoons from the sixties. Simon Bar Sinister is Underdog's nemesis. We've been watching the shows after gaming nights and they're awesome."

"Whatever works. Thanks."

Sidney said from her desk, "I've got nothing significant. Do you want me to put the Workers' Comp investigation on hold and keep going?"

"No. Now that Zane's saving my bacon on the Prepper search, I'll take over the twin hunt."

"Emailing you what I came up with so far. I stopped at Memorial Day."

Giulia opened the Word doc. So much for her expectations of quirky or feel-good stories about twins. Didn't newspapers need filler anymore? How could Buzzfeed let her down like this?

But at Christmas, Buzzfeed came through with a heartwarming story about separated at birth twins reconnecting at a *Messiah* sing-along. Then a lot more nothing until she adjusted the search parameters and found a college research call for adult twins back in September.

A rabbit trail at last. She opened parallel search windows and ran identical searches on both names. A cartload of results filled the windows: the research abstract. Articles on the psychological makeup of twins. Twitter posts from both men in the article. Reunion photos on Instagram. A burgeoning side research trail on a mythology Giulia was unfamiliar with. She bookmarked the trail as Zane knocked on her doorframe.

"I found something, but it's from *The Scoop*."

Giulia groaned. "That show is punishment for sins I don't remember committing." She typed in the show's web address. "What day?"

"Two months ago today. I'll keep looking. Will there be foul language?"

Sidney laughed at the same time Giulia said, "How long have you been working here?"

"Good point." Zane retreated.

For this episode, *The Scoop* pre-empted its usual histrionic opening. First a compilation of atomic bomb explosions followed by footage of destroyed Hiroshima. Then lingering shots of ebola victims. As the crowning touch, the Twin Towers collapsing on 9/11.

"Kanning," Giulia said to her monitor, "you are a festering sore on the cable TV landscape."

Ken Kanning's mellifluous voice crushed her muttered invective.

"Disaster! Doom! The end of civilization as we know it! Scoopers, today we're introducing you to the *Alice in Wonderland* world of Doomsday Preppers."

A shot of Kanning's back, his head of brown hair with its perfect off-center wave bobbing as he walked into a massive department store. The camera bobbed in the opposite direction as his cameraman followed.

"Doomsday Preppers are convinced the world as we know it

will end at any given moment. The Bomb. An Electromagnetic Pulse frying every circuit on the planet. The Plague." He stopped in front of an outdoor kayak display and affected shock. "The end of the world as we know it, indeed, Scoopers. Any one of those scenarios would mean no more of *The Scoop*."

An older couple passed him without bothering to glance at either him or the camera. A twenty-something woman stopped, looked, and snapped a picture of Kanning with her cell phone.

Kanning continued. "Because *The Scoop* is dedicated to giving our viewers everything they need to know, we're heading into the Pittsburgh REI to price out what you'll need to survive the inevitable apocalypse."

He headed straight for the camping section. As he held up price tags on tents, sleeping bags, cooking gear, and more, a ticker ran across the bottom of the screen with a running total.

"Your kids won't need their college funds when civilization collapses," Kanning said after completing his fantasy survival list. "It's a good thing, because otherwise you'll have to take out a second mortgage to make sure your bunker is zombie-proof."

The show cut to the sidewalk in front of a gun store as the owner refused to let the camera inside. The ticker added prices for guns and ammunition as Kanning advised his audience to buy a few hundred sand bags to barricade their fortified house against floodwaters and bullets from hostile neighbors. Giulia made a face at the screen at the knowledge she and *The Scoop* used the same research sites.

"What's that you say? Storage is a problem for that many sand bags? Use your garage. Cars will be obsolete once gasoline can't be pumped because the electrical grid has failed. And if you haven't found that special person to share the scorched earth with—" An inset appeared next to Kanning's face. "There's always the Doomsday Prepper dating sites." He mimicked the iconic *Home Alone* mirror scene.

The last segment began with Kanning walking along a tall hedge made of ivy and something deep green with berries.

"We're in the woods near Beaver Falls," he whispered. "We don't know who owns this property, but we'll find out. The Keystone State's very own homegrown Doomsday Prepper compound may lurk behind this hedge, or it may be nothing more than a family's private campground. But true Scoopers know no one builds a fence like this unless they have something to hide."

His finger pointed to a brown spot in the deep green leaves. He reached in with both hands and created a hole. The camera lens closed in on the hedge. A spider scuttled away to the right. The lens entered the improvised opening. The image blurred, refocused, and Giulia saw people.

Off to the far right, a man chopped wood. In the center, a woman worked a spinning wheel. Behind her, two people weeded a garden. Giulia reached for her mouse to enlarge the video. The picture went black. Then leaves and twigs slapped the lens followed by the sounds of multiple rounds being chambered into shotguns.

Kanning's face returned in Serious Reporter Mode. "We apologize for this abrupt ending to our search, Scoopers. Four bullies grabbed us and smashed our camera lens, but not the camera. They claimed we were on private property and chased us all the way out to the road. They may think we're intimidated, but they don't know *The Scoop*. We won't rest until we learn what's really happening in those woods."

Giulia paused the video. Was that a whole pound of pancake makeup on Kanning's sculpted cheekbone? Why yes it was, plastered on top of a massive bruise. She tried not to smile as she rewound the video to the quick shot of the people on the inside of the hedge. One of the women in the garden resembled Joanne Philbey, but she was thinner than the photos Giulia had seen and a complex tattoo decorated her left arm.

"Zane? Sidney? Did either of you ever use a dating website?"

Eighteen

Giulia's staff appeared in her doorway as if by magic. Sidney's brown eyes were as big as an anime character's.

Zane's pale hair was trying to stand on end. "What did you say, Ms. D?"

Giulia couldn't answer him for a moment because she was laughing too hard.

"Guys." A deep breath to forestall the hiccups. "What kind of opinion do you have of me? I'm a married, pregnant, former nun."

Sidney tottered to Giulia's right-hand client chair and sat. "Don't scare us like that, even though we should have known better."

Zane leaned on the back of the other client chair. "My sister uses dating sites. The juxtaposition of what those sites are like with the question coming from you," he smoothed his hair with one hand, "it shorted out my synapses."

Giulia tried a few more deep breaths. "I admit I didn't think through the implications of the question when I asked it. However, I am serious." She typed as she talked. "Joanne Philbey registered on three different dating sites, and I need to create a false profile for all of them." She touched her bouncy curls. "Zane, you have Photoshop skills, right?"

Zane and Sidney started to grin.

"This is going to be fun," Sidney said. "The captain of my college swim team met her last two boyfriends online. "

"Excellent," Giulia said. "Do you have time to help me with this right now?"

Zane picked Giulia's phone off her desk. "Smile, Ms. D." He took several pictures.

"You have a mad scientist look on your face."

"All in the name of a successful case." His grin widened. "How do you want me to change you?"

"I want to resemble Joanne. I should be thirty to forty pounds heavier, with straight hair and not much makeup. Small earrings."

"Right, like you're repressing everything," Sidney said. "The fake you should wear a button-down shirt in a neutral color. Like you used to wear when I started working here."

Giulia shook her head. "It's a good thing I'm not too vain."

Zane elbowed Sidney and the imaginary light bulb appeared over her head. "Oh, wow. I'm sorry. I didn't mean anything by it, honest."

"I know. And I know I used to dress like the world's biggest frump. For this experiment we should recapture the old me."

Zane walked out. "Magic will happen. Don't go anywhere."

Sidney moved her chair next to Giulia. "Let's create low self-esteem Giulia."

"With a new name."

"Oh, yes, right. A neutral name too."

Giulia logged on to the first site, the mainstream one with the largest TV and internet presence. The home page tried to lure her in with bright, upbeat copy. "I need a name before I can go anywhere. What about Maria, like in *The Sound of Music*? The last name should be something less suspicious than Smith."

"Rogers? Olson? Martin?"

"Martin, yes. Like Mary Martin the actress. I can remember that."

She filled out the form using the separate Visa card she maintained for undercover work. "Blast, I need an email address."

"Yahoo," Sidney said.

"No, they want a phone number for verification." A few

minutes later, "Aha. Found a free email that won't check up on me."

"Maria Martin's" dummy email completed the entrance form and the full site opened to her. "Good Heavens. So much required information."

Sidney pushed her chair against Giulia's "Let me take over. I've seen these places before. Zane," she yelled. "What color are you making Giulia's eyes?"

"Hazel."

Sidney filled out screen after screen, Giulia listing Joanne's preferences for activities, reading, and movies. When they reached the personal statement page, they both worked out a lure for people Joanne may have dated.

"I'm into the outdoors. Hunting with bow and arrow and shotgun, plus fishing and camping. I like to cook. I like cats. A lot. Sex is important too. So are sci-fi and kooky comedies. Make me laugh. Satisfy me."

"Oh, wow, you're going to get major creeper activity."

Giulia smiled. "Good. If Joanne got involved with a sex offender or a general creeper, this profile is engineered to lure him out."

"Zane, we need the new Giulia picture," Sidney called.

"Your wish is my command," he called back.

Giulia's email notification popped into the lower right-hand corner of her screen, followed by Zane in person.

"If you don't like it, Ms. D., I can scrap it and start over, no problem."

Giulia opened the attachment. "Maria Martin" had chipmunk cheeks and a double chin. Her flat blonde hair had dark roots and needed a trim. Her smile tried to be attractive but instead projected nerves and, yes, low self-esteem. Her tan button-down shirt washed out her face and hair.

"Someone get this woman a life," Giulia said. "She's perfect."

Zane grinned again. "I have skills."

"Oh, stop preening," Sidney said.

"Jealous."

"We're all working together, class," Giulia said. "Do I have to get out my Ruler of Doom?"

As one, Zane and Sidney said, "No, Sister."

"That's better. Zane, I'm glad you chose an honest career. You could have made a fortune in fake IDs."

Silence. Giulia looked over the top of her monitor. A ghost of color flared on Zane's cheeks.

"Which you did in college?"

"Maybe."

Sidney said, "I wish I'd known you then. I paid stupid money for mine, and the first night I tried to use it I got laughed out of three different bars."

Giulia face-palmed in mock despair. "I never expected Driscoll Investigations would also be a rehabilitation center for minor lawbreakers."

"You should tell your brother you're doing such charitable work," Sidney said. "He might approve."

"Not a chance. He'd find a way to make my hiring you despite not knowing your past indiscretions a sin on my part." She waved away thoughts of her brother. "Zane, this photo looks enough like me and enough unlike me not to arouse too much suspicion when and if I meet with someone from one of these places."

"Meet?" Sidney said.

"Why else would we go to all this work? Our client is certain her sister is alive. I'm almost certain. Since Joanne signed up for these meat markets, trying to find the men she may have met is my next logical step."

Zane came around to Giulia's side of the screen. "Did you upload the photo?"

"Doing it now." A moment later, the site's first ten suggested matches came on screen.

Zane pointed to each in turn. "Creeper. Drunk. Creeper. Underage. Has a record. Him too. Possible. Creeper. Also possible. Lives in his mother's basement."

Sidney and Giulia studied the photos. "I agree," Sidney said.

"Me too," Giulia said. "Let's see what the creeper quotient is on the next site."

They set up the same profile for the site restricted to twins and triplets and for the site catering to Preppers and off-gridders. Zane's opinion of the first set of suggested contacts did not differ between all three.

"I'll check back tomorrow morning. What I'm really looking for are personal messages. Thank you both for interrupting whatever you were working on."

Sidney put the chair back, laughing. When she caught Giulia's quizzical look, she shook her head and said, "Later."

Zane said, "Everything was worth dropping for this." The phone rang and he picked it up at Giulia's desk. "Good morning, Dris—"

A high, hysterical voice cut him off. "I have to talk to Aunt Giulia right now!"

Nineteen

Giulia held out her hand for the phone. Zane closed the door behind him.

"Cecilia, it's Aunt Giulia. What's—"

"You have to stop dad! You have to come over here right away!" Sobs muddled the last words.

"Cecilia." Short and sharp. The sobs cut off. "What is happening?"

"Dad's making us pack up all mom's clothes and things and he's going to take everything to the St. Vincent DePaul shelter. That means he won't let mom come back home." Behind her voice, Giulia heard a car drive by and a door slam.

"Cecilia, stop and think. Your dad is angry. Give him time to calm down. Your mom's stuff can always be replaced."

"But he tore up their wedding pictures and buried them in the compost pile. He made Carlo throw the engraved wine glasses from their wedding into the garbage bin. It's like he's trying to erase her from our lives."

"Where are you calling from?" The last thing her niece needed was an enraged Salvatore overhearing this conversation.

"I'm in the garage with the camping stuff. Dad says we're getting rid of it all because we're not going to do anything mom did with us ever again." The sobbing restarted.

A light bulb of her own popped on over Giulia's head. "Cecilia, is any camping gear missing?"

Through the sobs, the sounds of boxes and nylon bags moving around. "Um, yeah, maybe. The Scouts stuff is messed up and the cooking gear isn't where it used to be." More cardboard and metal sounds. "The wok is gone. That was a present from Grandma. Dad's gonna be piss—um, mad. Oh shit."

"What's wrong?"

"Who is this?" Giulia's brother said.

Giulia closed her eyes. "Hello, Salvatore."

"You disgusting heretical whore. How dare you sully Cecilia's ears with your foul mouth?"

"What a Christlike example you're setting for your children."

"What?"

"You're told to find the lost sheep and bring her home. Instead you're locking the doors to keep her out."

Her brother's voice cracked as he spewed out-of-context Bible verses at her. She cut him off.

"If you don't stop this Saint Pius the Tenth insanity, your kids will run away just like Anne did."

"Only if you put that disrespectful idea into their heads. They are obedient and devout, unlike you. You spit on the Cross with every breath you take."

Giulia slammed down the receiver. So much more satisfying than pressing "End" on a cell phone. She rubbed her eyes with the heels of her hands. All three of those kids would appear in her kitchen one morning if her brother kept this up.

She pushed back her chair and pressed her forehead against the window screen. Traffic noises cleared the rage out of her head. When she could think again, she returned to her desk and wrote: Anne → Camping → Prepper supplies → Unknown drugs → Where did she run to? → Who did she run to? → Who did she run with?

The phone rang again. Zane buzzed her. "Potential new client, Ms. D. Do you want to pick up?"

"No. Please get our standard intake information." Whoever she talked to might get blindsided by leftover fury at her brother.

She grabbed her purse and opened her door. Zane and Sidney

were both on the phone. Although she didn't want to look at even a picture of food, she mimed eating and left.

Ten minutes later, she arrived at the triangular downtown park. A panicky day care worker was cajoling a three-year-old wearing an Ariel dress out of the elaborate fountain. Six more three- and four-year-olds leaned on the rim, giggling. Three others were feeding peanut butter sandwiches to the pigeons. Two more day care workers tried to corral the pigeon feeders and the fountain gawkers to a picnic table where juice boxes and watermelon slices were set up.

She sat on the edge of the fountain after the day care worker fished out the *Little Mermaid* cosplayer. July sun warmed away the chill of her brother's phone call. She leaned her head back and spread her arms like a lizard sunning on a rock.

Anne probably wouldn't have logged on to a dating site from her church job. Not from her phone either, since Salvatore would likely have monitored her phone usage. Therefore, when she sneaked out at night, she met up with a sympathetic friend or with whoever supplied her the mysterious drugs.

Giulia sat up. She needed to go back to Joanne's apartment and try to channel a drug-sniffing dog. No, first she needed to hack into Joanne's dating site accounts and see whose profiles she'd saved. All three of these incidents were connected; she was ninety percent positive. Well, maybe eighty-three percent.

Zane to the rescue.

Twenty

She returned to Sidney on the phone talking baby talk to Jessamine. While she waited for Zane to get back from lunch, she plowed through emails and read over the latest intake form. It had been a smart choice to let Zane field this one. The caller danced around the "d" word, but at the core he wanted DI to catch his wife doing the nasty with her boss.

She called the number and left a message of polite refusal. DI was no longer taking divorce cases.

Zane saw the crumpled note in Giulia's recycle bin when he returned. "I knew you'd see the hidden divorce language."

"It's one of our only rules."

"Far be it from me to request a rerun of drunk cheater scumbags busting in here to try to beat us up." He stared at her staring at her screen. "Can I help you with anything?"

"Actually, yes, but how many times can I disrupt your schedule before we start falling behind?"

"Ms. D., you worry a lot. I've put work on the back burner several times to help you with something more urgent." He inhaled and sang. "And the culminating pleasure that we treasure beyond measure is the gratifying feeling that our duty has been done."

Giulia gave the only possible response: "I shall begin calling you Giuseppe."

Zane high-fived her. "Nobody knows Gilbert and Sullivan anymore."

Giulia spread her hands. "Musician, remember? Every so often community theater expands its repertoire." She smiled a wicked smile. "I will find something to quote at you to mess with Sidney. Okay, to work. I need access to Joanne's accounts on those three dating sites we signed me up for. Here is her email address and a list of her possible usernames. I place them in your skilled hands."

Hollow laughter came from the same throat that produced the baritone song. "Hush the gallery. The maestro is about to conduct a symphony."

"I'll get any incoming calls."

From her own desk, Sidney said, "Thanks, Giulia. I didn't have time to pack a lunch and I'm starving."

The phone remained silent for the next forty-five minutes while Sidney left and returned with a sandwich bulging with cheese and sprouts. At minute forty-six, Sidney said from her desk, "Check your own profile on all three sites."

Giulia leaned left to see around her monitor. "It's been less than three hours."

"Trust me."

She logged in to the off-grid site first. "Fourteen? Already?"

"Not bad. Any D-pics?"

Giulia fell back in her chair. "You have got to be kidding me."

Sidney and Zane ran in. "You did?"

Giulia reached for the keyboard. "I was reacting to the idea. Now I'm afraid to click any of these mug shots."

Her loyal staff said, "Do it. Do it. Do it."

She reached for the mouse. "I'm sending you two out for eye-bleach." A click. "He's fully clothed. I'm safe."

Sidney pointed to the screen. "Click the other tab."

Click. "Oh, my dear God."

Zane peered at it. "Photoshopped."

So did Sidney. "Sure?"

He outlined the length. "See that edge? Look behind it. The wallpaper pattern is smeared."

Sidney leaned in. "Son of a gun. What a loser."

Giulia said in a plaintive voice, "May I delete him now?"

"Yes, with extreme prejudice," Sidney said.

Giulia clicked through eight more profiles without genitalia assaulting her eyes. The tenth, however...

"Whoa. That's real," Zane said.

"I need to lie down in a dark room," Giulia said.

"Every comment in my head is not safe for work," Sidney said. "Except this: My swim team captain got twice that many, but she showed mega cleavage in her picture."

"All right." Giulia straightened up and grasped the mouse. "I am an adult. I can handle this."

She clicked again and again. Six more photos appeared in her queue, three with movie camera icons next to them.

"Videos, oh, yes, videos," Sidney said. "Zane, you should probably leave the room."

"I have seen the nadir of masculine crassness. Besides, you couldn't drag me out of here without seeing these guys in action."

Giulia said a quick mental prayer to St. Jude, the patron saint of hopeless causes, but in her heart she knew she wouldn't get out of the office today without seeing shaky-cam of some stranger's naughty bits. Then she clicked the first video.

A black light. A mirror. A thumping bass soundtrack. A camera panning at its leisure up the length of a tall, hairy male.

"Oh, my God."

She clicked the big red X icon on the video at least twenty times in three seconds, just to make one hundred percent certain it stopped. She believed in ripping a bandage off fast, so she clicked video number two right away.

This prospect wore a t-shirt at least one size too small to emphasize his sculpted torso. He tried the same effect with his jeans.

"Stuffed," Zane said.

"Totally," Sidney said.

The Vision in Musculature spoke. "Yo, Maria, I got what you want."

"I was sure his voice would be at least an octave lower," Giulia said.

He continued, "I bench 335. I fix stuff. I build stuff. I got a full-time job and I got this." He gestured toward the stuffed jeans. "You're gonna love hookin' up with me. Let's do it."

The video ended. Sidney's head was buried in her arms on Giulia's desk. Her body shook with laughter.

Zane made a dismissive noise. "Steroids."

"Being handy around the house is not enough," Giulia said. "Not remotely enough."

"Yo, Maria," Zane said in his natural Humphrey Bogart baritone.

Giulia laughed at the incongruous juxtaposition of Bogie and Stallone.

"All right, one more. Brace yourselves."

A stocky male of medium height and waist-length dreadlocks faced the camera straight on. "I'm twenty-six, blood type A, in good health, no STDs. The men in my family have strong male sperm, so we have a good chance at breeding several sons. Reply with your health record, blood type, and a list of the staple dishes in your repertoire. Include your pelvic dimensions as proof you're able to bear and raise strong sons."

Giulia couldn't speak for several seconds. Sidney had collapsed to the floor, laughing so hard she had trouble catching her breath. Zane clutched his chest and staggered to one of the client chairs like a bad actor in an overwrought death scene.

"Ms. D., you remember how I said I love this job? I take it back. This job is the best job on the planet."

Sidney gasped from the floor, "I wonder how many replies he gets?"

Zane said, "You caught a real survivalist there. He's looking to make the two of you into a breeding pair for the apocalypse. A new Noah's Ark might be on scaffolding in a hidden cave as we speak."

Giulia's stupor shattered. She closed the dating website. "Out, you two. I'm morally bereft at the present moment, which makes this the right time to send past due invoices to our few recalcitrant clients."

Twenty-One

After supper, Giulia walked Frank through the dating site research. He reacted exactly the way Sidney had. Giulia sat back against the couch, arms crossed, and waited.

A few minutes later, Frank clawed himself up off the floor and put his ginger head on her shoulder. "Babe, this is priceless. Show me the videos, please, I'm begging you."

"Not in your wildest dreams. I deleted them."

Frank raised clenched fists to the sky. "Noooooo."

"Yes. They were horrific. However, the last one, the one who hoped the future of humanity resided in my hips, gave me a lead."

Frank's arms dropped. "You contacted the nutcase?"

She gave him the stink-eye. "Be serious. My client's missing sister might have gone Prepper. I know which pits of virtual depravity she joined, and I spent my afternoon in said pits."

She opened the first site. "Tonight you will be my moral support as I see who's attracted to my alter-ego, and we will hope at least one of them went for Joanne too."

"Hold that thought. I need a beer for this."

Giulia groaned. "Sure, drink a Murphy's in front of me. Your progeny has stopped my intake of alcohol and caffeine."

Frank stood in the archway between the kitchen and living room, took a long drink from the cold bottle, and said, "A good Catholic would offer it up."

Giulia threw a soccer ball pillow at him.

Frank became positively giddy as Giulia navigated the sites. On the mainstream site, the one with the least hits, men were determined to charm her with their pets. Giulia counted nine photos with dogs, four with cats, one with a ferret—"Didn't ferrets go out of style in the 1990s?"—and two with boa constrictors.

"One of those snake guys should have posed himself like that Nastassja Kinski poster from 1982."

"You know the year it went on sale? You were," she calculated, "four years old."

"Certain images are generational. Every male of my acquaintance owned that poster. It was a twelfth birthday rite of passage."

"There is still so much I don't know about you." Giulia kissed him on the temple.

"How else can I keep you interested? I have to compete with your first husband." He waited a beat. "Jesus? You know, The Big Guy? Hard sandals to fill."

Giulia laughed so hard she choked. Frank set her laptop on the coffee table and thumped her back.

"I will—ha ha ha—say a rosary—bah ha ha—for you."

Frank said, "Only one?" which sent her off again.

He made another trip to the kitchen and came back with grapefruit juice. She sipped it until her breathing returned to normal.

"All right, sir, you are charged with protecting my wifely honor while I navigate these cesspools." She closed the animal-heavy page and opened the site for twins and triplets. "This one will probably have D-pics too. Fair warning."

"I will endeavor not to make personal comparisons."

With a Herculean effort, Giulia didn't lose another five minutes laughing. "Clicking on the first one."

Frank raised his eyebrows. "*Cac naofa.* This one is a 911 call waiting to happen."

Fourth in the row of six photos was one of a smiling male whose message said, in part, how much he loved his dogs and coaching Little League. In the photo, he had his arm around a petite blonde. The blonde's face was obliterated with black marker gouges.

"I will now back away from the internet." Giulia deleted the contact. "Oh, look. A video."

Frank riffed on the one-minute video in the best *Mystery Science Theater 3000* tradition. Giulia deleted it, opened the next one, and deleted it after two seconds.

"What are these people thinking?"

"*Muirnín*, you know exactly what they're thinking."

Giulia made a gagging gesture. "Only the Prepper site to go."

It treated her to four junk photos and three videos.

"The videos are my last hope."

Frank set down the empty beer bottle. "My razor wit is up to the challenge."

A shivery little Chihuahua yapped counterpoint to a nineteen-year-old's attempt at stoicism. His jeans hung low on his hips, giving Giulia an unobstructed view of the acne encroaching on his junk.

"I like walking in the woods as long as we're there to hunt. You should be able to grow everything we can't shoot or catch for ourselves. I can render deer and pluck game birds. You need to know how to cook them in multiple ways. I like natural blondes, but you're cute so I'll try you out. Message me if you're serious."

Giulia clicked back to his profile. "He claims he's twenty-five."

Frank snorted. "If he's a day over nineteen, I'll buy those brats down the street a new vuvuzela."

"Heaven forfend."

Frank bounced on the couch cushion. "Play another one. Play another one."

Her smile was indulgent. "You are easily amused."

"You know it. Come on, click that guy who claims he's twenty-nine."

"Yes, dear." She clicked. "At least he's dressed."

This one wore a polo with a hardware store logo on the pocket.

His buzz cut might have hidden some gray at the temples. His tanned face had the wrinkles of either too many years in the sun or too many years chain-smoking cigarettes. His muscles looked legitimate. His voice did not indicate steroids.

"I have half an acre of vegetables and fruit that see me through every winter. You will have canning skills as well as cooking skills. We have to have similar reading tastes. Romances are a deal-breaker. If you can play a musical instrument which doesn't require electricity, you'll have a leg up on the competition. I expect a sensible, strong woman. Message me if you're that woman."

To the tune of the Monty Python Viking skit, Frank sang, "Men, men, men, men. Testosterone men, Butt-headed men."

"Got it in one." Giulia replayed the video. "This one has possibilities. Something about him seems the type my client's sister would gravitate toward."

Frank reached over her arm and clicked on the manly man's profile. "He's got at least two red flags."

"At least. I might want you as bodyguard when I set up a meeting with him."

"What about the mama's boy?"

Giulia gave him a side-eye. "Please. If I needed backup over a cup of coffee with him, I should turn in my license. All right, last one."

His black hair and blue eyes were striking. He had to be six foot four or five. His voice resonated like a street corner preacher's.

"Your profile fits the required parameters. I will presume truthfulness regarding your hunting and agriculture skills, but I will commit to nothing without an in-person meeting."

Giulia said, "Three in a row who didn't make me want to gouge out my eyeballs."

"Are you serious?"

"It's all in the comparisons. After defaced girlfriend pictures and a barrage of male anatomy, men who keep their clothes on are a win. Even if what they're really saying is they want a woman to stay barefoot, pregnant, and in the kitchen."

He leaned away from her. "The sentiment comes from thousands of years of dominant male genes. Or classic TV sitcoms. Donna Reed cleaning the house in high heels and pearls was hot."

"I refuse to honor such a viewpoint with discussion. Look at this guy's eyes." She enlarged the paused video. "He's on something."

"He spoke at a normal rate, so not cocaine."

"He's not haggard or covered with sores, so not meth." She restarted the video.

"You may choose the place and time. Include your religious affiliation in the message. If you adhere to Scientology, do not reply."

"I know what his voice reminds me of," Giulia said. "The guy who does the movie trailers. "'In a world where' and all that."

Frank said from his diaphragm, "In a world where strange men are flapping their junk at my ex-nun wife and she's making me watch..."

Giulia laughed. "Oh, hush. You're enjoying it."

"True. You want me to check this guy's record, assuming he used his real name?"

"Yes, please. All three of them, actually. If I have to carry my gun to a first date, my choice of clothing will require alteration." She opened a reply window. "I'll need to buy tinted contacts and temporarily go blonde. When they ask why I'm thinner, which they all will, I'll say I used an older picture to see who'd be attracted to me for more than my body."

Frank didn't reply, but Giulia felt him tense up.

"Do not tell me I have to think of the baby. You have to trust me to do my job and take care of little Zlatan, or we are going to have to have a discussion."

She sent text-only replies to all three. To the "twenty-five-year-old," she offered a local coffee shop that was not Common Grounds. To the patriarchal wonder who hated romances and played musical instruments, she suggested the public library.

"What do you think?" she said to Frank as she typed a

response to the fanatic who wanted her to prove her gun and farming skills. "Someplace public, but not a coffee shop. Someplace, I don't know, rugged?"

"Home Depot."

Giulia gazed at him with raised eyebrows.

"I'm serious. It's open all hours. Do-it-yourselfers practically live there. There's a perception that girly-girls won't set foot in there. Try it."

"Why not?" She sent the third message. "I've told all of them to wear a blue shirt and I'll be wearing a floppy sun hat." Her computer played *deedle-dee*. "The first reply already. Desperate, much? The teenager agrees to the coffee shop tonight because he's working early tomorrow." She looked at the clock. "I need hazel contacts and blonde hair dye now. Walmart, here I come."

"I'll be married to a blonde."

"Your mind follows interesting channels."

Twenty-Two

Two and a half hours later, a blonde Giulia with a hint of brown roots walked into a coffee shop on the other side of town. She'd chosen her plain blue skirt and the gray shirt left over from her early post-convent days. Combined with tight braids and pale makeup, the overall effect augmented her natural power of invisibility at will. She'd even removed the bright red ribbon from her floppy straw sun hat.

She ordered a peach smoothie, since she'd consumed her allowed caffeine intake for the day. As she waited for the barista, she looked around at the tables. Her contact sat at a window with an iced tea, wearing a blue polo with a lawn care company logo.

A moustached young man sat in one corner texting with one hand and drinking cappuccino with the other. Two middle-aged women hovered in front of the dessert case, debating the caloric doom of cheesecake versus jelly rolls. The speakers played Spyro Gyra.

Frank came in the back door as she took her smoothie over to the window table.

"Hi. I'm Maria."

He gave her the once-over.

Giulia copped an attitude. "Yeah, I lost a bunch of weight. I want men to ask me out for what's in my head, not what's stuffed inside my bra."

He blushed. He might have tried not to if he knew how it turned his acne into a dot-to-dot puzzle.

"You look, um, good."

Frank sat at the table behind them. Her date spoke in a thin voice about self-sustaining crops and large families to make a working farm the center of the new Cottonwood. Ten minutes of this lecture without him once asking Giulia about her wants or needs or even her taste in music.

All at once, Giulia reached her limit. "Driver's license, please." She laid her hand palm up on the table.

He jumped. "Why?"

"I'm sitting at a table with a complete stranger I met on the internet. I want proof you are who you claim you are."

He must have gone to Catholic school, because he produced his license without hesitation at her peremptory Sister Mary Regina Coelis voice. She inspected it.

"Tell the next person you buy a fake ID from to use better materials. This one wouldn't fool the greenest bouncer at a low-class strip club."

Behind her, Frank coughed into his drink.

The teenager stammered excuses.

"Please. Did you think you were going to impress me with your Prepper knowledge? Did you think I would leap at the chance to travel into the new world with you because of your youth and stamina?" She gestured with her smoothie as though it were a ruler. "I'm reporting you to the site moderators. Go call your mother to come pick you up."

Since she never raised her voice above a whisper, neither customers nor baristas looked in her direction. She walked out the way she came in, sipping her smoothie in a show of unconcern. Using the spare car keys, she unlocked the Camry and drove it into the next parking lot.

A few minutes later Frank opened the passenger door. "Honey," he cringed. "I swear I almost peed my pants. If God is good, my phone caught it in full color."

"What a waste of time. If my client's sister met up with him, she would've reacted the same way." She drove home and popped out the contact lenses first thing. "Little Zlatan will not be pimply and pale and living in our basement when he's nineteen," she called downstairs. "His sister or brother will kick his butt into gear first."

"As well he or she should," Frank called from the living room. "Hey, babe, more total strangers want to meet the sexy blonde I'm married to."

Giulia came downstairs and sat next to him. "You're not going to think this is sexy when it wears off and I look like 1980s Madonna in need of a dye job."

Her husband adopted Rodin's "The Thinker" pose. "You know how I said the Kinski snake poster was a rite of passage? Fantasizing about easy-access Madonna was the other rite."

"I so enjoy learning more about your young, impressionable mind." She opened the message. "The one who hates romances has to come into Pittsburgh tomorrow for supplies and suggests eleven a.m. You'll be asleep. I'll get Zane to be my muscle."

Frank's foot beat time on the carpet. "I should be your muscle."

She pecked his nose. "Not when you're on all-night stakeouts. Why have minions if I'm not going to use them?" She spoke as she typed: "Eleven a.m. good. Western Allegheny Community Library NF section."

"It's the closest to Cottonwood," she said to Frank. "If he wants to scope me out as a potential apocalypse mate, he'll make the trip."

"I'm not happy, but"—he forestalled Giulia's impending speech—"you trust Zane and I trust you."

Giulia grinned like a loon. "It's good to hear you say it. Now let's see what number three has to offer." She clicked. "Well. We have competition for the Overbearing Patriarchal Attitude trophy. Listen: 'If you're serious, meet me at the Home Depot on Ben Avon in Pittsburgh at six-ten tomorrow morning by the seed displays.'"

"That's it?"

"That's it. At least he's consistently domineering." She typed: "Will be there."

"I can do abrupt too," she said to Frank.

He was texting. The reply buzzed a moment later. "Okay, VanHorne says he can finish the last hour of our stakeout on his own. I'll meet you at the Big Orange Box."

"Yes, dear."

Twenty-Three

Wearing the same outfit as the night before, Frumpy Giulia walked into the Home Depot main entrance at five minutes past six the next morning. As she reached the spinning seed racks, Frank entered through the garden department door and began studying the hardiness information tags on various shrubs.

Giulia went right for the heirloom seeds. She'd never grown tomatoes other than plum and Big Boy, and she wondered what kinds of sauce purple or yellow tomatoes would make. Next to the tomato packets she found Lemon Cucumbers.

A resonant voice behind her said, "The lemon cucumbers have a disproportionate amount of seeds."

Giulia kept control and didn't startle. "Too bad. They look like fun."

Her black-haired, blue-eyed date towered over her. "Fun is for children younger than the age of reason. Good morning, Maria. I'm Alexander."

"Good morning. Have you ever made sauce with these types of tomatoes?"

They discussed fruit and vegetable husbandry, one-upping each other with stories of full canning shelves and compliments received. Frank moved from the shrubs to the potted plants one aisle nearer to them.

"What are your religious affiliations?"

Again, Giulia parried the abrupt question. "I was a Cradle

Catholic, but now I only show up on Christmas and Easter. It keeps the parents happy. What books do you like to read?"

He played right along with her. "Nonfiction. I'm always reading about better ways to grow food and raise animals. I like staycations."

"Have you had any success planting multiple colors of bell peppers and not having them all come out green?"

They discussed planting strategies as a few early risers entered, chose shrubs and pots and fruit trees, and left. Giulia asked about camp cooking and they compared fire starting methods and the best way to gut fish.

It might have been the way she described filleting trout that made him bite. "Would you like to see what I've done with my property?"

Frumpy Giulia made her mascara-free eyes big and eager. "I'd like to, but I'll have to check my work schedule. I work two jobs. One is in a nuns' retirement home and the other with a cleaning service."

He nodded.

"The Catholic Church knows how to educate its followers. I respect them. Are you free Sunday morning?"

Giulia took out her phone and made a small show of checking her calendar. "Yes, that will work. What's your address?"

"I'll pick you up." He stopped himself. "No, of course not. You shouldn't trust someone you've only known for twenty minutes." He gave her a rural address. "It's less than an hour north of here, near Beaver Falls and close to the Beaver River itself."

Giulia struck a balance between self-effacing and pleased. "I'll dress for tramping around in the woods."

He didn't even shake her hand as they parted. When he left through the garden door, Frank sprinted to the windows to catch his license plate. Giulia went back through the store proper and waited for Frank to pull the car around, in case the preaching farmer hadn't left yet.

"You hussy," Frank said when she got into the car.

She batted her eyes. "He was quite polite and non stalker-ish. No physical contact at all."

"I was prepared to chuck a potted ficus at his head if he tried anything. He drives a pickup, maybe six years old. He's no poser. That truck works hard. I'll run the plate as soon as I get on a computer."

As they turned onto their own street, Frank said, "Nuns' retirement home?"

"Who'd lie about that? Besides, I told him I was raised Catholic." She typed a note into her phone.

"Nevertheless, you've added the sin of lying to your list for your next confession."

"Always, unfortunately." She saved the note. "If the Church still sold the corrupt Medieval version of Indulgences, I'd have to purchase so many we'd be too poor to buy a pack of gum."

"You do know I plan on riding into Heaven on your coattails, right?"

"We have to talk about your Catholicism."

Frank hit the garage door opener. "Oh, look, we're home. Don't you have to get to work, dear?"

She took out her car keys. "We have our whole lives to finish this discussion."

"So many more chances to dodge this issue." He kissed her.

"One of the perks of married life."

She hopped into the Nunmobile and ended up purchasing Real Coffee Number One of the day at a different coffee shop since she was still in disguise. The extra driving got her to work half an hour later than her usual time.

Zane looked up from his keyboard. "Welcome to Driscoll Investigations—oh my gods."

Sidney squealed. "It really is the old you, back when Frank hired me as his admin. You haven't worn that skirt in years." She dug into her combination diaper and messenger bag and came up with her phone. "I think I still have a picture of you in it. Jessamine...Olivier and Jessamine...Just a second...Here." She handed the phone to Giulia. "Your hair wasn't blonde, but it's the same skirt."

Giulia passed it to Zane. "Dowdy was my middle name back then."

Zane handed the phone back to Sidney. "I value my continued employment and will therefore not comment on my boss' choice of clothing."

Giulia started to rub her eyes, but thought better of it. "Zane, you will go far in life. Today I need you as my bodyguard again."

"Will there be catfights with casseroles of food like at Mr. Silk Tie Convicted Killer's apartment?"

She blinked several times and the contact lenses re-centered themselves. "Heaven forbid. I'm meeting one of the dating contacts at the Allegheny branch library at eleven. He comes across as a complete Neanderthal. If he tries to club me with a book, you have my permission to go, what did you call it? Super Saiyan on him."

"Awesome."

At eleven o'clock Giulia was browsing the gardening books in the library's nonfiction section. Zane stationed himself within eyeshot by the graphic novels.

At two minutes past eleven, the romance hater in a plain blue polo shirt walked through the door and nodded at "Maria's" tentative wave. As he came nearer, she confirmed her impression from his dating site picture: He'd been creative with his age.

"I'm Maria."

"I'm Dyami. Dan will do."

Giulia waited for a comment on her weight in the photo compared to the person who stood before him. Nothing. She gave him a point for tact. In library voices, they discussed much the same topics as at her six a.m. meeting.

"I play tuba and harmonica," he said. "I like to call it my mouse and elephant repertoire."

"Flute, guitar, and piano," she said with a polite smile at his attempted humor. If this had been an actual first date, she would've already tried to end it. Even if she cut him slack for being nervous, his stodgy conversation highlighted the lack of any spark between them.

As she thought this, he closed the distance between them and plopped his hands on her hips. She froze before she dislocated his kneecap; shrieks of pain would violate the "library voices" rule. Zane slipped into the end of the aisle, running a finger along the Dewey Decimal System labels on one of the rows of books.

Giulia said, "Remove your hands." He didn't rate a "please."

He rolled her hips with his palms. "Good pelvic spread. You should have many easy births."

"Remove. Your. Hands."

His head jerked up. "What's the matter? You know the baselines have to be established before we can make further overtures." But his hands left her hips.

With a prodigious effort, Giulia stayed in character. "The rules don't change the fact that I decide when touching happens."

He grinned, showing hockey-player teeth. "I like you. My last two contacts were prissy bitches. What do you say to a hike in the woods and a picnic? Can you forage or do you want to bring garden harvest?"

Zane took a book from the shelf and sat facing Giulia at the nearest table.

Taking an educated guess at his interpretation of "forage," Giulia said, "My foraging skills aren't as sharp as I'd like yet."

"We'll use cultivated then." With that he turned as eager as the nineteen-year-old poseur from last night. "What do you say to this Sunday? The weather's supposed to be good."

Giulia held out both palms.

"I work a second job on the weekends. I won't have a day off until a week from tomorrow."

"Let me check." He took a small calendar from the back pocket of his jeans. "I teach a woodworking class every other Saturday morning. How about we meet at the Commonwealth entrance to

Point State Park at one o'clock for a ten-mile hike and a late lunch after?"

Good thing she kept in shape. "I'll send you a message through the site."

Another gap-toothed grin. "Great. Want to get some lunch now?"

She pointed to the clock. "I have to get back to work."

He glanced over his shoulder. "Yeah, okay. Good first meeting. I'll look for your message." He shook hands with her like she was part of the club.

Zane hauled it outside a step ahead of Dan. When Giulia met him at his car, he said. "Got his plate number. Did he seriously have one of those checkbook-style pocket calendars?"

"He did. That man is in major prep mode for the day an electromagnetic pulse sends us back to the stone age." She got into the passenger seat and texted Frank. "Good job on the license plate. Frank will run it for me when he wakes up."

Back at the office, Giulia took out the contact lenses while Zane regaled Sidney with his version of the library meeting.

"He grabbed Ms. D's hips and shook them. Ms. D. got this 'mayhem approacheth' look on her face."

Sidney said with glee in her voice, "I've seen that look."

"I really wanted to let her bust him up, but those librarians are scary. When I was a kid, I used to think they kept axes behind the desks to chop off our heads if we talked too loud."

Giulia came to the bathroom doorway, blinking a third set of eye drops into her dry, tired eyes. "The librarian nun in the Catholic school I went to adopted a perpetual expression of 'No court in the world would prosecute me, so go ahead and try.' She kept the best-behaved library in the state."

"How did you get his hands off you?" Sidney said.

"The Voice," Zane said. "She never raised it, but he'd been measuring her hips with his hands and eyes. When The Voice spoke, it was like someone tied a string to his head and yanked."

Giulia laughed. "You can take the private eye out of the

convent, but you can't take the convent out of the private eye." She dabbed her eyes. "Sidney, if my next meetings with domineering jerks give me any leads to Joanne Philbey, I might need Olivier's insights on the mental makeup of these end of the world types. Could you have him email me his rates?"

"You don't need them. You can ask him anything."

"Nope. He's a professional psychologist, and he'll get paid like every other professional we consult."

"Yes, ma'am."

"The next person who calls me 'ma'am' will take a trip back in time and witness the wrath of Sister Mary Regina Coelis."

Twenty-Four

Frank called at three.

"I ran both plates. The library guy got two tickets in the past year for minor infractions: An expired inspection and a tail light out. Zero tickets for the garden department guy, but here's the interesting part: I ran a traffic cam archive search for both plates. Between the two of them, they got snapped only a dozen times in the past year."

"They're mapping routes to avoid the cameras."

"That's what I think."

She hung up to chew on that idea and Zane buzzed her. "Jasper Fortin would like five minutes."

Doomsday Preppers and clairvoyants. *The Scoop* would devour this combination like Sidney at an all-natural dessert bar. Still, she respected Jasper, a decorated war veteran whose partnership with his eccentric Tarot reading aunt made for a thriving business.

"Please send him in."

He wore his usual working clothes: black jeans and shirt, tattoos that were works of real art, multiple piercings, long dark hair pulled back with a strip of beaded leather.

"Ms. Driscoll." He held out his prosthetic hand. "Sorry to interrupt your workday, but Aunt Rowan saw danger for you in her sunrise Tarot reading. I couldn't get away from the shop until now."

Giulia shook hands. "Did she see anything specific?"

He smiled in his self-deprecating way. "You know what Tarot readings are like. It's the cards combined with their interpretation combined with the subject of the reading. Taking all three elements into account, Rowan says four things: First, lost is in the eye of the beholder. Second, herbs have many uses. Third, the gods are no danger to us but their disciples can be whack jobs." He stopped while Giulia did her best to suppress a smile. "Fourth, take your prenatal vitamins every day without fail."

Every so often, Rowan spooked her. Then again, she or Jasper could have overheard a conversation somewhere, or spied on her to gain her confidence, or any number of standard shyster tricks.

Jasper's dark eyes held hers. "We're not trying to pull a con on you, Ms. Driscoll. Aunt Rowan only cons the cheaters and liars." He winked.

Giulia wasn't the least embarrassed. "I suspect everybody. It goes with the job. Please thank Rowan for her concern and her advice." As an olive branch, she said, "We enjoyed *The Scoop*'s unceremonious exit from your shop on Monday."

His smile hardened. "Bloodsuckers. I would've done more, but I had the business to think of. They claim they're filming an exposé of frauds and predators. The only thing they want to expose is themselves to a bigger TV market."

"No argument here."

The outer door crashed open. Ken Kanning's voice followed in full-on announcer mode. "We're here at Driscoll Investigations on the trail of yet another psychic predator trying to suck money from the pockets of hard-working professionals."

Giulia jumped out of her chair an instant before Jasper leaped out of his. They reached the doorway together. All Zane's muscles bulged as he shoved Kanning's cameraman back out the door. The cameraman spread his legs and braced his heels against the doorframe. He switched his lens from the top of Zane's head to Jasper at a signal from Kanning.

"Jasper Fortin." Kanning dodged Sidney and thrust his microphone at Jasper. "Isn't it true that you claim you lost your right hand in a battle with a demon from hell? What do you have to say about the rumor that your Tarot cards are marked? What about the claim that your aunt goes dumpster diving for information about the victims she targets?"

With an inarticulate noise, Jasper lunged at Kanning. Giulia and Sidney held him back. Zane hooked his foot around the back of the cameraman's knee and shoved him out the door when he lost his balance. Then he turned on Kanning. The voice of *The Scoop* looked at white-hot, bulging-muscles Zane and hustled after his cameraman.

Jasper stopped fighting Giulia and Sidney. They released him. He assumed a yoga pose and took several slow, deep breaths.

Zane turned and faced the room. His pale hair began to return to its normal straight-down position, but all the veins in his arms and forehead still throbbed. As Jasper calmed himself, Zane mirrored his deep breathing and posture until his circulatory system retreated to its usual subcutaneous position.

"I'm all right now," Jasper said.

"They're not worth the jail time," Giulia said.

Sidney said, "They'd take it that far too. You know they would. More news coverage for them."

"Zane, you're a life saver," Giulia said.

"It's all in the timing. I'd just gotten up to replace the cyan ink cartridge in the printer, so I was in the optimum place when those douchenozzles barged in."

Everyone laughed.

"That's the perfect term for them," Giulia said.

Jasper rubbed his temples. "If Kanning's mouth is open, he's lying. I know damned well they have access to my war record, but I'm not going to defend myself. It would bring me down to their level. My unit, too, by proxy, sort of. But if they keep attacking our business, I'm going to lose my temper."

Zane said something in Estonian. His tone conveyed all the translation anyone would need. "The ink cartridge broke. I must've knocked against the printer table when I kicked them out."

"A small price to pay." Giulia looked at the floor by Zane's feet. "I'll get towels and floor cleaner."

Sidney said from the window, "Their van is a block away and moving south."

"Time to make my escape," Jasper said.

"Thank you for passing along your aunt's warning," Giulia said.

Zane locked the door behind Jasper. "Warning?"

Giulia finished blotting ink and sprayed wood cleaner over the area. "If we end up with a blue stain on the floor, we'll consider it our anti-*Scoop* badge of honor."

Zane brought his trash can over and Giulia threw several soaked, colorful paper towels into it. While she started on a second round of cleanup, she told them Lady Rowan's four messages.

Sidney groaned.

Giulia said, "I'll believe her when she tells me the nickname we have for the baby."

"What? Tell us."

She concentrated on a stubborn spot. "Nuh-uh."

They booed her.

Twenty-Five

Frank woke Giulia up from a nap at five o'clock.

"What's wrong? You don't take naps."

She stretched. "I'm stocking up on sleep for little Zlatan's two a.m. feedings. Sidney's advice."

Frank sat next to her. "I'm serious. Are you sure you're all right?"

"Of course I am." She pulled her laptop over. "Come check out the dating sites with me."

The rest of the day's harvest of messages made yesterday's look like grade-schoolers passing notes in class. The first two men made her explicit, vulgar offers. A man who could've been Giulia's grandfather wanted to know if she'd be willing to meet for a coffee and book discussion once a week, or even once a month.

Giulia bookmarked her message. "When this case is over, I may put him in touch with Marjorie the Cat Lady. I counted three cats in his profile picture plus another tail off to one side."

"You are still a bleeding heart."

"I beg to differ. Compassion is a necessary character trait for Franciscans. In or out of the convent, crabgrass is easier to uproot than the core Franciscan values. Besides, Crazy Cat Lady plus Crazy Cat Guy has to be a perfect match."

In the last of a deplorable string of videos, an average guy with average looks, hair, and clothes turned on a karaoke machine and sang, "I like big butts and I cannot lie..."

Frank grasped Giulia's hands, pulled her off the couch, and

danced her around the room, singing along with Maria Martin's musical suitor.

The silliness defused Giulia's rising anger. Frank patted her definitely not big butt and they resumed sitting side by side on the couch in front of her laptop. Giulia deleted every single message.

"Aw, honey, even our troubadour?"

"He might have been the least rude, but he doesn't fit the criteria. I don't know which are worse: The perverts trolling for sex or the judgmental *cavones* who think only size zero women are worthy of them. Tonight was a complete waste of time." She pushed the laptop away. "Only Alex the garden guy and Dan the library guy hit my top trigger points."

Frank stood. "Come supervise me grilling the fish and tell me your triggers."

"That sounds wrong even though it's not." In the kitchen she whisked together brown sugar, hot mustard, and soy sauce while Frank rinsed the salmon.

"I'm working from the premise that if Joanne's body isn't decaying in a shallow grave in the Pennsylvania woods, she ditched everything to join a Prepper group." She daubed the sweet-hot mixture on the salmon with a generous hand.

"Why?"

"The running theme in all my interviews with coworkers, relatives, and friends is how giving Joanne was. Or is, depending on whom I talked to."

"Good grammar is so sexy. Hold that thought." He elbowed open the back door, set the fish on the grill, and returned. "So she's everybody's friend. Why is that your neon sign?"

Giulia opened a bag of frozen dinner rolls. "Her personality as characterized by everyone who knew her reminds me of me back in my convent days. She breaks her back to be everyone's problem solver, everyone's listening ear, everyone's advice columnist. I would guarantee that her own wants and plans kept moving further back in the queue of everybody and their cat clamoring for her to take care of them."

Frank set out dishes and silverware. "I'd want to kill myself if I couldn't shut out the world like that."

"No, Mr. Police Detective, I'm not saying she killed herself." She set a cookie sheet with four rolls in the oven. "That is, if she's dead, which I don't really think happened. I give it eighty percent to twenty she's still alive."

"Gut instinct?"

"Yes, bolstered by evidence from her apartment." She poured lemonade into two imitation Depression glass tumblers. "We also found a video from *The Scoop*. They were trying to sneak into a Prepper compound and I thought I saw someone who resembled Joanne in there. Therefore I'm pretending to be her clone on those dating sites, looking for men in my trigger profile. First, they have to be True Believers, the kind who make bug out bags for their dogs."

"Who make what?"

"Not important. Second, they have to want her skill set because she's valuable as an equal."

Frank opened the back door. "Those cavemen were not looking for an equal life partner." He tested the salmon and came back.

Giulia set butter on the table. "No fooling. I meant an equal the way men and women were in pioneer days, both working the land and sharing the chores because they had only themselves to rely on. Third, they have to be overloaded with testosterone."

Frank turned a chair backwards and sat spread-eagled. "Tell me more."

Giulia made a wry face. "Joanne likes, as her twin sister puts it, major schlong."

Frank leaned his forehead on the chair back. "You women. Never looking above the waist."

"Would you be more complimented if I said I married you for your brain? Don't answer that."

"You're blushing."

"Am not." But she felt her cheeks heating up.

He stepped over the chair and came around the table to hug

her. "You are complex and adorable and"—he looked down—
"barefoot, pregnant, and in the kitchen. I will be the envy of every
cop in town."

"Go check the salmon, caveman."

"Yes, ma'am."

As they washed the dishes after supper, Giulia made up her
mind. "I'm going to go to the scheduled meetings with the library
guy and the gardener guy. I told them I would, but that was only to
escape their clutches. The gardener gives me a weird vibe, but he
hit two trigger points right off the bat. The library guy seems
normal, aside from his caveman-itis, but I'm not clueless enough to
assume good intentions."

Frank closed the dishwasher. "The psycho ax murderer's next-
door neighbors always say, 'But he was so quiet.'"

"Sometimes they say, 'We knew all along something wasn't
quite right about him.'"

"Hindsight. If they really think the neighbor's planning to go
American Psycho on them, they're spying on said neighbor and
making six panicked calls to 911 per day."

Frank closed himself into the game room for the weekly Driscoll
brothers' family bonding night. Giulia put in a DVD of the Peter
Cushing/Christopher Lee version of *The Hound of the Baskervilles*
and heaved the box of Joanne's papers onto the coffee table.

Right about the time the action of the movie switched to
Baskerville Hall, she slammed the lid on the box, fetched her Glock
from the nightstand drawer, and sat at the kitchen table to clean it.
Frank came out of the gaming cave and opened the refrigerator, his
wireless headset pushed back from his ears.

"What's bugging you?" he said as he removed a Harp lager.

"Hm?" Concentrating on her alter-ego strategies, Giulia heard
his voice, but not his words.

"You only clean your gun late at night when you're stuck on a
case."

He got her complete attention then. "I didn't know I was that obvious."

"Need help brainstorming?"

She shook her head. "Go slaughter space aliens. I'm about to brazenly deceive two complete strangers."

"My wife always makes me proud."

Giulia finished cleaning and returned to the living room where Holmes was being his usual brilliant self on the TV. She opened Maria Martin's messages and replied to Dan: "Switched shifts with a friend so I could take a vacation day. Open for a hike tomorrow?"

A reply appeared within thirty seconds. "You bet. I'll bring sandwiches."

She answered, "I'll bring homemade pickles and canned peaches." To the screen, she said out loud, "And my gun."

Twenty-Six

Pregnant Giulia did not like humidity. Pregnant Giulia's ankles in her hiking boots and snug socks promised escalating retribution with every mile hiked. Weren't these problems supposed to hold off until the third trimester? She made a mental note to ask her three sisters-in-law. One of the benefits of marrying into a big family: Lots of advice to draw on.

Maria Martin compartmentalized Giulia Driscoll's life and continued her foraging discussion with Dan.

They'd been walking uphill and down and sometimes blessedly level for half an hour. The sun bled through the trees in pockets of golden hellfire. The monotonous buzz of every insect native to western Pennsylvania waxed and waned, sometimes loud enough to frustrate conversation.

"I'm looking for wild plums," Giulia said.

"There won't be enough in these woods to make a decent canning batch." Dan's hiking uniform—his term—of jeans, boots, and a long-sleeved athletic wicking kind of shirt, reminded Giulia of childhood Paul Bunyan illustrations.

"I know. I've been experimenting with jam mixtures this summer. Currants and gooseberries should be ripening too. I haven't seen them in these woods. Have you?"

"Haven't looked. I'm not into berries. They don't pack enough nutrients to offset the effort of picking and cleaning them." He shifted his portable cooler from his left hand to his right and slapped his neck again. "I have to find a decent mosquito repellent recipe. I'm using the internet while it still exists, but the level of idiocy increases the longer I search."

Giulia pictured her medicine chest in the spare bathroom at home. "Let me guess: They all recommend a certain hand lotion."

He made a frustrated noise. "People who use commercially made products should be banned from serious preparation sites." He turned on her. "What are you using?"

Giulia affected embarrassment. "Unscented Off. Mosquitoes hone in on me like someone rang the dinner bell."

A disappointed head shake. "Not good enough."

"I know, but I haven't perfected a homemade recipe yet either." They passed a cluster of bushes. "Gooseberries. I knew it." She brought out a resealable plastic container from her backpack and picked all the ripe ones she could stuff in.

Over lunch, they discussed American history and current politics. When he brought out dried violets to sprinkle over the canned peaches, she almost revised her opinion of him.

On the hike back, his tone of voice changed from challenging to cozy. He must have approved of her hiking and canning skills. Giulia adopted the meme "Cynical Giulia is Cynical." Cozy didn't suit him, but when he wanted to be friendly, he wasn't an unpleasant companion.

"Got any family?"

"My parents both passed several years back. My younger brother lives about as far north in Canada as you can and still access the internet." Once again, Giulia Driscoll the detective lied like a rug. Thank God for Father Carlos and his understanding of her job constraints.

He shuddered. "Too cold for me. I like hot, sweaty summers. My folks are snowbirds now."

"Florida has giant flying cockroaches."

"Palmetto bugs aren't the worst thing I've eaten. They taste like greasy chicken." He glanced sideways at Giulia, perhaps to see if she was grossed out.

"Given the choice, I prefer foraging to throwing a handful of termites into a frying pan." She opened her water bottle and drank.

"You might not have a choice."

Giulia said with a tight smile, "Let's make a deal. I won't lecture you on the classic roots of modern democracy, and you won't lecture me on my preparedness preferences."

They walked in silence. Perhaps none of Dan's contacts had ever spoken back to him before.

As they reached the parking lot and unlocked their cars, he said, "We've got a connection, don't you think? What about coming out to one of my neighborhood slow pitch softball games? My team is composed of Preppers only. We're putting together a working group for post-EMP times."

Giulia thought fast. "I have to check my work schedule since I juggled to get today off. I'll leave you a message on the site."

"Yeah, okay. I don't own a computer or a cell phone, so it's not like I can give you another way to contact me. I check email at the library and at work."

Giulia drove home, blasting eighties glam rock to drive the idea of eating a palmetto bug out of her head. What if Joanne was hiding in plain sight in some off-grid community? Hard on that thought: Real life problems seldom tie themselves up in neat Disney movie plot ribbons.

Seven point three minutes after she walked through her own door, her feet were soaking in a tub full of cold water. She watched one of the Benedict Cumberbatch *Sherlock* episodes on her phone while her lower legs turned into beautifully shrunken prunes.

Twenty-Seven

"I am not happy," Frank said early Sunday morning as Giulia dressed for her outing with Alex the gardening guy.

"That's because your body's natural cycle is shot. You should be sleeping the sleep of hard-working law enforcement officials who've successfully completed a stakeout." She laced her hiking boots.

He lunged at her from his seat on the bed and dragged her into his lap.

"No, it's because your location is too rural for me to follow you as backup."

She buttoned her short-sleeved shirt. Forced to wear jeans and boots to church because she wouldn't have time to change and still make the meeting, she hoped St. Thomas' ceiling fans would work a miracle this morning and do more than merely move the hot air around. Last Sunday she was sure the Hosts in the Tabernacle would spontaneously combust.

For a former nun, her Catholic jokes edged close to heresy. She'd said so to Father Carlos, who wanted the Host joke repeated. He laughed loud enough in the Confessional for three old ladies to be staring at Giulia when she opened the wooden door afterward.

"Husband of mine, I repeat that I am taking care of the baby while I perform my job."

"It's not just Zlatan. I'm worried about you too."

She kissed him. "My gun is in the glove compartment. My keys will be in my pocket. If by any remote chance this goes south, I'll trigger the retrofitted auto-unlock and shove his nasal cartilage up into his sinus cavity. After that I'll either floor it and get out of Dodge, or he'll have a chance to admire my meticulous gun barrel cleaning."

Early Mass finished at nine thirty. Giulia procured salted caramel dark roast and hit the road. As she drove the Nunmobile north into cow country, she recited all the Prepper lore she'd crammed last night after pruning her feet and making dinner on a modern gas stove with store-bought sausages. Which they ate while streaming the rest of *Sherlock*.

Why Giulia Driscoll would never make it as a Prepper, reason number one: She had no desire whatsoever to live off grid.

An hour later, the entire world seemed to drop away as she drove out of the last of the suburbs. Corn fields and apple orchards replaced cookie-cutter two-story houses with golf course-worthy lawns and streets with no sidewalks. Half a mile northeast, she reached the crossroad indicated in the directions and turned right. Another mile through air permeated with manure and she turned left. A third mile past horse paddocks and more corn, and she turned right again into a dirt driveway marked by a mailbox shaped like a largemouth bass.

The driveway curved back and forth for another quarter mile until it ended at a small farmhouse. Chickens wandered the yard. Over to the right, rows of potted herbs grew in a fenced-in garden four times the size of Giulia's backyard. Between the garden and the woods beyond, beehives and the beginnings of a patch of corn.

She tapped the horn. Alexander came out from the woods. He too wore jeans plus a long-sleeved shirt and a straw hat. Weeds dangled from the hoe in his hand. Giulia got out and locked the car. He waved.

"You didn't stiff me." His voice carried across the beehives and vegetables without effort.

"Did you expect me to?" Giulia asked when he came nearer.

"It's happened. One woman saw the beehives and backed out

of the driveway so fast she sprayed dirt all over the chickens. Guess she was allergic." He wiped his left hand on his jeans and reached toward her. Giulia envisioned a repeat of Dan's pelvic width test and kept space between them. His dark, straight eyebrows merged into a single entity. He dropped his hand.

Giulia remembered her character. "Sorry. I had a trial meeting with someone else who didn't understand boundaries." When the eyebrows didn't separate, she said, "He treated my hips like they were his personal property."

His face cleared. "Amateur. I can tell you're good breeding stock by your stance and proportions. I wouldn't have asked you here if you weren't."

Giulia gave him the only possible reply not involving physical violence: "I've never thought about keeping bees. Does it require a significant initial investment?"

"Can you work with wood enough to build and join several boxes? You can't cut corners on lumber, screening, and beeswax to build the hives, so that's a few hundred dollars. Some people purchase bees, which can be expensive. I brought wild bees into my hives."

She admired the stamped metal borders on the hives. One with maple leaves, one with a Greek key design, a third with ivy, and interlocking animal horns on the fourth.

"I worked in a metal stamping plant in high school." Alex held out his right hand. A thick scar puckered the base of his thumb. "When I moved up here I bought some used equipment and created my own designs. Our tools in the new world should have beauty as well as usefulness."

They passed the herb garden. Giulia saw the usuals: parsley, oregano, basil, marjoram, chives, thyme, lemon balm, coneflowers, and several plant leaves she couldn't identify at a glance. Morning glory vines covered the entire side of the fence next to the beehives.

"I bottle most of the honey. It's the only sweetener I use. I've got two acres here, but growing sugar cane this far north isn't practical. Besides, with honey I can make mead."

They discussed drying herbs and canning in greater detail than at their first Home Depot meeting. Giulia held her own for this part of the conversation with ease. He led her past the hives and onto a wide expanse of tilled land.

"Wow."

His grin became proud. "It's enough for three or four people to live on for years. I worked out a grid system to rotate the crops. The fruit trees are the exception, of course. Do you spin?"

Giulia was quite sure he didn't refer to a specialized class at the gym. "No, but I sew."

He made a wry face. "No one's perfect. You should acquire the skill. There's a learning curve, but department stores will be looted or torched or both within a month of the cataclysm."

Preppers appeared to be prone to mansplaining. Giulia let this one slide.

"I thought hemp was more durable than wool."

He shook his head. "Why draw unwanted police attention? When flyovers happen out here they're not reporting on rush-hour traffic."

Giulia turned her head toward the hedge beyond the beehives. "Do I hear sheep?"

"You do. Also goats. Cows are great for manure, but sheep and goats serve the same purpose and take up much less room."

"And sheep have wool. I've eaten goat cheese but not sheep cheese."

"It's quite tasty. Both animals provide milk and cheese and fertilizer. As an added bonus, they're our garbage disposal for what doesn't go in the compost pile."

Giulia was pleased he considered her one of the gang, but she had a creeping sense of time warp. When she got home, she was going to challenge Frank to a game of Tomb Raider to regain her sense of the modern world.

"You've got a baseball bat growing under the zucchini leaves," she said.

He followed her pointing finger.

"I was sure I harvested them all yesterday. Show me."

They walked the rows and found two oversized zucchinis. Giulia made the standard joke about leaving them on the neighbor's doorstep at midnight. He laughed. She gave him a point for being polite on a first date.

She met the sheep and goats, avoided the bees, and inspected his hand-carved bows and arrows. "My grandfather would have approved your hedge over there. When we were kids, we swore he used a level to trim it."

"My neighbors keep pigs. The hawthorn hedge keeps my crops safe, plus I make jelly from the berries."

"What do you use when the zucchini and cucumbers get attacked by white powdery mildew?"

They discussed cayenne-based natural pesticides and the importance of planting marigolds around the vegetables to keep rabbits out.

"What does your family think of you going off grid?" Giulia said after he made the standard joke about how quickly rabbits multiply.

"I have two younger sisters, identical twins, who live in New York City," he said. "They think I've taken preparedness to extremes. We don't speak much now."

Maria Martin's inner Giulia Falcone did a happy dance. A twin connection. Luck or coincidence, she didn't care.

"Who would've thought? I don't talk about this much, but I had a twin. She died in a car accident in high school. Drunk driver."

"That's rough."

Silence. Giulia didn't want to overplay her hand, so she didn't elaborate on her fake sob story.

"My sisters have a pretty close connection," he said after deadheading several marigolds. "They say it's a twin thing. Does it feel like part of you is missing?"

"Yeah. That's a good way to express it. For the first few years it was pretty bad, but it's eased up now. Sometimes I still reach for the phone to call her when something we shared comes on TV or when I reread a book we both liked." Her next Father Carlo confession list was shaping up to be the length of an epic poem.

Awhile later, as he worked with the hoe and she weeded the smaller sprouts by hand, he said, "Have you ever visited an actual preparation community?"

Giulia sat on her heels in triumph as her dating site persona reeled in the mark by virtue of knowing how to grow one's own food. "Not yet."

"I belong to one not too far from here. Would you be interested in joining me for a visit?"

Giulia pulled more weeds under pretense of considering the idea. "Yes, I would. It'd be good to meet with like-minded people. None of my friends are willing to acknowledge the current world reality."

He stepped over the broccoli, easy for his long legs. "Your two jobs. When do you have a day off?"

She couldn't make it seem too simple, so she brought out her cell phone and poked buttons. In her peripheral vision, she saw his frown of disapproval. At the use of technology? Probably.

"I switched shifts with someone this weekend, so I have Tuesday off starting at noon."

He took out a pocket calendar and pen. "A perfect opportunity. I'll clear it with the leader of our community and let you know, but Tuesday should be fine." He wrote. "Shall I leave you a message?"

Giulia refrained from pointing out the dichotomy of how all these anti-technology Preppers had no problem using evil internet tech to find women. "Yes, thanks. Just for now, you know?"

"Not a problem. Not everyone is trustworthy, not like us who understand."

Giulia went into full-on rant mode when she got home.

"These guys all seem to think my earthly value rests in my pelvis. As long as I can be their brood mare, my farming and cooking skills and ability to work from before sunrise to after sunset are an added bonus in their beautiful new technology-free world. That is, after they prostitute their values enough to hunt for the perfect pelvis."

Frank refilled her lemonade. "But, honey, don't you want to shovel sheep manure on hot summer days and brew mead at night by the light of a whale oil lantern?"

"After I cook three meals over an open fire and clean the dishes using homemade soap, which I'll also make. In my spare time, of course, between spinning wool and sewing clothes and keeping radioactive dust out of the beehives." She drank the entire glass of lemonade without taking a breath.

"I thought these guys were into the EMP version of the fall of civilization?"

"What's the difference?" She opened the refrigerator. "Burgers for supper?"

"Anything you want, my hardworking wife."

Her head poked around the open door. "Do I detect a touch of trepidation in your voice?"

He joined her. "I was merely trying to show you I know the value of my life's partner."

She handed him the hamburger buns. "A sentiment which garners my complete approval." The barbecue sauce and onions came next. "I want to find evidence these extremists are using the internet to lure and seduce underage women."

"Nobody's underage."

"That we know of. Maria Martin's dates this weekend are all about making a new generation of Preppers. Younger women provide more childbearing years. It's been that way for millennia in the Church. Remember, Juliet was fourteen."

"*Romeo and Juliet* is fiction."

"Based on current practice in Shakespeare's time." She took the barbecue seasoning from her spice rack, but held onto it instead of putting it on the counter. "Maybe we do know they're targeting underage girls."

Frank said with his head in the lettuce drawer," How?"

"The teenagers in the park and behind the convenience store."

Frank's head reappeared. "Based on?"

"Are you really asking me that?"

Out came the lettuce and the rest of Frank. "Drugs are drugs. Runaways are runaways."

"Frank, Frank, Frank. Just because a connection isn't a blinking neon sign..."

He peeled off lettuce leaves. "Based on skin discoloration, both teenagers had an allergic reaction."

"Not that simple. If they'd had a standard allergic reaction to the usual suspects, the toxicology reports would've pinpointed the culprit sooner."

Frank bit off the end of a carrot. "When fanatics go off grid they also grow their own versions of their favorite hallucinogens? Possible. Harder to detect, too."

She separated three burgers from the bag of frozen ones. "And what are all the men of the future seeking in their women?"

He pointed the carrot at Giulia's hips. "The ability to birth strong sons and hardy daughters."

"Very good, class. You've been paying attention. And what do teenagers think about?"

"Sex, drugs, and rock and roll." He chomped more of the carrot. "No rock and roll off grid."

"Not necessarily. Dan the Neanderthal plays the tuba."

"Like Opus the penguin in *Bloom County?* I hope I never meet this guy. I'll bust out laughing."

Giulia punched in a microwave thaw cycle for the burgers. "Extrapolating from the relevant points, we have discontented women of childbearing age ready to be convinced they're special and chosen."

"Your client's sister." Frank tossed the carrot end in the trash. "Those teenagers."

"My sister-in-law."

Twenty-Eight

Frank called Giulia at work the next morning with all three toxicology reports: The teenagers' and Giulia's sister-in-law's.

"You are a miracle worker," Giulia said. "How did you get access to Anne's information?"

"I made a vow never to reveal the inner workings of the police department."

"Which means you convinced Jimmy of the connection between all three women and he worked his magic."

"You used to be much more gullible." A sigh. "You were right. They were all on homegrown junk. Most of the concoction is natural. The reports show valerian, hyssop, and fennel, but get this: it also shows traces of tannin and a ton of sugars."

"Tannin? As in tea leaves?"

"Tannins also appear in fermentation, according to the lab guys who brew beer in their basements. Because of the sugar content, they think a sweet wine was used to hide the kicker ingredient: LSA."

Giulia opened a search window out of habit. "Define LSA, please?"

"You started to Google it, didn't you?" The smile in his voice came over the receiver. "LSA is a home-grown version of LSD. Now, class, who can tell me the number one problem with home-grown illegal substances? Ms. Driscoll, I see your hand up."

"Incorrect extraction, Mr. Driscoll."

"You're my favorite student, Ms. Driscoll."

"You can also add the side effects of mixing it with alcohol." Giulia typed as she talked. "Oh my, yes, such a bad idea."

Frank's voice changed. "Your sister-in-law's tox report showed traces of LSA as well as thebaine, papaverine, and a few other -ines, all derived from opium."

Giulia's mouth tightened. "Is she dead?"

"No, no. She's out of lockdown but still in intensive care. She hasn't woken up yet. Don't worry, there's still brain activity."

Giulia suppressed with difficulty the curses she wanted to bring down on her brother, her sister-in-law, and the irresponsible idiots creating their own version of *Breaking Bad* with their gardens.

"So the teenagers didn't have the extra drugs in their systems, but they did have alcohol indicators?"

"Correct, but their LSA levels were quadruple your sister-in-law's. Still think all three are related?"

Giulia clicked over to a "how to use LSA safely" discussion board. Good Heavens. "Yes," she said, reading posts from several people in major denial about their addiction.

"I can hear in your voice you're already in clue-hunting mode. See you tonight."

"Thanks, honey." She hung up and drilled deeper into the drug user blog, then found another, and another. The hardened users fell into two categories: People whose brains were so fried they couldn't even spell "extract" half the time, and people who posted useful information about portions, how-tos, and potency. If one discounted the inevitable cumulative effect of LSA, one could almost believe the logical-sounding advice about counteracting a bad trip. The discussions of those still having flashbacks after weeks and months belied the pseudo-medical advice, though.

"Anne, you idiot. Salvatore may be a bully and a psychological abuser, but you should've thought of the kids before you swallowed that first dose. Plus, you have me talking to myself again."

If Anne had been a prize idiot using Salvatore as justification, what had been the teenagers' excuse? Disaffection or abuse or plain old rebellion? The idea of Anne and the teenagers and Joanne in the same Prepper cult took deeper root in her mind. She drew an arrow on the corner of her legal pad.

→ Anne:
• Trouble at home
• Sneaks out multiple times
• Runs away with camping gear
• Weeks later comes to DI
• High on something unusual and natural
• Regrets change of lifestyle
• Nearly dies

→ Teenagers:
• Trouble at home?
• Sneak out? Multiple times?
• Run away
• Weeks(?) later regret change of lifestyle? Are afraid?
• Try to return to civilization for help but drugs too much for their younger bodies and die before help acquired
• If afraid, what were they afraid of?

She'd written around the margin of the legal paper and flipped to the other side.

→ Joanne:
• Trouble at home/work
• "Sneaks out" in the sense of finding strangers through dating sites
• "Runs away" either on her own (voluntary disappearance) or a date attacked her (Mugged? Car jacked? Worse?)
• Happily tripping on LSA and baking cakes in a cast-iron pan over an open fire?
OR
• Regrets change of lifestyle and hides even deeper off grid?

Zane knocked and brought in the mail. "Three checks at once, Ms. D. We're rolling in wealth today."

Giulia shook herself out of the drug culture and took the checks. "For certain definitions of wealth, yes. Specifically, this covers the health insurance premium for five months."

Sidney said from her desk, "Jessamine's pediatrician thanks you."

"I aim to retain my employees, and health care helps."

"A lot." Zane cleared his throat. "So does the occasional day off. May I put in for a four-day weekend around Labor Day?"

Giulia calculated Zane's hire date. "Your vacation time doesn't reset until November fifteenth."

"I'll trade off for any Saturday, no restrictions."

"Let me check the master calendar." She opened the ginormous Excel doc and clicked the sheets for July through September. "Nothing is worth the trade at the moment. Are you willing to keep the offer open-ended?"

"Yes. This one's important."

"Ooo-OOO-ooh." Sidney's singsong mirrored Giulia's curiosity.

Zane didn't react to Sidney, interesting in itself since he bantered with her much more than with Giulia. Which wasn't saying they'd become a Vaudeville team, but still.

"All right. An extra day before the Labor Day holiday in exchange for a Saturday to be named later."

She wanted to know why, but she was the boss, not a friend. Boundaries she understood, unlike Mr. "You've got good breeding hips."

"Breeding hips," Giulia said out loud. "Thank you."

"You're welcome?" Sidney said.

Giulia took out her phone. "A chain of ideas connected in my head. Joanne's friend Marjorie the Cat Lady may be the only person I interviewed who doesn't have an agenda. Joanne visited her every Sunday, which creates enough of a time gap to notice changes."

*   *   *

An hour later, she parked the Nunmobile in front of the flamingoes and their siege engines. The front door opened when she stepped on the sidewalk. Groucho and Tallulah zipped out and tried to kill her by weaving around and through her legs as she walked. From Marjorie's smiles and tee-hees, she considered attempted murder endearing. Inside, Giulia sat in the same chair inhaling the same ammonia/poop/flower odors as cat hair glommed onto her skirt. She managed not to check for cat hair in the glass of iced tea Marjorie handed her.

After the polite preliminaries, Giulia played the ex-nun card.

Marjorie ate it up and gave Giulia even more in return. She took a velvet-plus-cat-hair picture frame from the top of the piano and detached the backing.

"This is my mother, God rest her, on her wedding day in 1952." The photograph showed a smiling, petite woman in a cathedral train wedding gown with a veil composed of yards of netting and dozens of orange blossoms. Marjorie then produced a second photograph from behind it, of the same petite woman in a plain white gown and plainer white veil. Her smile in this photograph appeared uncertain.

"What Order?" Giulia said.

Marjorie bounced on her sofa cushion, causing the fox-tailed tabby to leap from around her shoulders with a screech. "I knew you'd get it. She joined the Carmelites, but escaped before her final vows. She never said 'escape' though."

"She jumped the wall."

More bouncing. "Yes, yes, that's what she used to say. Is it a secret code?"

"Something like that. Your mother looks lovely in both wedding pictures."

"You're very kind." She set the frame and photographs on the coffee table. "Mama always said to trust nuns, and especially to trust ex-nuns. How can I help you?"

Giulia explained about her sister-in-law and the Society of Saint Pius the Tenth lockdown and how she may have detached from her home cult and attached herself to a different cult. She placed great emphasis on Anne's dramatic collapse at Giulia's feet and the multiple drugs in Anne's system. Marjorie made sympathetic faces and sad noises.

"The deeper I look into Joanne's life the last few months before she disappeared, the more I see signs of similar behavior. Since you knew her so well and saw her outside of her work setting every week, I hoped you could tell me if she showed signs of cult-like behavior or drug addiction."

Marjorie sipped her tea, the lines on her forehead deepening. "I don't know anything about drugs, really. I wouldn't know what to look for. Do you mean like people who take cocaine and their eyes get all crazy and they zoom around at super speed eating everything in sight like on cop shows?"

Giulia held her iced tea glass without drinking from it. "No, nothing that extreme. More like clichéd hippie behavior. Everything is soothing and easy and wonderful."

Marjorie laughed. The identical calico cats on either side of her growled and resettled themselves. "I was born a few years too late to tune in and turn on, but my older brother wasn't. I spied on him and his friends often enough to know those signs." She stroked both calicos simultaneously. "I've been thinking more about Joanne since your last visit. Did you know she was passed over for a promotion early in January?"

"Do you think that was her turning point?"

"Yes, well, that and the boyfriend who broke up with her before Christmas. For three Sundays running I listened to her complain about how she lost out on everything because she was a fat woman."

"I know too many women who think they'll never have a life until they're supermodel skinny."

Marjorie patted her thighs and got two handfuls of cat. "I like apple pie with cinnamon ice cream and I buy pants with elastic waistbands. Joanne, silly thing, was sure her problems would be solved with the right diet. When she came that Sunday with no makeup and in Army surplus clothes, she looked hard. Not the sweet Joanne I knew." Marjorie tried to scoot the cats off her legs, but they dug their claws into her pants and purred. "If you tell me Joanne found some concoction of drugs that would make her fit and skinny, I believe she would have followed it like a new religion."

After the drive home, Giulia the pacifist understood why people erupted in road rage. First the construction, then three student drivers, then when she finally got off the highway, the little boy in the minivan at the red light who rolled down the window and whizzed onto the asphalt. In a breeze. Blowing the stream onto Giulia's windshield. Good thing she'd rolled up her driver's side window when she realized it was indeed a tiny little pecker sticking out of the minivan's back window.

Frank made immediate plans to teach little Zlatan that skill as soon as he was potty-trained.

Giulia walked out to the patio and turned the hose full force onto the broccoli. A moment later, she relented and switched the spray to "shower" setting. Only a thoughtless gardener ruined perfectly good broccoli over a temporary snit.

Frank came out with ice water. "I put the laundry in the dryer. All the cat hair appears to have been scrubbed away."

"I like cats, but I'm still phantom itching." She shifted the spray to the tomatoes.

"I want to go over some self-defense basics with you tonight," Frank said, eyes on his phone.

Giulia pinched her lips together for a second. "I don't expect this Prepper to get me in a headlock and tie me up in a storage bin until I agree to give up flavored coffee."

"You're going to an extremist's stomping ground. He might be a crunchy naturalist who preaches against the evils of iPhones. He might also be a Jim Jones type who wants to brainwash everyone for the cause."

She turned off the hose. "Point taken. If I'm not home by midnight tomorrow, call out the militia. I'll leave my phone on and stash it in the glove compartment."

Frank's jaw clenched. "The more I hear about this, the less I like it."

"I'm not a fragile flower." Giulia advanced on her husband. "I am a successful PI who has repeatedly proven I can take care of myself. Correct?"

Frank inclined his head. "No argument there."

"Thank you. My Glock will also be in the glove compartment. Remember with the car's remote unlock I can have it in my hand in fewer than thirty seconds."

"That makes me feel better." He took her hand. "Come inside and show me all the different ways you can kick my butt. I'll sleep better."

Twenty-Nine

Giulia met Alex the gardener next to his pickup at the same Home Depot Tuesday at noon. Wild eyes, she thought.

"Ready to follow?" he said. "I was told not to give you the exact location because you're not yet a member of the community."

"I understand." If the leader of this community handed her a tin foil hat upon arrival, she'd never be able to keep a straight face.

They got on the highway and off again after only a few miles and began a winding trek north. Giulia missed her small house with its extra-large garden more every mile she followed. She wanted to sit next to Frank on their couch and read a romance novel while Frank watched the Manchester United game.

To business. Cases didn't get solved blowing the weekly budget at Barnes & Noble.

The city gave way to the 'burbs. The suburbs slipped into cow country. Cow country changed into woods and back again. An hour and twenty minutes into the drive, Wild Eyes led her through four more turns and down a dirt road through thick woods. They parked on more dirt next to an older Volvo and a newer pickup.

She locked the Nunmobile (never trust strangers not to paw through your unattended vehicle) and stretched. First she touched her toes and checked out the bumper stickers on the other vehicles.

"I brake for Bigfoot."

"Bambi: He's what's for dinner."

The go-to meme for hunters, apparently. Joanne had a t-shirt with the same phrase.

She stretched backwards. As much of the surrounding area as she could scan in a three-second glance was covered with trees. Birch, pine, spruce, cottonwood, chestnut; more she couldn't identify in that snippet of time.

When she straightened, she faced the hedge. It looked familiar. Not in this context, but she'd seen it.

"Are you ready to meet the community?" Alex said.

Maria Martin put on her signature tentative smile. "You bet."

Giulia Driscoll, formerly Sister Mary Regina Coelis, heard the way he said "community" and erected mental siege walls.

They walked through a concealed opening in the ten-foot ivy and hawthorn hedge and entered a fairy-tale village. Giulia remembered her parents once taking a young Giulia and younger Salvatore to a kids' theme park based on nursery rhymes. The condo-sized high-button boot of The Old Woman Who Lived in a Shoe and The Crooked Man's Crooked House would've fit right in among the irregular circle of Tiny Houses. Some were restructured mobile homes, some looked like two or three elaborate sheds bolted together. One was octagonal. One was a perfect gingerbread-fretted Victorian home scaled to doll house proportions. All of them were painted to blend with the trees.

A vegetable garden fronted every house. Looking down the narrow paths between each house, Giulia saw signs of more gardens in the back. A fire pit with a square grill over it dominated the central area. Chickens wandered among the beehives off to Giulia's right, behind a long herb garden fenced in with wire. Alex had apparently modeled his own garden and land after the design of this community.

Between the fire pit and the gingerbread house's garden, a middle-aged woman sat at a traditional spinning wheel, working fluffs of off-white wool into yarn. Two teenage boys ran from the woods between two of the houses, the first carrying a football.

"Hey, Alex," they shouted as they ran off.

The spinner raised her head and nodded without breaking her rhythm. Giulia was relieved on one point: No one wore "Little

House on the Prairie" clothing. The boys wore shorts and t-shirts with some kind of slogans. The woman wore a tiered cotton sundress.

"Come on," Alex said to Giulia. "I'll give you the grand tour of my own place. It's pretty typical of what we've chosen to bring into the new world."

Giulia heard goats and sheep now. At least she thought she detected two different types of baas and bleats and maybe grunts and snorts as well. This pre-post-Zombie Apocalypse world would need Febreze.

Why Giulia Driscoll would never make it as a Prepper, reason number two: She had no desire whatsoever to grow her own lamb chops the way her great-great-grandparents did on the farm. Shearing sheep for wool, certainly. Slitting their sheared throats to drain the blood after scooping out their sheepy viscera? Thank you, no.

They climbed two steps to a miniature house similar to the one Joanne's ex Louis Larabee lived in. A metal sign above the door read "Home of the Horn." Giulia wasn't surprised to see Alex's decorating scheme ran to horns. Lots of horns.

"See the headrests on my chairs? They're carved from the base of stag antlers, where the antlers meet and form a cup."

Giulia picked up a candlestick from the mantelpiece. "Is this carved from an antler as well?"

"A goat horn, actually. I carved it myself." He graciously acknowledged her compliment.

The painting over the mantelpiece illustrated an ancient cult dancing and drinking around a fire with stags and rams watching from the trees. Druids, Giulia thought from their robes and the runes carved on their drinking horns.

Alex wasn't merely admiring pioneer back to basics. He was looking way, way back. Mr. Peabody and Sherman's Wayback Machine back.

At the first mention of "sacrifice" she would be in the Nunmobile and halfway home.

No, that worry was silly. She was touring a survival cult with a hip fetish. They weren't going to sacrifice the Pelvis of the Future.

The photos Diane had given Giulia didn't show Joanne's hips to their best advantage. The image of Joanne buried somewhere in these dense woods kept poking at her.

Alex gestured at the floor-to-ceiling bookshelves flanking the fireplace. "We all have as many books as we can cram into our houses." He pointed up to the loft, which was lined with bookshelves instead of wallpaper. "We all possess the essential volumes for survival after the dirty bombs or the EMP destroys this corrupt and lazy modern world. Farming, woodworking, preserving, hunting, and medical care are the main ones. We stock guns and ammunition, but one of the entrance requirements is knowing how to carve and fletch arrows. Those two football players you saw earlier are our best bow makers."

Giulia ran her fingers over the spines of the books. Mythology from a dozen different cultures. Ancient Greek and Roman history. American history and politics from the Revolution to present day. Not a single mystery or action-adventure or even a political humor. Everyone needed a laugh at some point. Especially if one of the many end of the world scenarios came true. Even gallows humor would be useful.

She played disingenuous. "I don't see any place for storage. I mean, I've never been inside a Tiny House before, so I don't know how they work. Where are the preserves and dried meat you're preparing for the winter?"

His long arm pointed to the back of the house. "Let me show you the wonders of my stone cellar." He led her into a kitchen narrower than the galley kitchen in both of her tiny post-convent apartments.

A cast-iron stove stuck its antique glory much too far into the available space. Alex's personal choice for Pelvis of the Future would have a heck of a time maneuvering her pregnant self around it.

Why Giulia Driscoll would never make it as a Prepper, reason number three: Gas stoves were a gift from the cooking technology gods. Giulia Driscoll was no Luddite.

Maria Martin, on the other hand, praised the stove, the compact cabinets, the design of the hidden trap door at the end of the kitchen. Following Alex, she climbed down the ladder into a stone-lined fifteen-foot square cellar.

"I expected cinder block." She shivered. The temperature here was at least forty degrees cooler than the air above ground.

"Stone is much more durable. Why would we use something man-made when the earth provides us with what is best for our needs?"

Giulia feigned embarrassment at the mild rebuke. Alex patted her shoulder.

"Don't worry. We all make rookie mistakes."

They climbed up and out the back door onto an entire farming complex. Wheat and barley in tall rows grew between old-growth maple trees. Enough vegetables to feed three times the number of Tiny House families hunkered between birches and cottonwoods. Apple and peach trees alternated with maples, the latter showing signs of having been tapped for syrup.

"I would never have guessed the community possessed this much land."

"Our leader keeps it well hidden from spies. The government doesn't like its cash cow taxpayers going off grid. Over the years we've pruned the tree cover to let in enough sun to grow our food yet still disguise our true purpose. When one of our members flew over it in a commercial airplane, he couldn't see the farm at all."

They walked the narrow path between his house and the next and came upon the football players in thrall to the spinner. One wound the spun wool into skeins, the other weeded the garden.

The woman winked at Giulia.

"They both hate me right now. I'm quite sure they're planning a catalogue of woes for their father's arrival tonight." She brought the spinning wheel up onto her porch. "I'm Cheryl. You're Maria, right? Come feed the pigs with me."

Maria Martin joined her with a happy smile. Giulia Driscoll noted how expertly the new recruit was being herded.

Giulia's great-great-grandmother would have been proud as Giulia spread grain and table scraps. The enormous pink and brown beasts snorted and grunted as they shoved their noses into the feeding trough.

"Would it be rude of me to think of them as bacon on the hoof?"

Cheryl winked. "You wouldn't be the only one. Who wants to live in a world without bacon? Did you know it contains a nutrient that helps prevent Alzheimer's?"

They talked about the work required to run the many aspects of the community. Giulia's compliments were genuine. She'd worked in enough huge schools and spent three years in a Motherhouse filled with more than one hundred nuns of all ages. Both places required exhaustive levels of organization.

Fortunately for Giulia, Maria Martin could ask any number of questions without being considered rude. When they filled the trough, Giulia got a close-up view of the intricate tattoo running from Cheryl's elbow around her lower arm to the back of her hand.

"Your tattoo is lovely. What is its significance?"

Cheryl rotated her arm as she explained. "We're all marked when we become full initiates of the community. I chose blackbuck horns, because I once traveled to India as a little girl and one of these lovely animals let me pet it."

"Do you have a job outside the community that accepts tattoos?" Giulia feigned embarrassment at her forwardness.

Cheryl patted Giulia's shoulder. "I run a home-based spinning business, so I'm my own boss. My husband's tattoo is completely hidden under his work shirts. He's an accountant, so he can't live here all summer like the boys and I can."

"What would happen if the worst occurs and he's in the city?"

Cheryl smiled and shook her head. "I'm afraid detailed plans are only open to members of the community. You understand, I'm sure."

"Oh, of course. I didn't mean to pry."

"It's natural curiosity, my dear. Come check the coffee plants with me."

Giulia was surprised at this. "Coffee?"

"We are a sensible community. We understand that no world, old or new, is complete without coffee. One of our other members discovered that coffee can be grown just about anywhere, even in a pot on a desk." She led Giulia to the brightest corner of the compound. A loose grouping of bushes with shiny green leaves and cascades of red berries sucked up unfiltered sunshine. In a conspiratorial whisper, she said, "It's not Starbucks quality, but it's much better than instant. The one part of today's world I'll miss is Starbucks. When I leave the compound, my first stop is for my caramel macchiato fix. It's my weakness, but I've taken my caffeine addiction into my own hands." She caressed the trailing leaves.

Hers was the first sane statement Giulia had heard all afternoon.

Thirty

"My parents aren't happy about our lifestyle choice," Cheryl said as Giulia sat at the spinning wheel to try her hand. "They don't get their grandchild fix often enough, they say."

Giulia made sympathetic noises as she attempted to control the spinning wheel plus the raw wool. First the wool broke. Then it tangled. Then it broke again.

"Why can I use a sewing machine but not this?"

Cheryl made a dismissive gesture. "We all start out the same way. If you're fortunate enough to become a member here, I'll show you all the tricks I've learned over the years."

Giulia gave up after three yarn breaks in a row. "I knew I had another question. What about vaccines for the children? The last thing the new world needs is to be wiped out by an outbreak of measles."

"You're so right. Our leader has a stockpile of vaccines stored in a lead-lined safe. They'll last us for years, he assures us. We have penicillin and other essential medical supplies in there too."

Maria Martin said approving words while Giulia Driscoll's thoughts were all about refrigeration and viability and expiration dates. The community had perfect faith in their leader's wisdom. Cult mentality at its finest. Giulia wouldn't want to be around them when they injected their outdated vaccines into the children. Into the adults as well, possibly, if some of their members indulged in the luxury of vaccine denial. That would be an interesting argument...for certain definitions of interesting.

The sound of cars driving onto the dirt parking area came through the hedge. Giulia rejoiced. More tin foil hat wearers prepared to be charming and helpful to a complete stranger, none of whom had the least clue she was mining them like her personal vein of ore.

Today was turning out to be a very good day.

The teenagers crashed through the hedge opening. "Dad! Dad! Mom busted up our football game again!"

A deep male voice answered them. Three other voices joined the conversation, the bodies attached to the voices appearing through the hidden entrance one by one. The men loosened neckties. The women slipped off high heels and pulled off earrings and wristwatches.

"Home at last," came from everyone in a ragged chorus. Two German Shepherds, a Rottweiler, and a Border Collie came in with the new arrivals, barking and running everywhere except near the beehives.

Alex introduced Giulia to the humans and the dogs. So many names. At least the dogs' names were easer to remember. The collie was Lassie, of course, and a humongous Rottweiler was called Pepin. The dogs accepted her and the humans were kind and welcoming and helpful. Giulia kept herself from making Jim Jones Kool-Aid jokes in her head by brute force.

The aroma of roasting pork came from two of the houses. The men opened doors and returned to the central area now wearing jeans and sandals or work boots. The football players and two teenage girls set up wooden tables next to the fire pit. Giulia helped with dishes and utensils, cucumber salad, zucchini pickles, and cups of water. The talk turned to a broken water purifying system and ways to repair it. No one mentioned calling in a certified repair technician. Giulia most definitely did not suggest the community recruit one.

Cheryl and Alex brought out roast pork and big flat loaves of bread. Everyone sat and ate. Giulia's welcome never faltered. She talked politics and history across the table, canning techniques to her right and homemade spice blends to her left. Each community member added a nugget of information specifically given to them by their leader. Not only did this as yet unseen leader appear to know everything about everything, his flock seemed to take every word from his lips as Gospel.

Giulia clamped a death grip on her legs before they tried to run through the hedge back to normalcy. Cheryl offering her mead distracted her.

"I have to drive home soon." She was always pleased when she could make a plain, truthful statement while undercover.

Her driving comment led to several humorous stories of encounters with police while transporting pigs and goats and trees.

Everyone at the tables was under the age of forty. So many Pelvises of the Future. An equal number of Schlongs of the Future, therefore. Giulia stopped that train of thought before she started to giggle for no reason she dared explain. She blamed Diane Philbey for planting the "s" word in her head to appear at inappropriate times.

The spices on the pork made her lips tingle. She would've added a good, thick barbecue sauce to dip the chewy bread into. Yeast wasn't allowed in the new world? That didn't make sense. Somebody in this community must know how to maintain yeast. Since Joanne hadn't arrived for this communal supper, drat the luck, Giulia would have to wangle another invitation here. Bringing an offering of a yeast starter might tip the scales, if the judgment of these happy, welcoming Stepford people wasn't completely in her favor.

Meals appeared to be the way these busy pioneers of the future relaxed. All the adults were leaning back in their chairs, smiling. Multiple conversations slowed from the pace of a ping-pong match to a leisurely game of catch. Even the teenagers mellowed enough not to gripe when told to milk the goats.

Giulia applied her crack detective skills. All clues pointed to the mead. She might not be familiar with the brewing process for mead, but she did know the legal drinking age in the United States.

These teenagers did not meet it.

After everyone helped clean up—Giulia tacitly approved the workload sharing—Alex corralled her to try her hand at archery. The day-long audition continued.

Giulia discovered the skill set to aim and fire a gun did not transfer one-to-one upon picking up a bow and arrow. When her third shot flew over the target into the trees, she said, "A whole family of squirrels is in that chestnut tree, laughing at me."

Alex coughed. "Have you ever fired a gun? Oh, wait. You're a hunter. What am I thinking?"

Maria Martin gave him her self-deprecating smile while Giulia Driscoll thought at him, "You didn't forget a thing in my profile, you weasel. And what happened to your preacher voice? Now you're all about how fun this first date is."

They detoured into his house to get pistols, since a hunter wouldn't need to prove her skill with a rifle. Giulia's ankles sent her nasty messages as they walked all the way to the end of the barley. She promised them the Nunmobile's air conditioning turned on high and another tub of cold water as soon as she got home.

Giulia decided not to fake this and hit the bull's-eye seven out of eight shots. Alex shut up. Maria Martin made sure to deprecate her skill without quite calling it luck. When Alex's powers of speech returned, his hands expressed their approval as well. Giulia turned in an Oscar-worthy performance of pretending to enjoy his mead-laden kiss and butt grope.

"You're wasted out in the world, Maria. Would you be willing to tell me if your finances are robust enough for you to become a functioning member of the community?"

"Well, really, that's a really personal question. I mean, I don't mean to sound like a goofy teenager or anything, but I don't know..."

What Giulia "really" wanted was mouthwash and a shower and more mouthwash. Also her phone to take pictures of everything. There ought to be a way. She needed to figure out the way before her next adventure in the land of tin foil hats.

She looked at her bare wrist and dithered. "Oh, no. How can I find out what time it is? I have to get up at four thirty for work tomorrow."

Alex wrestled his octopus persona into submission. "We all learn to tell general time by the sun." He backed up several steps to look through a long gap in the tree cover. "I'd guess about eight o'clock. I'll walk you to your car."

When they reached the circle of houses, Giulia thanked Cheryl for her spinning lesson. Cheryl was still a good deal mellower than she had been before supper. The teenagers were on the octagonal house's porch. One of the girls was reading out loud. One of the boys was asleep with his head in her lap.

"The rest of us are putting the animals in their sheds for the night," Alex said. When they exited through the hedge he said, "You fit in so well. The community will discuss a return visit, if you're amenable."

Giulia chose a strategic push back. "Today gave me a lot to digest. I'm going to need to think hard about everything a complete lifestyle change requires."

Ding-ding-ding. Alex the wild-eyed evangelist shoved aside Alex who got turned on by a woman with pistol skills.

"I respect your desire to analyze your fitness for the community. I will leave a message informing you of the community's decision."

They shook hands as a G-rated conclusion to the day. Alex gave her reverse roundabout directions to get back to Pittsburgh. Giulia popped the glove compartment as soon as she was out of sight and pulled to the side of the road. Her paranoia level infected by the day's events, she took out pen and paper plus her cell phone and made a show of writing directions. One of the happy, helpful people might have binoculars trained on the Nunmobile. After the show she unlocked her phone and dropped a pin on her current location before heading home with the air conditioner blasting arctic air on her throbbing feet.

Thirty-One

Frank opened the garage door before Giulia turned off the Nunmobile's ignition.

"I was half an hour away from coming up there to rescue you."

"O ye of little faith. No, don't touch me until I gargle with a gallon of Listerine. Wild Eyes rewarded my accuracy with a pistol by mashing his lips on mine and grabbing my butt. I feel utterly violated."

Frank performed some lip-mashing of his own. "You wanton hussy. Your butt is mine alone to grope." Another kiss. "I will fling my gauntlet in his face." Another. "Did you find your missing person?"

Giulia kissed him once more before unlacing her boots. "No, but only a handful of the community—yes, you heard me—was around today. I have to soak my feet and then I want to use as much technology as possible for the rest of the night. We used more modern conveniences on my long-ago six weeks of total silence Final Vow retreat. Come up to the bathroom with me."

She ran cold water in the tub and sat on the edge. "This is paradise." When the water covered her ankles she turned off the faucet and turned on her phone's voice memo function. "This way I don't have to remember it again tomorrow when I type it all up."

She started with the hedge and its hidden entrance, paused to add more cold water, and moved on to the houses and gardens, football and spinning wheels.

"Good God. Did the women all wear prairie dresses?"

"No. I was surprised too. If I looked at the surroundings one way, I saw happy workers on an old-fashioned sustainable farm. If I looked at them another way, I saw paranoid cyberphobics indulging in the equivalent of stuffing their money in their mattresses." She checked her shrinking feet for levels of prune. "Did I mention the mead?"

"Homemade hooch? They'll all die of botulism."

Giulia opened a search window on her phone. "No they won't. It's something to do with the honey...here it is. Honey is all about good bacteria. My grandfather used to make wine in the basement. He taught us kids how. We should return to my peasant roots and brew some mead. Little Zlatan will be born by the time it's ready and we can toast his birthday."

She opened the stopper and the water started to drain. "The tattoo interested me the most. It looked like henna, but I know ink can be made from walnut shells and blueberries and tree bark, so I wouldn't want to guess what her horns plus wheels was made from."

"The mark of the beast," Frank said.

"I got more of a hero-worship vibe of their yet-to-be-seen leader than a religious one." She chewed her lip. "I need to get back in there and find out if Joanne is still inside."

"Are you sure that was pork you ate? Was anyone named Donner?"

Giulia made a horrified moan. Frank took her phone, laughing, so she could dry her feet.

"You have an evil streak, Mr. Driscoll."

"It keeps our marriage exciting."

"Are you sure you didn't marry me for my Pelvis of the Future?" She paused the recording, then changed her mind. "One last thing: I'm certain that particular mother and her boys were hand-picked to make me feel comfortable. I'm also certain she gave my date a report on my aptitude for pig feeding and spinning the minute I left."

"Logical and creepy."

"Yes and yes." She stopped recording for real this time. "It is now time to use an excess of technology simply because I can."

Frank said, "Assassin's Creed? Madden? I've got it: Halo 5. You turn on the air conditioner and I'll drag out the ice cream maker Sidney gave us for the wedding."

Thirty-Two

Giulia lay awake at two a.m. lamenting her lack of a personal drone to fly over the compound and take surveillance photos. The community members would probably consider it more Big Brother spying and use it for target practice. Ultra-light stealth technology was no match for multiple firearms in skilled hands.

She laid a hand on her stomach. Five weeks was too soon to feel the baby move. She squashed an irrational fear of turning into a fanatical religious parent like her brother.

They ought to think about real names for the baby, because Zlatan was not happening.

Maybe an invitation to return to the happy-happy community waited in her dating site inbox. She'd check it before leaving for work tomorrow. Rather, today. She had to get some sleep.

Frank rolled over, flopped an arm over her chest and a leg over her knees, and snored.

Giulia relaxed.

At 8:40 a.m. Giulia logged in to her dating site account. No message from Wild Eyes, but two videos graphic enough to sour her coffee, plus three that seemed boring and normal by comparison. A trickle of worry inched along her spine.

Zane knocked on her doorframe and held out a sheet of paper.

Giulia took it. "Is this the fruit of your super-sized cranium?"

"It is. You did not hire me in vain."

She ran a finger down the list of Joanne's usernames and passwords. "You bet I didn't."

Cup of coffee number one sustained her through the videos and messages Joanne received on the twin site. Most were similar enough to Maria Martin's offers to make Giulia pretty sure a website existed with come-on scripts for the taking.

One hour in, Giulia tried the mainstream site, the one that hadn't gotten her own alias much action. Not so for Joanne. An entire football roster of males fitting the target profile wanted Joanne. She scrolled through several messages from sallow, whiny young men in gamer t-shirts sitting on identical couches in identical basement apartments. Only the upholstery and wallpaper differed.

When she entered the Prepper site, Worried Giulia and Grossed-out Giulia faded away. Into their place stepped Snap-to-Attention Giulia. This Giulia stared at a photograph of Chef Eddie, magically slimmer and with the start of a chin-strap beard. Was he trying to create a real-life *Shop Around the Corner/You've Got Mail* romance?

Chef Eddie brought more magic, because three clicks later Giulia found a familiar photo of Alex the gardener in full Wild Eyes mode. Confirmation that Joanne also possessed The Pelvis.

She read through the messages between them. Diane didn't snag all the street smarts in the Philbey family. Joanne's replies mirrored Giulia's: Polite caution and no personal contact until after a preliminary mating dance.

Larabee of the cow neighbors left messages and his profile picture shaved five years and ten pounds off his actual self. At least he stopped a centimeter short of a D-pic. Now there was a term Giulia could have lived without knowing.

She backtracked to Chef Eddie's string.

Ouch. One reply couldn't be called a string. Joanne's words were careful and polite. Double ouch. The next few mornings at work must have been the epitome of awkward.

Larabee's string. Hold it. Larabee and Joanne actually dated. Why resort to this online business?

Joanne's first reply reflected Giulia's perplexity: "Louis, what's this all about?" An embarrassed and convoluted reply followed, amounting to "You only look at me like a hunting buddy. I need to make you see me outside your comfort zone."

So that was the start of the brief relationship. They'd stopped messaging after that, unfortunately for Giulia's investigation. Score one for Larabee not lying, at least.

Her reading had taken her nearly to noon. Maria Martin had to have a second invitation to the happy tattooed bacon farm by this time. She opened another tab and logged in to her undercover account. Success. The message informed her that the community invited Maria Martin back to experience the life of the world as it would be sooner than anyone thought. With that in mind, they would expect her tomorrow afternoon. If she could not get the entire day off work, she should let them know what time in the evening she could reasonably get out to the community.

She patted her hips. Thank you, Pelvis of the Future.

After a series of stretches, she opened her door. "Is anyone going out to lunch?"

"I am," Sidney said. "The barbecue truck is by the park fountain today."

A beat.

"What?" Giulia and Zane said.

"What do you mean, what? They make a great Southwestern salad."

"You had us worried." Giulia handed her a ten. "Take my money, please. The baby wants pulled pork."

Giulia left the office at three and drove to her brother's street. Her slim hope of catching her niece outside on a summer afternoon playing with her babysitting charges withered like the patches of phlox around the streetlights.

A group of grade-school kids kicked a soccer ball and four preschoolers ran squealing through a sprinkler on lawns in various stages of chemical perfection. Two old women rocked and talked on a front porch. The soccer ball headed for the street. A mail carrier in standard issue gray-blue shorts kicked it dead center into the miniature net. Half the kids cheered. The other half groaned.

Her brother's lawn needed mowing. Verdigris bloomed in Christ's armpits on the gigantic bronze crucifix obscuring the front door. The blinds were closed, but so were the blinds of the houses on either side, now that the afternoon sun hit the windows like a battery of lasers.

She gave it up after turning and casing the block a second time. For all she knew, her brother had the family on high alert for the Nunmobile and had barricaded them all inside. If that was the case, he probably had them on their knees praying another rosary. What a memorable summer vacation.

Since she couldn't get new information from her niece, she rounded the corner and pulled over to the curb to text Frank.

HEADED BACK TO PENN HILLS OVERNIGHT. IS THERE ANY WAY YOU CAN GET ME INTO MY SIL'S HOSPITAL ROOM LATE TOMORROW? I WANT TO ASK HER SOME QUESTIONS.

Just because today's long shot failed didn't mean her backup plan would necessarily fail too. She signaled left and pulled into traffic. Another left and she aimed for the highway and a second overnight stay in Penn Hills.

Thirty-Three

According to her notes, Larabee worked the second shift at a distribution warehouse. An alarm for six a.m. should get her to his house at the optimal time to wake him up too early and guarantee he'd be tired and punchy.

She opened a SoBe, a result of Sidney's influence. Her sometimes unreliable taste buds approved the melon flavor, although the amount of processed sugar in this version would rate a long Sidney lecture. Giulia leaned against the queen bed's headboard and logged in to the Quality Inn's Wi-Fi.

Larabee's Facebook page no longer came up in a search. Diane had turned her own Facebook page into a multimedia Find My Sister event. The header mimicked those Missing Person flyers people stapled to telephone poles: The single word "MISSING" in capital letters next to the picture of Joanne and the birthday cake.

First on the page was a short video of Joanne talking about her wedding cake business. Below that, a video of Diane explaining how long her sister had been missing. Below that, Joanne's physical description and the last places she was seen, followed by a plea from Diane for any information at all. Such a post was bound to bring the trolls a-running, and Giulia wasn't disappointed. "Never read the comments" was a rule she created long ago, because it kept her blood pressure in check. Now she had to break it.

"I saw her in the airport boarding a flight to Paris."

"I saw her last week on a bus headed to Canada."

On and on, vague and useless, giving Diane false hope. Then the sick puppies came out. Three people posted photos of dead women in the morgues of three different cities. Another five posted graphic descriptions of how they killed Joanne.

In her convent days, Giulia would've said a prayer for such people. Now she wanted to track them down and practice her self-defense techniques on them.

More fodder for confession time with Father Carlos.

Farther down the page, an edited post informed Diane's readers of her decision to remove photographs of Joanne's last few boyfriends.

"No matter what I really think, I don't want the police knocking on my door asking why I'm in essence accusing those men of kidnapping and murder. So let's pretend the police are doing their jobs and looking for my sister instead of telling me over and over and OVER how my sister 'wanted to vanish.' We all know that's a big, steaming pile of crap, right? Keep the leads coming. I'm tracking down every one of them when I'm not at the Day Job."

The replies to this post were lots of cyber hugs and prayers. A few people claimed to be psychics with a message from Joanne from "beyond the veil." An argument started, creating reply strings dozens of messages long.

Giulia read them all. They got her precisely nowhere on the case, although they did decrease her estimation of the American education system's ability to teach grammar and punctuation.

She wondered what Lady Rowan would have to say about Joanne.

With a bang, she closed the Facebook tab. She would not bring a psychic in on a case. She was a professional. Calling Lady Rowan would show almost as much desperation as calling *The Scoop*.

At six forty the next morning, she parked the Nunmobile across the street from Larabee's Tiny House and sipped Italian roast with Dulce de leche creamer. Larabee's Jeep was parked in the driveway.

Remembering his history of violence, Giulia banged the deer head knocker twenty times, then stepped five feet back on the dirt path, out of arms' reach.

"What the hell do you want?" His eyes had sunk into dark circles and he smelled of beer. His camouflage sweatpants needed a wash and his hand scratched his hairless chest. Giulia thought with fondness of Frank's morning look, which originated in a universe in which people showered.

"We met a few days ago, Mr. Larabee. I'm investigating the disappearance of Joanne Philbey."

Score one for years of experience at reading people. Larabee must not be called "Mr." too often. His mouth curved upward on the left side a quarter inch. He didn't abandon his defensive posture, but his arm muscles ramped down their level of clench.

"Yeah, I remember you. The Bible-salesman detective. What do you want at this hour? I work second shift, and I'm not in the mood for an interrogation."

"This won't take long. May I offer you a cup of coffee?" She extended the extra cup she'd bought at the local coffee shop.

The steam floated toward his face. "Yeah. Thanks." He popped off the plastic lid and took a long drink.

Giulia's tongue curled at the thought of his scalded taste buds, but he didn't blink once. "One cream and one sugar. Good guess."

He didn't invite her inside this time either, despite the early hour and the neighbor three doors down taking a long time to close his garage door while looking their way.

She kept to the half-truth, half-lie she'd chosen while waiting in the car. "I see your Facebook page is down."

All his muscles clenched again. After treating Giulia to several seconds of his opinions of Joanne's friends, he downed more coffee.

"Getting doxxed would cause that reaction in most people," Giulia said.

"No shit. So far you're the only one who seems to have figured out that limerick. I haven't seen any fat women hiding behind the cows next door or posting signs on my lawn."

What a charmer. Giulia put on her polite yet neutral smile. Would that be Polite Smile Number Three or Four? She really should keep a list.

"I'd like to ask about the online dating site geared to Preppers. It's so hard to find the right person these days, isn't it? You wouldn't believe some of the photographs and video clips I've received." She made a disgusted face. "My mother keeps telling me about the nice young men at her church, but never again. Been there, done that, still drinking away the memory."

Three...two...one. The wall between them didn't crumble but it thinned enough to allow conversation.

"Heh. I don't know if you're an uptight broad, but I got four striptease videos. They were all skanks, but they gave me a great free show."

Giulia didn't even grit her teeth or count to ten in Latin. She must have been getting better at this detective gig.

He finished his coffee. "I needed this. My car cooler has a leak and the beer I stashed in it yesterday got lukewarm. My mouth tasted like last week's garbage all the way home." The neighbor across the street dragged her trash can to the curb, her eyes on Larabee and Giulia the entire time.

"Nosy cow," Larabee muttered. "You done with your coffee?"

"Yes."

"Gimme the cup." He shook the dregs out of both cups and tucked them in his back pocket.

"I can take them back to my car and throw them away later," she said. DNA possibilities existed on his cup.

He might be thinking the same, if she was reading subtext in his answer. "Don't you compost your paper?"

Without missing a beat, Giulia said, "Sure, once I rinse them out."

He nodded. "Next time, run them under hot water and separate the seams. They layer better. We won't have the luxury of hot water when the world falls apart, but we won't be using paper cups after that anyway."

Two girls in Catholic school uniforms piled into a black SUV in the next driveway, followed by a woman in a business suit and running shoes. The girls waved out the windows. Larabee didn't acknowledge them.

A barely audible woman's voice came from the meadow side of Larabee's house. He must have had a window open, because the noise sounded like one of the actors on the local TV channel's all-night cop show marathon. Larabee had a hidden TV. So much for his stated intention of going off grid if he wasn't stuck living here and forced to use city power.

"So, yeah, you want to know about me and Josie online. It's like this. I don't go for fat chicks, but Josie was great to hang around with. Then she dropped some weight, and I figured it was time to make my move, but she wouldn't look at me except as a hunting buddy." He bared his teeth at a dog being walked by yet another neighbor. "So I contacted her on that Prepper site. She was kind of surprised, but we had a real date. Played laser tag. Stupid game, only for amateurs, but it was fun to pretend we were amateurs for a couple of hours." He squatted in front of a dandelion with leaves a foot wide and dug around it with his fingers until the entire plant came up by the roots. "We went out for a while. It was pretty good until her bitchy friends decided she was too good for me." He held up the leafy weed. "These are good when they're boiled."

Giulia could match him in cooking lore. "Only if you use plenty of water to counteract the bitterness."

He made a "point to you" gesture with the dandelion.

"Why didn't you tell me about dating Joanne via the internet when I was here the other day?" Giulia said.

"I don't know you. Private eye is one step removed from cop. I don't want the cops here again. It's bad for my career."

"It's bad for Joanne. She's still missing."

"Josie's dead. Her sister should have used her money to hire one of those dogs trained to sniff out corpses instead of giving it to you."

"What about the Beaver Falls Prepper community? The Home of the Horn."

He flinched. Another successful long shot. Larabee fit the "stud looking for his personal Pelvis of the Future" profile.

"It took me months of proving I was good enough before they'd give me a trial. They're a closed group. They kicked me out; said I wasn't a team player." He described Alex's bunch in a succinct unflattering phrase. "How'd you find out about them?"

"I'm a detective. It's what we do."

He stepped backward into his living room. "Get off my property. I'm fed up with strangers accusing me of shit. I told you everything you needed to know last time."

Giulia stood her ground, pleased with the extra space between them. "Thank you for your assistance, Mr. Larabee."

"Bitch." The door slammed. A cow mooed.

She didn't laugh until she'd driven around the corner out of sight.

Thirty-Four

The white-haired crocheter at Sunset Shores' reception desk remembered Giulia's name after two attempts.

"Our morning chef should be free before nine. Why don't you look at the lovely handmade items in our craft room while you wait?"

Always ready to maintain goodwill, Giulia entered the glass-walled craft area, but positioned herself to intercept Chef Eddie as soon as he appeared. She admired lacy blankets, shelves of matching gloves and hats, endless slippers, and some imaginative knitted neckties. Before she gave in to the temptation to purchase a metallic silver tie covered with Kelly green shamrocks to startle Frank, the kitchen door opened and Chef Eddie came out.

The receptionist waved her multi-ringed hand at him as Giulia advanced. In such a public situation, he couldn't pretend not to see her, but the look on his face implied he'd rather be at the dentist.

Giulia put on the smile she reserved for clients and witnesses she needed to charm. "Good morning. I promise this will only take a few minutes."

His answering smile was not a success.

"May we go out to the gazebo?"

He glanced at the receptionist, whose crochet hook held a loop of pink yarn suspended in mid-air. The woman winked at Eddie. His smile faltered and tried to regroup.

"Sure." He led the way out the back door and didn't speak

again until they were under the gazebo roof. "Evelyn thinks you're chasing me."

"She seems to approve."

"Unfortunately, yes. I mean, not that you're not good-looking, I mean..." His hands floundered in the air.

Giulia's smile widened. "I know what you mean. She's the matchmaker of the place?"

"One of them. Every morning they huddle like vultures over a fresh kill, planning the lives of all the staff and residents they think need romance. Or the ones whose current romance doesn't meet their standards."

"If they only could keep a dozen cats apiece, right?"

He shuddered. "I'm allergic to the hell beasts. The manager's found three illegal cats in this place because I started sneezing when a cat hair-covered old lady sat near me." He looked over at a group of men and women in shorts and t-shirts doing modified yoga on the lawn in front of one of the condos. "What else can I tell you about Joanie? There's no other reason you'd come back here."

"Have you ever seen the Jimmy Stewart movie *The Shop Around the Corner*?"

For a moment his body language said "fight or flight," but only for a moment. He dragged off his chef hat. "How'd you find out?"

Giulia said for the second time that morning, "I'm a detective. It's a job requirement."

Eddie picked at an invisible piece of food on the hat brim. "I didn't kill Joanie."

"I'm not accusing you. You don't see the police here with me."

His head jerked up. "You're serious."

"Yes. I'm still working from the premise that Joanne is alive. What happened between you two when you contacted her through the dating site?"

The sight of the strong man cringing opposite her said more than he realized.

"You're right. I tried the *Shop Around the Corner* thing because Joanie was always too busy to notice me. I was her colleague, but that was it. We didn't have anything in common outside of work. My cat thing was a deal-breaker, plus I don't hunt." He twisted the hat around one hand, then untwisted it. "I sort of altered a picture of me to look buff, because I knew Joanie was working out. She recognized me and sent me this God-awful message."

The joys of letting the witness think she knew nothing. "She was angry?"

"No, she was...kind. It sucked. The next morning, she winked at me when she came in, like we were friends sharing a secret. Friends. Neither of us mentioned the messages again. It was like they never happened."

If anyone had ever looked like someone kicked their puppy, Eddie was that person.

"Did Joanne ever talk to you about other men she met on dating sites?"

His laugh was bitter. "Oh, yeah. A bunch of hunters and a couple of guys who were all about how the world was going to end any minute now. One of them came to pick her up here at work, and I recognized him from some group hunting weekend pictures she showed me." His hands smoothed the hat out on his lap with little success. "You're a woman. Maybe you know. Why was Joanie so insecure about herself when at least two of her friends were all ready to take it to the next level?"

"Every woman is different. I can't speak to Joanne's reasons for lack of self-confidence, other than she thought she was too heavy."

The hat got another wring. "I hate Hollywood and supermodels and fashion designers."

Giulia stood. Maudlin was her signal to exit. Eddie raised his face to hers, which emphasized the kicked-puppiness. "You really think Joanie's run off with some rifle-toting jerk with a big dick? Excuse me."

"I think it's a strong possibility."

Hope erased some of the plaintiveness from his face. "That

would be awesome. You don't want to know all the nightmares I've been having of her body sliced up and dumped in the woods."

"I might advise watching fewer *CSI* reruns."

"Yeah."

She recorded the interview on her phone while still in the parking lot. Chef Eddie might be further down on her list of suspects, but he wasn't off it. The lost little boy act meant nothing to her after ten years of teaching high school.

Joanne's landlord gave Giulia no trouble about letting her into the apartment on short notice, but since he was out of town he sent his minion to unlock the door. His hungover minion. Giulia thanked him in a low voice. He grunted, keeping his head still. When they got out of the elevator on the third floor, *SportsCenter* on maximum volume slammed into their ears. The minion whispered something unprintable.

"I'll be in the first floor office." He winced and lowered his voice below a whisper. "Knock when you're done."

She closed the door on ESPN and started with the kitchen. First the cabinets above the counter, then the drawers below it. Nothing hidden in the dishes and silverware. Nothing secreted in the complete set of high-end pots and pans.

Oh, how Giulia coveted those pots and pans. But she moved on without Googling the manufacturer's website and fainting at the prices. Nothing hidden in the oven or broiler or refrigerator or freezer.

On to the bathroom. Sink, cabinet, towel shelves, toilet. Nothing in the tank or under the tank lid. You couldn't trust movies to give you useful clues anymore.

Bedroom. She ripped apart the bed and shoved the mattress off the box spring. Again, the movies lied to her. Nothing hidden between them or in the pillow cases. Nothing tucked in the boots in the closet or the pockets of the shirts or jeans or the few pieces of clothing in the dresser drawers.

At this point, Giulia wasn't sure whether she was grateful for only one more room to search or aggravated at coming up blank. She must be right. She must have missed something. She was going to find it.

Into the living room. She opened every single DVD. A plastic sandwich bag containing three hundred dollars was taped inside the cover of *Disaster Movie*. She made a note in her phone to let Diane know about her sister's emergency money.

All the other DVDs came up blank. So did the picture frames when she took them apart. So did the first two bookshelves.

But when she shook out a paperback titled *A Devil in the Details*, a folded invoice for cake decorating supplies fell to the floor. A flow chart covered the back.

"Giulia Driscoll, you need to recognize the obvious when it's beating you over the head."

She sat cross-legged on the carpet and unfolded the paper. A hand drawn grid covered the back of the invoice.

The name "Joanne" with a red line through it headed two lists of words. The first: Bean, Muscles for brains, Challenge, House, Prepared. The second list: Cucumber (with a star after it), Charismatic, Land, Charm, Honest, Allure. "Joanne" without a line through it topped the third list: Zucchini?, Ego, Hard work, Talent, Future, Shift.

Giulia's first thought was how to break to Diane that the police were two-thirds right about Joanne wanting to start a new life. Her second was how even naïve Giulia a few years back would've figured out what "bean," "cucumber," and "zucchini" stood for.

Her third was to thank Joanne in her heart for keeping all her secrets in one place. All three vegetables' names and phone numbers were on the bottom of the sheet: Lou Larabee, Alex Sila, and Kurt Warfield.

She un-pretzeled herself and grabbed her iPad from her messenger bag. The stiff kitchen chairs didn't do much for her back, but she stayed at the table to get on to the internet. Not five minutes later, the money Driscoll Investigations spent on the complete Whitepages phone plus address lookup site proved its value again. "Lou Larabee" and the Louis Larabee Giulia had twice interviewed were indeed the same person. Hooray for day jobs requiring their employees to have a phone.

"Alex-with-a-star Sila" might be Alex the wild-eyed gardener. Better than a fifty-fifty chance for that because of the Larabee match. She could research this Alex back home on a real computer, so his name went into the hold queue.

"Kurt-with-a-question-mark Warfield" had a number that led to a cell phone with the carrier's canned voice message. If Kurt thought not recording his own voice message kept him anonymous, he was about to lose faith in the concept of privacy.

She stepped around the stack of books from the successful shelf and took a closer look at the photographs themselves, not at what might be hiding behind them. No clues there. All the pictures were of Joanne and Diane or Joanne hunting, but not with any men.

Where else would a photograph hide? Giulia had stopped her search when she found the chart hidden in the paperback with the pointed title. Like the money hidden in the DVD with the pointed title. Therefore...

She read the rest of the titles on the shelf with the chart in her hand. Ego and talent. Hard work. Not Jane Austen, she failed on ego. None of the erotica titles were suggestive enough. At the far end, a werewolf romance and a ghost mystery sandwiched a biography of Oscar Wilde. The only biography on the entire bookshelf. Thank you, Mr. Wilde, for being talented and possessing a massive ego.

The picture fell out from between the tipped-in set of glossy photos of Wilde in the middle of the book. Joanne standing next to a tall blond dressed in an extravagant military uniform. For half a second, Giulia thought, "Armed forces?" until she saw the stage makeup. The back of the picture read, "*Carmen*, closing night, March 6th."

And thank you, Joanne, for labeling your photographs. She

returned to her iPad and searched for local opera companies performing *Carmen* this past March.

Cottonwood didn't have its own opera company, only the local theater where she and Frank still played flute and cello in the orchestra pit on occasion. However, Pittsburgh boasted two and, yes, one of them ran *Carmen* from February twentieth through March sixth. A few clicks brought up the cast. Don José: Kurt Warfield, Tenor.

Never trust a tenor. Every musical theater director had said this during rehearsals, and all the tenors had high-fived each other.

Noon. The tenor might be at lunch now and have his phone on. She called again.

"Hello?"

"Mr. Warfield, I'm with Driscoll Investigations. We're looking into the disappearance of Joanne Philbey."

"The what?" His voice cracked. He coughed twice, and when he spoke again Giulia understood the continual warnings. Even half-awake and froggy, this voice was meant to seduce. "Who are you and what are you talking about?"

At quarter to one, Giulia sat kitty-corner from the tenor at his kitchen breakfast bar. She sipped chilled orange blossom tea and nibbled a lemon cookie. The tenor dunked Oreos in milk.

"I can only indulge my childhood on days I'm not performing." He held the cookie in the milk to let it soften. "Dairy coats my throat and cuts half an octave off my range."

They talked musical theater, favorite pieces, closing night pranks they'd pulled, and ones they'd been the victim of. Kurt's voice remained impressive even when sabotaged by dairy products. Framed posters of his shows hung on every wall Giulia could see. The apartment's decorating scheme consisted of black, white, and crimson. Checkered tile. Three white walls and one black. Crimson area rugs. The stark contrast made Giulia restless, but the colors suited Kurt's easy, modern clothes, poster frames, and hair.

Kurt stopped at five cookies. "Oreos are the perfect indulgence, but my fans don't want to see a spare tire on Otello." He sealed the package of cookies. "You're patient. I like you. You didn't jump down my melodious throat as soon as you walked through the door."

Giulia sipped tea. Charmers, in her experience, didn't do well with silence.

He unfolded his napkin. "You remind me of the nuns in the boarding school my parents tossed me in when they got divorced. They were decent."

Giulia didn't offer any of her own personal information. She recognized the double meanings in his words. She used the technique herself. He re-folded the napkin. The current moment of silence lasted less than five seconds.

"You're probably wondering why I was asleep at noon on a Monday. I teach high school chorus and give private voice lessons. In the summer it's only private lessons. I get to sleep in." He drank the rest of the milk, complete with saturated cookie crumbs on the bottom of the glass. "You may not believe I didn't know Joanne disappeared, but that's not my problem." He paused. "Maybe it is my problem. Do the police think she's still alive? Are they looking for kidnapping suspects?" The cookies appeared to stick in his throat. "Do they think I'm involved?"

Without a smidge of guilt, Giulia played him like he was her flute. "I'm not in the confidence of the police. How long has it been since you spoke to Joanne?"

His long, thin hands picked at the defenseless napkin. "Months. It's been months. She stopped returning my calls after *Le Nozze di Figaro*. That was the end of March. I sent her flowers for her birthday and when she didn't call to thank me I gave up." He saw the napkin confetti and placed his hands flat on the narrow table. "Joanne bakes cakes. Have you seen them? We have a new stage manager who came from someplace in Ohio, and for our Christmas party she ordered this incredible cake decorated like the ball scene from *Die Fledermaus*. We were so impressed we offered the baker tickets to any opera of her choice. When she came, our stage manager brought her back to introduce her to the cast. She brought cupcakes for us and they were almost better than sex."

Giulia kept her face impassive. "I am aware of Joanne's side business baking cakes."

He spoke faster. "I like women with meat on their bones, so I asked her out for a drink. She was shy; I'm your classic extrovert. She's tone-deaf, can you believe it? She could only appreciate one of my talents." He winked, but his hands refused to stay still.

"How long did your relationship last?" Giulia stiffened her spine to convent posture and projected Teacher During Exam Time.

Kurt looked around at his framed posters as though Rossini and Mozart could give him inspiration. "A few months. Only off and on, you know? She had two jobs with wacky hours. She'd come hear me sing when she could and we'd shack up for a couple of days. She cooked everything I challenged her to. I tried to educate her on opera. She tried to get me to watch those parody movies, the really dumb ones."

"Is that why she cut off contact? Because you tried to educate her?"

"No, no, it wasn't like that. You make it sound like I thought I was better than her or she was stupid. She's smart and talented and so am I. I used to watch her cook. She could make magic with eggs and bacon and herbs and French bread."

Interesting. Giulia had been wondering how the three of them fit into bed: Kurt, Joanne, and Kurt's ego. While the question still applied, Kurt seemed to be the one person in Joanne's life who wasn't in take-take-take mode.

"The last time you saw Joanne, what was she like? Secretive? Worried? The same as usual?"

He frowned. "No, not worried. She came to closing night of *Carmen* and we went to the cast party. The chorus complained when she didn't bring cake, but I shut the idiots down. We went back to my place for the night, but she left right after breakfast." He opened the Oreo package again and ate two in a single bite each. "I was going to talk to her about sticking together long-term. When she never called me back after about ten voicemails, I figured she wasn't into me anymore. Funny, but I thought she wasn't the type of person who dumps and runs." He looked straight at Giulia. "When did she disappear?"

"The first week of April."

He tapped a third cookie on the counter, each tap spraying chocolate crumbs. "Rip off the Band-Aid for me: Do you think Joanne's dead?"

Giulia gave him an honest answer. "I'm not sure. She may have chosen to disappear or she may have been abducted, or she may have been robbed and murdered."

He flinched. "I asked for that."

"Thank you for your assistance." Giulia set down the tall tea glass.

He started. Perhaps he expected further interrogation. Perhaps he wondered if her next stop was the local police station to report on him. Both ideas pleased her. She didn't get a negative vibe from him, except for the Texas-sized ego, but he might think he was safe because he thought she couldn't access his phone records.

He ate the remains of the cookie. "When you find her, will you tell her to call me?"

Thirty-Five

Back home after checking in with Sidney and Zane, who reported a normal busy day, Giulia composed a reply to Alex's order to appear at the Hedge of Separation.

She'd better stop thinking in video game terminology or she'd laugh at the wrong time and things would get awkward.

"It's short notice, but I'm able to switch shifts with two different people for the next two days."

His reply icon dinged on the screen within two minutes. Alex wasn't completely off grid either.

"Very good. Here are the rules for a longer stay:

1. Immersion is required. This means you are expected to help with any and all chores as needed.

2. You must agree not to divulge any details regarding the community to outsiders.

3. No technology of any kind, including cell phones.

Do you agree to these rules?"

Giulia chewed her bottom lip. The no cell phone rule could be part of Technology Bad, Simple Life Good, if one ignored the plain fact of Alex using an internet dating site to find new pelvises. Pelvii? Her Latin had gone downhill in a big way since she'd left the convent. Although she'd never been asked to conjugate "pelvis" for her students, not even in Sex Ed.

No cell phones could also mean some members of the community didn't want themselves outed. To their friends? On the internet? The mom of teenagers said her parents knew of their participation, but she could be the exception.

If she tried to sneak her phone in, would they search her? She couldn't afford to risk getting the boot. She had her answer, then. The cell phone was a deal-breaker. Time to play hard ball.

"I can only switch shifts at such short notice if I stay on call. I'm really sorry, but I can't afford to lose my job. Thank you anyway for the invitation."

She sat back and watched the screen. How valuable was her Pelvis of the Future to him and his leader?

Thirty seconds later, she had her answer.

"I'll contact the others and get back to you."

Giulia grinned. Who would have guessed her skeletal dimensions possessed such value to total strangers? Not her, certainly. Where would it have belonged on her resume? Not under experience or education or professional awards. Such an asset deserved its own category.

No instant reply this time. She went into the kitchen to prepare her own sourdough starter as a sacrifice to gain the goodwill of this almighty community leader. When she located her sixteen-ounce glass measuring cup behind the milk in the fridge, she covered it with plastic wrap—the horror! Machine-processed kitchen supplies! When she checked her screen again, a message icon waited for her.

"The community agrees to make a temporary exception for your cell phone because the need is work-related. Make certain it is completely charged as none of our houses are wired for electricity. Immersion for two days includes not returning to your car to use its battery. When you arrive, please mute the ringer and set it to vibrate only so none of the other members are disturbed. Because this is a trial visit, you will not be expected to provide any supplies other than your own sleeping bag and toothbrush. The community members will share their toothpaste and soap with you so you may see how we will be living in the near future. Reply with your approximate time of arrival."

Giulia's reaction to this series of totalitarian dicta proved she was not the all-passive-all-the-time person she used to be. She was conscious of a strong desire to beat Alex and his community leader with a wooden ruler until it snapped.

After supper, she sat Frank on the couch and explained what she'd be doing on this sleepover.

"I've set them up to expect my evil, greedy corporate employers to wreck my visit to the future. Can you text me at eleven o'clock Wednesday morning with an urgent summons to go into work? I want a real message to show these people."

Frank rubbed his buzz-cut. "Do you know how much I want to send VanHorne and me in there with you as your bodyguards?"

"And destroy this cover I've spent so much time on?"

"Hold it. We have the same last name. They'll suspect something's wonky."

She shook her head. "So young and so forgetful. My name for this adventure is Maria Martin."

He echoed the name as soon as she got out the first syllable. "I'll go download one of those apps that improve your memory."

"Besides," Giulia said with mock relish, "bodyguards would seriously cramp my style with all the males who want to be my new best friend and bed companion."

Frank's smile was less than sincere. "Part of me is proud of my hot wife. Every other part of me wants to smash heads." Conversation stopped for some kissing. "I told the guys about your dating site experiences. I never saw grown men laugh so hard."

"There's no privacy in my life at all, is there?"

"Think of the unexpected joy you're bringing to the hard-working men and women in Precinct Nine." His smile faded. "Please tell me you know the exact location of this miniature Utopia."

She snapped her fingers. "I knew I forgot something." She unlocked her phone and checked the pin she'd dropped when she left the hedge the other night. "Well, well, well. Look at this." She turned the phone so Frank could see.

"North-northwest from here in the middle of farms and woods. You don't have anything more specific?"

"I don't need to." She enlarged the map, which revealed only Rural Route numbers. "The directions Alex of the wild eyes gave me for their Prepper community had me circle up and around to find the entrance. His two acres of land are right along here." She pointed to an empty space on one of the routes. "Alex and the almighty leader are in each other's pockets."

"This Alex sold land to the dictator, you think?"

Giulia shrank the map to see more of the surrounding streets, except there weren't any. "Cow country. You have to love it. Wait; I got distracted. I was going to say something."

"Selling land," Frank repeated.

"No. Oh, I remember. An anomaly keeps appearing in my research on this case. I've been shelving it because it won't slot into my data."

"You can't figure out how they make tin foil hats without using tin foil?" He held up a hand before she replied. "Better yet, you've found secret data proving all the Preppers are chipped and tagged like wild animals on those nature shows, and their new Utopia will turn out to be a covert government experiment in hive-mind research."

Giulia grinned. "Video games are warping your brain. I'm talking about twins. My missing person is a twin. Alex asked if I was a twin. I made up a backstory about a twin sister killed in high school by a drunk driver."

"You hardened sinner."

She scrunched her face at him. "Father Carlos understands me. My point about twins, assuming their appearance is a legitimate aspect of my search, is: What if the community leader is Alex's twin?"

"And they're recruiting only twins because of deep-seated whatevers in their psychological makeup?"

Giulia stared through the walls. "I'm trying to recall if the teenage football players were identical."

"Won't a group of twins intermarrying twins do strange things to the future gene pool?"

"Don't ask me. I taught sex education, not biology. I should talk to Olivier about cult mentality before I immerse." She dialed Sidney's number.

"You're going to Sidney's family farm in July? I married a brave woman."

Thirty-Six

Five hundred feet before the alpaca farm entrance, Giulia remembered why visiting the farm in July was a triple threat. It smashed together a field trip to a petting zoo, a farmer's market, and a Christmas village.

Custom signs with the alpacas dressed as Santa, Mrs. Claus, and various elves lined the road. As soon as she turned into the driveway, she heard Christmas carols playing from speakers mounted on the gift shop porch. Every window, door, and square inch of land twinkled, spun, glittered, or bobbed.

The seven alpacas all wore jingle bell collars. They looked less than pleased, but Giulia made allowances for their full coats in this heat. Shearing wasn't until the first week of August so all the Christmas in July visitors could see fluffy adorable alpacas, not shaved alien beasts.

Nine cars were parked in front of the gift shop. Three small children clung to the fence and squealed as they read the alpacas' collars.

"Mama, they all have Christmas names. Aren't they pretty? Can we take one home?" The alpacas projected disdain. The parents changed the subject.

Giulia drove past the gift shop and barn to the back cottage. Sidney's husband Olivier was weeding a vegetable garden three times the size of Giulia's. Sidney was weeding the flowers surrounding the cottage and talking nonstop to Jessamine sitting in a stroller next to her. Giulia parked and walked straight over to the baby, who cooed and held up her arms.

"Hello, sweetie." Giulia unstrapped Jessamine and tossed her in the air. The baby giggled. Her bright yellow dress floated around her ears and the sparkling red and green bows in her dark hair wiggled. Giulia caught her and kissed her chubby cheeks.

"I just fed her," Sidney said. "Be careful she doesn't spit up on you."

"I'll have to get used to it soon. Her hair is curlier than the last time I saw her."

"Do you like the bows?" Sidney stood and bent in half backwards. "Ah, spinal cracks. So good."

"Has she pulled any out yet and given herself a meal of glitter?"

"We haven't caught her yet. The customers love it."

"If you don't need a light tonight to change her diaper, you'll have your answer." Giulia cradled Jessamine in one arm and tickled her with the other hand.

Sidney took out her phone and typed. "Why didn't we think to add glitter to the fertilizer bags for the Christmas market? I'm texting dad right now."

"Sparkling unscented alpaca poop. What every gardener wants in their stocking on Christmas morning."

Olivier walked through the corn toward them, hoe in hand. Next to Sidney, they became a copy of the famous painting *American Gothic*, if those farmers had worn *The Avengers* and *X-Men* t-shirts. Olivier gave his daughter triple raspberries on her belly. Jessamine shrieked and wiggled with laughter.

"Will we be feeding the delightful beasts glitter or will we add it in the gathering stage?" he said.

Sidney typed into her phone. "Only if I can find some in bulk from an organic florist." She tried to enlarge the website on her screen. "Forget it. I need a real computer for searching." She took the baby from Giulia. "Let's pick flowers for Aunt Giulia to take home while she and daddy talk shop."

The inside of their cottage was Christmas-free. Not a Christmas elf herself, Giulia found the return to midsummer relaxing.

Olivier poured water for them both. "Let us discuss the mysterious inner workings of the cult mentality."

"Olivier, have you forgotten I spent ten years in the convent?"

"I have not. However, convents are celibate. This place you're investigating is set up as a colony. They perceive themselves as the founders of a new America. Or a new theocracy. Did you get a strong sense of religion when you were there?"

"Let's call it hero-worship." She paraphrased the series of messages she received today. "How else do you explain a varied group of sensible adults who relinquish their mental and physical freedom with a smile?"

"Did they smile?'

Giulia shuddered. "All the time. Everyone was happy and helpful and welcoming. Even the teenage boys who had to give up their football game did chores without whining."

"I wish I could use those techniques on the wooly beasts out there."

"Are they still spitting at you?"

"Not as often. They like Jessamine, so they treat me better when she's riding on my shoulders." He smiled. "I could work up an entire case history on them involving antisocial tendencies, gender intolerance, and social anxiety."

Giulia pictured lawsuits. "They don't spit on the kids clinging to the fences, do they?"

"No, thank God, even though no one pays attention to the signs everywhere telling visitors not to pet the alpacas." He got up and gestured to Giulia's glass. "Refill?"

"I'm good. If I were theoretically going to a Doomsday Prepper slumber party tomorrow, what survival advice would you give me?"

Tiny lines gathered around the corners of his mouth. "Don't."

She smiled. "Part of the job."

The lines deepened. "Do you have an exit plan?"

"Yes. Frank is going to text me with a work emergency at eleven a.m. Wednesday."

The lines retreated. "I respect your brains. All right, here's my generalized analysis of cults and Preppers and why sharing my life with seven aggressive mounds of walking fur is preferable to living with either." He passed her a pen and paper. "First: Groupthink."

"Shades of *1984*."

"Actually, no. The term sounds Orwellian, but it was coined by William H. Whyte three years after *1984* was published."

Giulia clutched an imaginary string of pearls. "I've lost the right to call myself a teacher of English."

"Sidney would blame it on baby brain. To continue. Cults foster exclusivity, setting themselves apart from the world, and the sense of being one of the chosen few. Members believe they're special and the leaders work to bolster that belief. Therefore, they happily imbibe the group's way of speaking, dressing, behaving, and thinking."

"And it's all good."

"In their eyes."

Giulia drank more water. "You realize you're describing my entire convent experience."

He hesitated. "I've never told you how tempted I am to ask you to be a case study in my ongoing effort to get published in *Psychology Today*."

"We'll talk after I extricate myself from the Stepford Doomsday Crazies."

Olivier's grin made her grin back. This kind, perceptive man brought out the best in almost everyone he met. But for now...

"Twins," Giulia said. "My client is a twin. One of the Prepper families possibly has twin sons. During my first date with one of the Preppers—don't laugh, it was research for this case—he asked me if I was a twin and talked about his twin sisters."

She watched Olivier regroup. "Fascinating. The only twin deities I can think of are Romulus and Remus, the mythological founders of Rome." He tapped a finger on his lips. "A twin fetish, perhaps. I'm inclined to the religion aspect, but I'd have to research more gods."

"Castor and Pollux, Apollo and Artemis." Giulia stopped herself. "Anyway, research is my job."

"Fair enough. If the place you're infiltrating is collecting twins, I would kiss all seven of those beasts outside for a chance to analyze their leader." He glanced out the window. "Maybe I'd kiss five of them."

"Only if you're prepared for YouTube fame." Giulia added twin god mythology—does Alex have a secret dominant twin?—to her notes. "In a perfect world we'd have the money to keep you on retainer."

"Speaking of perfect worlds, the second major point of my analysis is the divine mandate to create a perfect future."

A groan from Giulia. "Not more religion."

"It's always religion." Olivier leaned forward. "Either an established god has spoken to the cult leader or the leader himself is their god."

"Are you seriously claiming everyone who wants to establish a survival group has a god complex?"

Olivier shook his head. "No, but isolating and reconditioning the followers tends to make them look on the leader as their personal Jesus Christ. Continual worship works on the leader's mind until he starts to think he can walk on water and raise the dead. No offense."

"None taken. At least I have a secret weapon: I'm intimately familiar with Jesus Christ."

Olivier's laughter brought Sidney and the baby inside with a bunch of bright yellow jessamine flowers tied with one of the baby's glitter bows.

Thirty-Seven

The next morning, Giulia arrived at the office late and dressed for yard work. "I'm out of here before noon, guys."

Sidney was frowning. Zane looked from Giulia to Sidney and back as his face morphed from concerned to unsure to concerned again.

"What's the problem?" Giulia said.

"Don't go," Sidney said.

"I agree with Sidney," Zane said.

Giulia leaned against the door, arms crossed. "Say it."

Someone knocked on the glass at her shoulder. Giulia opened the door for Jasper Fortin, closed all four of them in, and cast suspicious looks at her hardworking staff.

"Jasper, it's always a pleasure to see you, but you must admit your timing is a touch too convenient."

"I couldn't get away before now, Ms. Driscoll. Aunt Rowan double-booked herself and I came to her rescue. Sidney and Zane said you'd be in this morning."

The smile Giulia favored her employees with was not her most pleasant one.

"Don't get mad at them," Jasper said. "Aunt Rowan did another Tarot reading for you and she saw coercion and bondage, both mental and physical. I won't tell you the exact cards and interpretations, but she says you have enough sense, and I quote, to keep your head out of your backside where the Tarot is involved."

Giulia didn't find Rowan's opinion amusing. "Please tell her I appreciate her concern."

Jasper glanced at Zane and Sidney. "I understand. I'll give her your message."

When the downstairs door squeaked closed behind him, Giulia waited until both her employees met her gaze. "I appreciate your concern also, but Lady Rowan is not in the private investigation business. I am, and I am capable of fulfilling my business objectives without advice from the Other Side. Specific to this case, I will point out that I survived ten years in a cult. I can survive another twenty-four hours."

Zane's expression changed from trepidation to confusion.

"The convent," Giulia said. "As for the Preppers, I have an extraction plan plus a backup escape plan if they try to graft a tin foil hat onto my scalp. Either way, I'll be out of there tomorrow, hopefully with our client's no longer missing twin sister."

Sidney said with unusual meekness, "What if she doesn't want to come out?"

"I'll give her the current total of what her sister is paying us to find her. From my research into her personality, the guilt would make her at least agree to a photograph and a voice message for her sister on my phone."

"A phone in an anti-technology Prepper compound?" Zane's natural Humphrey Bogart voice would never sound meek, but it did project "subdued."

"The dictator of this community has granted me special dispensation because my Maria Martin persona may get called in to work." She walked to her own office and paused with her hand on the doorknob. "I'm interruptable this morning."

Zane interrupted her exactly seven minutes later. "Ms. D., my girlfriend is hooked on *The Scoop*. She makes me watch their podcasts every time I go to her house."

Giulia saved her document. "Yes?"

She got the strongest impression he gathered himself to stand firm against her wrath. She must look angrier than she felt. Or else

Jasper's clairvoyance was rubbing off on her. What would her brother Salvatore say to that?

"She's been bouncing around their archive, picking episodes based on how much the titles make her laugh. Yesterday she found one from the middle of May. I think you should see it."

She opened *The Scoop's* website and found their archive. Zane pointed. "There. Fifth from the bottom."

Giulia clicked on an episode titled "Twinkies Will Survive the Apocalypse. Stock Up Now."

"Scroll to minute eight or so. The beginning is a recap of the episode where they stuck the camera into the bushes and the bouncers broke the lens."

"That was an enjoyable episode." She dragged her mouse to the eighth minute and clicked Play.

"...find an entrance, Scoopers, so we're in the woods around back. Have you ever seen anything that screams 'we've got a big, fat secret' louder than a ten-foot privacy hedge?" Kanning's idea of a whisper would reach to the last row of the balcony in the Cottonwood Community Theater. The trees around him glowed the unnatural green of things lit by a night vision camera. Kanning's face filled the screen, eyes dark and hair looking like phosphorescent seaweed. "We've returned to this camp of bullies to learn The Truth. It's almost dawn, but we can't hear any sounds from the eager pilgrims behind the hedge. Apparently Preppers don't get up early to work the fields. If they keep this work ethic, they won't survive their first winter in a technology-free world."

Giulia whacked her forehead. "I knew I forgot a connection. The hedge."

Phosphorescent Kanning sneaked along the hawthorn and ivy barrier, attempting to stick his hand in the dense cluster of branches, leaves, and berries. Giulia remembered a line from Mark Twain's famous review of James Fenimore Cooper's books: "Every time a Cooper person is in peril, and absolute silence is worth four dollars a minute, he is sure to step on a dry twig."

Clomp, clomp, snap, swish, snap, clomp, snap-snap-snap.

A dog barked. Another.

"He's toast," Giulia said. "Preppers keep big dogs."

Kanning and his cameraman detoured into the woods away from the hedge. The back of Kanning's seaweed hair bobbed and weaved as they ran, but his hairsprayed helmet never budged. The number of twigs snapping under their shoes sounded like Fourth of July firecrackers.

"Holy [*bleep*]." The cameraman's voice. The camera swooped away from The Hair. The night vision colors switched off and the regular spotlight illuminated a naked woman on a brown blanket of some kind. Her naughty bits were pixelated for television, as were her facial features. A crown of daisies lay askew on her short blonde hair. A henna-shaded tattoo of a grapevine trailed up her left leg and twined around a scaly horn, like some kind of lizard's. In the clashing sunrise and artificial light, both looked painted on rather than inked. Going by her smooth skin and general tautness, Giulia guessed her to be eighteen at the most.

Kanning photobombed the picture. "Miss? Miss, wake up."

"She's dead, Ken."

Kanning's Adam's apple bobbed, but he reached a steady hand down to the woman's—girl's—neck and felt her jugular vein. The camera gave the audience a close-up of Kanning's spine sagging. "No, she's not. I've got a pulse here." His head blocked her face and he sniffed. "I don't recognize the odor, but she's been drugged."

The camera zoomed in on the tattoo. Kanning's loud voice-over said, "We had to edit this out for television, Scoopers, but there are dried fluids on this young woman's legs. We didn't take a sample because it wouldn't stand up in court, but this recording is available to the Cottonwood police if they ever decide to stop stuffing doughnuts into their cake holes and investigate this underage sex slave ring."

"Leap to conclusions much?" Zane said. "I swear he believes his own hype."

"According to his website, he's the only hard-hitting investigative reporter in the Greater Pittsburgh area."

Kanning's face reappeared in his studio. "We got out of there fast, Scoopers, before the thugs found us again. There may have been a smile on that poor young woman's face, but we all know the drugs caused it. Not even our beautiful Cottonwood is safe from disgusting criminals, but never fear, loyal Scoopers. We will get to the bottom of this."

Giulia closed the playback window. "That man gives me a stabby pain right here." She massaged the back of her neck.

Zane shuffled his feet. "This podcast is why I called Jasper, Ms. D. Kanning might be sub-human, but you can't argue with the implications of him finding a naked girl in the woods. You're not staying at a geek retreat or a frat party hideaway. They've got weird drugs and women aren't safe with them."

Giulia smiled at him, all her annoyance gone. "I appreciate your concern. No, really, I do. This podcast gives me two more reasons to infiltrate their community: the dead teenagers and my sister-in-law. The pieces are starting to come together."

Zane opened his mouth but closed it without speaking.

"Thank you. I don't need you or Sidney to mother me. I'm capable of taking care of myself, and now that you've warned me about a whole 'nother aspect to their community, I'll be on my guard while I eat, drink, and breathe." She raised her voice. "Did you hear that, mom?"

"Yes. Fine. Sorry. Good."

Giulia had no trouble following Sidney's reasoning through those five syllables. She went over to the file cabinet and opened the bottom drawer.

"I can't sneak in fingerprinting supplies, but a few small Ziploc baggies won't show in my pockets. If I can find their drug stash, I'll sneak out a sample for the police."

"What if they search you?" Zane's foot tapped the floor.

"You're borrowing trouble. I learned a long time ago what a black hole that is." She opened the box underneath the fingerprint kit. "Here they are. These will go in my hiking boots, I think." She unlaced her left boot and slid two small bags under the insoles. "No matter whose house I sleep in, evidence can and will be hidden from prying Preppers. What time is it?"

"It's 10:57."

"I've got to get on the road." She shut down her computer and tucked her phone in her back pocket. "I might be back in here tomorrow afternoon. It depends on what I find and how exhausted I am after milking goats and shoveling natural fertilizer."

"I bet you'll appreciate our alpaca fertilizer a lot more," Sidney said. "If you'd told us you'd have to milk goats, we could've given you a lesson on the alpacas."

"Milking goats?" Zane said.

"They have sheep, goats, and pigs. No cows." Giulia picked up her purse. "I thought of it after I left your place, Sidney, but they don't expect me to know anything about animals except how to cook them, so I want to come in cold."

Zane patted his computer monitor. "You can have my technology—"

"When you pry it from my cold, dead hands," Giulia and Sidney finished.

Thirty-Eight

At ten after one, Giulia backed the Nunmobile into a spot close to the compound's hidden hedge entrance. The smart PI makes sure to plan for a possible emergency exit. Her Glock in the glove compartment was positioned for quick access. Her blonde Maria Martin hair was braided and wound around her head. The hazel contacts worried her. She'd stashed a miniature bottle of eye drops in with her toothbrush.

Her only unpreparedness: mosquito repellent. She hadn't found an all-natural recipe whose ingredients were already in her pantry or laundry room. Asking for some might be perceived as weakness. Maybe she could convince the most paranoid member of a theory she heard on the internet about how the government was conducting secret experiments in spy drone miniaturization. How she'd seen blurry photos like Bigfoot photos of a captured drone and they looked like oversize mechanical mosquitoes.

After dropping that rock in the pond, she would sit back and watch the paranoia explosion. Tonight's post-supper entertainment: Target practice on evil government spy-cam insects.

But for now she'd have to tough it out and look forward to baking soda plasters at home in the modern world. She took out her sleeping bag and well-worn canvas backpack (three dollars at Rowan's fourth husband's Army-Navy surplus store) from the trunk and locked it. Her keys went into her toiletry bag because she was still not naïve enough to think these Stepford people were too polite to snoop in the newbie's car. Finally, the car alarm could serve a purpose other than annoying everyone within a city block's radius.

Before she pushed aside the ivy curtain over the hidden opening, she smelled all-natural fertilizer. Tuesday must be shovel the poop day. Lucky her. She took a deep breath. Bad idea; find another way to get into character. She closed her eyes, counted to five in Latin, and opened her eyes into Maria Martin's Precious Moments figurine expression.

"Maria's here," the spinning woman called as Giulia pressed herself against the inside of the hedge, feigning uncertainty. Cheryl. The woman's name was Cheryl.

"Hey, Maria." One of the teenagers tossed his football at her. She trapped the ball between her hip and her sleeping bag.

"Not bad for a girl," his brother said.

Giulia dropped the sleeping bag and tossed a competent spiral pass back to him. The other one gave her a thumbs-up before snatching it from his brother's hands and taking off in a wide loop around the beehives. They were identical. One set of twins down; how many to go?

A short balding man sat on the porch step of the octagon house playing 1950s do-wop songs on an accordion. In a rocking chair on the porch, a redhead with retro cat-eye glasses mended a shirt. A basket piled high with ripped items of clothing waited next to her.

A skinny blonde—the blonde from *The Scoop*'s earlier show about this place?—carried a wicker basket with more clothes toward the woods. A hunk of yellowish handmade soap balanced on top of the clothes. An equally skinny redhead carried a similar basket.

The sound of an axe chopping wood came from behind the beehives. A teenage girl and a younger boy walked from one front garden to the next, spreading pungent manure. The expressions on their faces begged to become a meme.

Cheryl picked up Giulia's sleeping bag. "You're in Audrey's

house for tonight. She's on a business trip. She says welcome and enjoy and don't forget her Rottie thinks he's a one-hundred-fifty-pound lap dog."

Giulia ducked her head. "Thank you. I'm looking forward to a longer stay."

They walked up the single step into one of the trailer-style houses. The door opened without a key.

"I've never lived in a place without at least two locks on the doors."

Cheryl's smile got bigger. "I used to live in neighborhoods like that. It's so refreshing to find a place where everyone trusts each other."

Giulia made a thoughtful face. "You'd have to, if you all plan to create a safe haven for the future."

"Exactly. I told Alex you were the right kind of person to bring in. I do hope you'll like it here. Now," she pointed, "the bedroom is through the living area, and the galley kitchen is over to your left. All our houses are the easiest in the world to get used to."

Giulia set her sleeping bag and knapsack on the floor of the bedroom.

"Come out back and I'll call Pepin."

Giulia smiled. "For Pepin the Short. I remember from my first visit."

Cheryl clapped. "Yes. I'm so glad to meet another history buff. Alex is, but my husband and kids are all about gadgets and the insides of machines." They walked through a kitchen exactly long enough to squeeze in a half-size iron stove with two cupboards above it, plus a sink with an old-fashioned water pump. The screen door and storm door were closed. Cheryl opened both and whistled, then called "Pepin!"

The memorable black and brown moose galloped toward the house. A miniature moose, that is, with a flopping tongue whose steps rattled the dishes in the cupboard. Pepin stopped at the back step and *woofed.*

"Pepin, do you remember Maria? She's our friend. Say hello."

Giulia held out her left fist, fingers down. The moose sniffed it all over, considered for about three seconds, and bumped her fist so it landed on top of its head. Giulia scratched the top of Pepin's head. His muzzle stretched in a goofy smile and she walked down the step, brought up her other hand, and rubbed his ears.

"Get ready," Cheryl said.

The warning came only a moment before Pepin collapsed at Giulia's feet with a house-shaking *WHUMP*. All four legs pointed skyward and the barrel-like rib cage and stomach demanded pets. Giulia complied.

"If he lands on me in the middle of the night, you'll be able to use me as Soylent Green."

Cheryl laughed again but shook her head. "Don't mention that movie when Alex is around. He'll launch into a twenty-minute lecture on how our current world situation exactly mirrors the conditions that led to creating Soylent Green, and then he'll make us all take marksmanship refreshers."

Pepin slurped Giulia's face.

"Pepin, that's enough. Go chase squirrels. Go on, boy."

The moose rolled over and galloped into the woods.

"He's adorable." Giulia pretended she didn't care about dog drool drying on her cheek.

"To us he is," Cheryl closed the doors. "So are Rana and Boris and Lassie. But if a stranger finds the entrance, they won't get such a welcome. All our dogs are trained guard dogs."

A high-def image of Pepin's teeth clamped on Ken Kanning's butt sprang into Giulia's mind. To erase it, she said, "Have you seen Alex today?" A sensible question since Maria Martin was supposed to be Alex's date.

"Oh, yes, that's right. He said he'd be at the archery range because you need practice. Do you remember where it is?"

Giulia followed the repeated *thwip-thunk* sounds out to the targets. She anticipated more face-sucking action from Alex, but his body language conveyed otherwise.

"Maria. Welcome. I'm pleased you came here early enough to

experience more than recreation and supper." He handed her a bow and arrow. "Remember the skill set for archery differs in certain ways than the skill set for guns. There is no wind today. Set yourself, aim, and shoot."

Ten years in the convent, no matter how far in her past, made Giulia an expert in unquestioning obedience—on the surface. She was also an expert in the art of the poker face, because as much as she'd been a good nun, her thoughts didn't always merit scrutiny. Like now.

Her face smiled. She nocked the arrow, pictured Alex's narrow butt covering the bull's-eye, and released. Lower right cheek. Not bad.

"Not bad," he said. "Adjust your aim up and to the right."

For the next hour, as near as she could guess, she practiced enough to improve her average to one bull's-eye every four shots. Alex harangued her, criticized her technique, issued grudging praise, and in general showed himself to be the type of teacher Giulia hated the most. "Maria Martin" giggled at the praise, put on a serious face at the criticism, and ignored the harangues.

Reason number four why Giulia would never make it as a Prepper: She needed a clock to tell the time. Darn technology, making humans dependent on it.

Her fingers and shoulders ached and she wanted a tall glass of water, but she knew this was yet another test so she sucked it up.

At last he said, "Enough."

She lowered the bow and walked to the target to retrieve the arrows.

"Your technique has improved. But you are still a novice and if you are serious about becoming one of us you must bring your skills up to par."

Giulia pulled out three arrows from the imaginary Alex butt, in her mind hearing his didactic voice jump an octave with each yank. The satisfaction mitigated the shoulder ache.

Then again, she would much rather he lecture her than kiss her.

They stored the archery supplies in a shed behind the targets. The woods surrounded them on three sides. Rows of barley, then wheat and oats led back to the compound proper.

"Is this enough grain to support everyone over the winter?" she said.

Alex began another lecture about planning and equal distribution and how the only way for the community to lead the way in the upcoming new world was to use privation to grow stronger.

Blah, blah, blah. Giulia paid only enough attention to make the expected responses. She always, always wanted to duct-tape the mouths of people who preached unity and endurance through sacrifice. Her experience of these types usually ended with the discovery of their personal stash of whatever commodity was expected to be in short supply. Her first order of business therefore: Make the rest of the dogs remember her so they'd let her spy in the middle of the night.

When they reached the backyard gardens, she channeled her inner Sidney: "Oh, I almost forgot. I brought the community a gift. Let me run in for it. I'll only be a minute."

She ran to the correct back door before he could reply. The starter was expanding in the heat but it hadn't overflowed. Eager "Maria" ran outside with it.

"It's sourdough starter," she said, holding up the concoction like an offering. Easy to achieve since Alex towered over her. "When I was here the other day the flat bread tasted really good, but then I wondered if nobody remembered how to make this. I mean, it's possible because yeast is so easy to get in the grocery store. But the natural way is best, don't you agree? This will keep forever, honestly forever if you feed it right." She met his eyes with a shy but hopeful glance. "I know you said to bring only essential supplies but, well, is this okay?"

Channeling her inner Sidney was exhausting.

Alex smiled at her for the first time that day. "Very good. Our Cheryl brought the same natural bread starter when she joined us. I had worried you might be too concerned about making yourself fit in with everyone here, but I'm pleased to be wrong in this one thing."

He took the container and walked to the gingerbread house's back screen door. "Cheryl? Donald? Tim? Jim?"

"Coming." Cheryl opened the door, fluffs of wool dotting her apron.

"Look what Maria brought us." He held out the starter.

Cheryl clapped. "I told you, Alex."

Another smile, this time with a tinge of beneficence. "You did. I'm pleased you were correct. Would you put this in your cold room with the rest?"

"Would I? You bet. Maria, he means the special niche in our cellar lined with two layers of stone. My husband engineered it because he said the new world needs my bread." She glanced at Alex. "Is there room in the schedule for Maria to take a quick peek?"

More beneficence. It practically radiated from him, like a stylized icon of Our Lady of Guadalupe.

"Certainly there is. Besides, it's time to begin supper prep, isn't it?"

Cheryl leaned into the living room area. "Right as always. We'll take it from here."

She led Giulia into a kitchen exactly like the kitchen in Audrey's house. "We have an old-fashioned pull chain clock in our living area. I haven't yet mastered telling time by the sun like Alex."

Cheryl's house was fluffy. The gingerbread scrollwork on the eaves and porch outside repeated on every possible surface inside. Her house was also bigger than Audrey's. It had to be to accommodate four people.

"My boys made the clock. They both created the mechanism. Jim carved the wood and Tim painted it."

"They're very talented." Maria Martin's blandness was making Giulia itch.

"They are, aren't they?" Cheryl beamed. "I won't apologize,

because parents always brag on their children. It's in the rule book. You wait until you have kids of your own. You'll see."

She opened a trap door in the pantry off the kitchen and climbed down. "Come on. There's plenty of room for two in here."

Giulia descended the ladder and stood in a miniature version of fruit cellars she'd seen in regular houses. Supplies filled openwork metal shelving on all four walls. Canned goods and nut butters. Boxes of granola, bouillon cubes, and macaroni. Bags of beans and jerky. Cheeses hung from the ceiling in one corner, reminding Giulia of the provolone in her grandmother's fruit cellar.

Cheryl pulled one of the shelves away from the wall and opened a square door.

"It looks like a wall safe," Giulia said, thinking it also looked like a Tabernacle door.

"We got the door and the frame with hinges from an old wall safe. We don't lock it or anything in case someone needs to start bread and we're busy. See the beautiful flat river rocks my husband found for me?"

Giulia was able to make sincere compliments about the compact structure. Perhaps a cubic foot in total width, it held several glass jars of bread starter exactly like Giulia's.

Cheryl placed the new glass container in the front row. "Now a little part of you belongs to the community."

And with that Giulia was officially creeped out.

Thirty-Nine

If the community hadn't been technology-free, Giulia's first time milking goats would've become a YouTube "best of" video. Demon-possessed goat udder squirting warm milk up her nose? Check. Pointy goat horns stuck in her jeans? Check. Little goat hooves tripping her so she landed on her butt to the delight of her new friends? Check.

But none of those were reason number five why she'd never make it as a Prepper. Dinner prep was. Manipulating squishy hunks of venison wrapped in soggy brown paper gave her a new appreciation of meat in Styrofoam and plastic wrap in neat rows at the grocery store.

On top of that, the Fair Folk—an Irish tradition taught to her by Frank's grandmother—did not oblige her at supper. Joanne was not present. Instead, Giulia tested her ability to remember and match names to faces.

At the tables sat the accordion player and the clothes mender, Wild-Eyed Alex, Cheryl and her twins Tim and Jim, the goat milker and his wife the cheesemaker, plus two new couples, both in their early twenties. The first dressed and walked like seasoned outdoors enthusiasts. The second could have dropped into the compound from a 1969 wormhole. Tie-dye shirts, bell-bottom jeans, long hair. All of it perfumed with weed.

The outdoorsman possessed the community's whetstone. Supper conversation began with knife sharpening. It shifted to issues with a different water purifier. Giulia remembered this same discussion from her last visit. If the new world community had a weak link, their giant water treatment gizmos had been cast in the role of chief suspect. Tim and Jim talked technical machine jargon with the male half of the hippie couple. Alex presided over both tables, but didn't sit at the head of either. Everyone asked his advice or opinion about their topic of discussion. They queried him with deference but not reverence. Giulia chewed a piece of flat bread and wondered if this bolstered her theory of Alex's unseen twin being the real group leader.

No mead tonight, for which Giulia offered a silent prayer of gratitude. She didn't have the "driving home" excuse to avoid alcohol consumption. At least her admiration of the Celtic designs on the drinking horns from which they quaffed water was sincere. After supper, Cheryl and the hippie brought out coffee with the honey cakes. The twins passed around honey and goat milk for the coffee.

In the spirit of trying anything once, Giulia added both to the coffee and took her first sip with several pairs of eyes watching her.

It was vile.

She swallowed it anyway.

"Interesting," she said to the eyes.

Tim laughed. "Ma, that's exactly what you said."

"Exactly how you said it, too," Jim said.

Cheryl said, "It's an acquired taste. Once you get used to the goat milk, you'll be spoiled for cow's milk forever. Goat milk tastes so much richer."

"It's the mouth feel," said the hippie husband. "I work in advertising for now," he said when Giulia raised an eyebrow at the jargon.

She gave an honest compliment to the honey cakes and seized the opening. "I know this wonderful cake baker from a local discussion group about post-cataclysm cooking. She's an absolute magician with frosting. She once made a cake look like a swimming pool complete with a tiny person on a float." Giulia sipped more coffee to appreciate the next bite of honey cake. "I haven't heard from her in a couple of months."

Jim said, "You have to be talking about Phoebe. Ma, you remember Phoebe. She tried to show Alex a better way to make firecracker pickles, right Alex?"

Alex's smile seemed a little forced. "Phoebe knew her strengths. She wasn't always tactful in expressing them."

"I'm waiting until the bad weather hits so we can have a pickle competition," Tim said.

Cheryl kicked both her sons under the table. As a unit, they said, "We apologize, Alex."

Alex's forced smile became forgiving.

Two ideas fought for Giulia's attention. First, she rolled "Phoebe" around in her teacher's head until her memory pulled up Greek and Roman mythology. Joanne → Diane → Diana → Artemis → Too conspicuous a name for someone starting a new life → Scroll down the list of major gods and goddesses → Scroll down the list of minor ones → So much information squirreled away in her head → Try the Titans → Ah. Phoebe. So Joanne did drop out and start a new life. Sorry, Diane.

Alex said, "Phoebe's pistol skills were not up to the standards of the community. However, her rifle accuracy and genius for cooking more than made up for that lack."

Thus cementing the second idea: Alex wasn't simply their equivalent of an office manager. He was their priest. No wonder he'd asked Giulia about her religious affiliation. Casual observers, like she'd pretended to be, could be ripe for his cool new religion—Alex-worship.

Giulia sipped more goat and raw honey flavored coffee-like substance. She didn't want to push for the exact date Joanne left the community. Tomorrow for that, over breakfast. Food and Joanne were natural conversation companions.

If only Alex's use of past tense meant Joanne left here on her own and not in pieces for the coyotes to eat.

Supper dragged on until twilight when everyone gathered up

their dishes. Giulia relinquished the rest of her beverage without a qualm. Jim winked at her. As Giulia carried and washed and stacked alongside everyone else, she tried to predict what test Alex would throw at her next. Knife sharpening? Sheep herding? No one had yet handed her a shovel for her turn at manure collecting.

Speaking of Alex...She looked around, but he apparently bailed on the dish drying portion of cleanup, and no one had called him on it.

George Orwell was right: All Preppers are equal, but some Preppers are more equal than others.

Cheryl jogged between houses, whistling and calling "Rana! Lassie! Boris! Pepin!"

Pepin the moose led the galloping herd to Cheryl's feet. Cheryl lured them into the houses with bone-shaped goodies.

Giulia followed the rest of the gathering to the central fire pit. The outdoorsy couple lit the flame and nursed it with twigs.

Cheryl returned. "All the dogs are in for the night."

Everyone seated themselves around the fire, not too close since the night was warm. Someone passed around long pipes with bowls carved in the shape of a humanoid head with six-point buck antlers.

Giulia's first thought was: They're all *Lord of the Rings* cosplayers.

Her second: Smoking's bad for the baby.

Her third: *Lord of the Rings* didn't mention antlers. Pan, then? No, Pan had nubs of horns. Come on, mental storehouse of fiction and mythology, cooperate.

The goat milker opened a drawstring bag and stuffed loose herbs into the bowl of his pipe. He passed the bag to the accordion player, who did the same and passed it to his wife. Tim packed his own and his brother's bowls and passed the pouch to Cheryl.

Giulia cursed her inability to take incriminating pictures.

Cheryl handed the pouch to Giulia, who said with perfect truth, "I've never smoked."

"Don't worry. This is mild as can be. We grow it in the herb garden out front. I'll show you how this works." She stuffed herbs into Giulia's bowl with a practiced thumb. Giulia passed the pouch. The mixture didn't smell like weed, thank Heaven.

The cheesemaker took enough spills from the fire for everyone to light their own pipe. Cheryl got hers going, then turned to Giulia. "Suck in now, while the flame is on the herbs. Again. Once more."

Giulia got a nose full of smoke and coughed. Her nose was not having a good time at this overnight stay. She closed her throat and inhaled, holding all the smoke in her mouth.

"That's right," Cheryl said.

The instant Cheryl turned away, Giulia opened her lips a millimeter and let all the smoke stream out. Lavender and something bitter coated the inside of her mouth.

The fire puffed and shot sparks. Pine, cedar, and juniper mingled with the lavender in her nostrils. Something else too, something her students used to use when they thought the nuns didn't know about the school's unofficial weed-smoking areas.

The accordion player began to chant. The twins picked it up followed by all the men except the outdoorsman. All four women added harmony. Last, the outdoorsman came in with a bass drone.

The smoke from the pipes, the smoke from the fire, and the smoke from the incense enclosed the group in an undulating gray cloud. A fitful breeze swirled the mingled smoke among them for a chorus and Giulia could see only Cheryl and the red hair of the clothes mender. Where were Alex and the twins? The breeze shifted and she glimpsed Tim and Jim. She blinked. Her contacts clamored for eye drops.

The eyelids of every single person around the fire drooped. The twins began to sway, the others following their lead. Giulia too, even though she was freaking out inside. Little Zlatan was still in his first trimester and his mother was inhaling a concoction of who knew what kind of drugs. For the first time in her life, she wished she knew what opium smelled like.

She fought the encroaching mellowness and listened to the chant:

"By the circle and the flame
O Horned One
By the smoke and the oil
O Horned One
Come to us, live in us
Show us your power
Horned One, Great Horned One."

Standard invocation language. Simple call and response. Designed on purpose for mellow drugged worshippers, Giulia had no doubt.

Cradle Catholicism came to her rescue. Almost thirty years of daily Mass attendance made her an expert at worship planned for non-singers. She picked up the melody of the response and swayed in time with Cheryl.

Across the circle from her, the hippies took drags from each other's pipes. Tim and Jim's voices started to slur. The smoke slithered between them all, slipped away, and blew over their heads. The chant continued, not louder but more intense: Worshippers invoking their god.

Giulia stifled a yawn and saw him. A man with antlers. She didn't see where he appeared from, only between one "O Horned One" repetition and the next there he was within the circle. The flames picked out red and gold highlights in his long black hair. The polished antlers gleamed in the light. His skin, good Heavens so much skin, glistened when he moved. Oil of some kind. Giulia thanked God for the favor of the cosplayer's fringed loincloth.

He danced behind his worshippers. No lighthearted "let's have a good time after a hard day" frolic; a stately dance conveying power and authority. The triple layers of smoke gathered around him like a mantle. It made him grow larger in Giulia's eyes; stern yet protective; a leader to follow into the wild, uncertain future. He was their future.

Giulia reached out to the stones surrounding the fire pit and clamped her hand on a rough edge. Her head cleared. Her eyes stung. She remembered to keep singing along with the rest.

The cosplayer's voice began a counter-chant with the men. The women's harmony clashed against it, but in an odd way the accidentals were pleasant to the ear.

Or it was the drugged smoke. Giulia had to breathe clean air, but Maria Martin wouldn't leave this special event for any reason including nuclear war.

The cosplayer stopped dancing and walked around the circle, placing his left hand on each person's left shoulder in turn.

A ring of adults playing duck-duck-goose. Welcome to the future. Giulia bit both lips closed—*don't laugh don't laugh don't laugh*—before opening them again and picking up the women's part of the chant.

The antlers stopped behind the hippie's wife. His left hand rested on her shoulder. His right hand tilted up her chin. He slid his right thumb across his stomach and drew a four-pronged antler symbol on her forehead. It shone in the firelight. He helped her to her feet and they walked through a hole in the smoke into the woods.

The chant wound down after one more verse. Tim and Jim curled up next to each other on the ground and started snoring. The outdoorsy couple staggered to their house, undressing each other on the way. The hippie's husband imitated the twins.

Cheryl touched Giulia's arm, a loopy grin on her face. Giulia stood, her stagger not all put on for the community's benefit. Cheryl led Giulia to the absent Audrey's house. Giulia unrolled her sleeping bag but her fingers couldn't manage the zipper. Maybe it was warm enough tonight to sleep on top of it.

Forty

Giulia woke with a clear head and a throat dry enough to light matches on. A three-quarter moon shone on her legs. That window wasn't her bedroom window. Her nose was all stuffed. Weird. She had no allergies. She squeezed her nose between her finger and thumb and smelled lavender.

The Horned One ritual.

Her body jackknifed off her sleeping bag. She fumbled open her backpack and with her phone still inside it to hide the light, pressed the home button. Seventeen minutes after two. Panic surged into her Sahara-like throat. What had she inhaled? What would it do to the baby?

Stop.

She took a long, deep breath.

Think.

Panicking was a waste of energy. She needed the residue from her pipe and ashes from the fire and a gallon of water. First the water. She unlaced her boots and padded to the kitchen. From his bed on a throw rug in the living room, Pepin opened one eye and thumped his tail. Giulia patted his head and he was snoring a minute later.

The absent Audrey got a thank you from Giulia, because a clear stream of room-temperature water flowed into Giulia's cup when she held it under the gigantic water purifier contraption's spigot.

Giulia filled and drained the cup over and over and over, stopping only when her bladder threatened to go on strike. The toilet took up ninety-eight percent of the minuscule bathroom, but Giulia didn't care about her knees knocking against a wall.

Now that the emergency needs were handled, Giulia returned to the bedroom and tucked her phone into her jeans. She would've preferred writing a bullet list to help her snoop more efficiently, but the smart PI left no physical evidence.

She turned the back door handle without making a noise and squeezed through minimal openings in the house and screen doors. The moon shone on the entire compound. Fortunate for her. If she'd needed her phone flashlight, she wouldn't have been surprised to learn the dogs had been trained to raise an alarm around technology.

The hippie's husband and the twins were still asleep on the ground next to the fire pit. The twins' positions proved there was such a thing as womb memory. Before she stepped away from the space between the houses, she stretched her neck to see as much of the central area as she could. No lights shone anywhere. Hurricane lamps would be bright enough for her to see them through a window. She hoped. If someone was spying on the newbie, she could claim a need for fresh air after the smoke without adding it to her confession list for Father Carlos.

All the pipes lay on the ground in a ragged circle around the fire pit. She crept to her spot and dug out a quarter of the herbs from her pipe and Cheryl's. More than that might be noticed. Next, the ashes.

Maybe not. The heart of the embers still glowed red. Right, everyone had gone to sleep or to bed after the cosplayer and the hippie headed for the woods. Everyone...Giulia closed her eyes and pictured the group around the circle. Everyone except Alex. How convenient.

She poked the outside edge of the fire pit. The ashes weren't an option. The plastic baggie would melt if she scooped some in.

One eye on the twins and the hippie, she eased herself vertical while the idea coalesced in her mind. Alex disappeared before the pipe ceremony. Alex might have been the same height and weight as the glistening Horned One, as well as she could recall from behind the smoke and its effects.

Giulia whacked her own knuckles with an imaginary ruler. The experienced PI doesn't allow her pet theories to block the facts. She'd taken Joanne's twin obsession and run with it. Amateur.

After this evening, she'd suggest to Olivier the possibility of cults recruiting for inherent worshipper tendencies. An analysis of the incense and whatever they smoked might yield substances designed to make the cultists mellow and receptive. An ideal combination for the leader/god: With regular use, a content group of followers would approve anything he did. Three examples snored at her feet.

She rubbed her hand in circles over her stomach. Tomorrow she'd pay for a rush analysis of this herb mixture and make an appointment with her OB/GYN. Her doctor scheduled patients exactly like an acting cattle call, so Giulia wouldn't get squeezed in sooner than the return of the analysis results.

No panicking. She would not panic. Worry achieved nothing but elevated blood pressure and heart rate. Little Zlatan wouldn't benefit from mama pulling a Sister Frumentius the Freakout on him. Living with that woman at one of her school posts had been a daily trial.

She flipped a mental coin: Heads for house, tails for woods. Tails it was: Alex and the hippie in the ultimate back to nature experience. It wasn't really a fifty-fifty chance. Alex and his consort communing with nature via sex *al fresco* made perfect sense.

A nightingale warbled in the woods. She followed its song as she tiptoed past the beehives. Not a twig cracked beneath her feet as she looked down to keep her progress silent. Did these people vacuum the ground? No, silly her. Vacuums required electricity. The Mormon Tabernacle Choir of crickets helped her as well. It was a wonder roasted crickets hadn't been served as an appetizer tonight. Thank God for unexpected favors.

She seldom took her home for granted after her years in the convent, but after this immersion it would be difficult not to kiss the threshold when she returned.

A discarded daisy marred the obsessive cleanliness of the dirt path. It lay at the edge of the woods about a hundred feet from the clearing.

Giulia left the path to follow the beginning of a trail of unintentional breadcrumbs. The trees blocked some of the moonlight but she could still see her way clearly enough to avoid twigs and holes. Another hundred or so feet in, the trees opened to reveal a small clearing.

The couple lay asleep on a brown blanket. Giulia crouched behind a cluster of juniper bushes and squinted. Not a blanket; deer skins. At least four had been sewn together to accommodate Alex's height plus the width needed for his consort of choice. A daisy chain crowned said consort's disheveled blonde hair. Giulia took a moment to reconcile herself to the task of examining two stark-naked strangers for evidence of her theory. She opened the camera on her phone, turned off the flash, and centered it on the antlers. Then she zoomed it two hundred percent.

The antlers appeared real but the hair colored like shining autumn leaves was definitely a wig. At least the wig hadn't been a drug hallucination. The trailing end of a tattoo curled around his neck. The tip of a horn, it looked like. No surprise there. She'd never seen Alex's neck.

On to his chest with a quick left swing over to his arm before an inadvertent eyeful of his naughty bits.

And there it was. Her phone's extreme close-up showed her the puckered scar at the base of his thumb. The scar Alex had gotten when he worked at a metal stamping plant in high school. Alex, you dog. So your wild-eyed preaching of the Gospel of Doomsday survival was merely an excuse to gather hard-working, willing women to use in every sense of the word.

Giulia snapped several pictures in the hope one would be clear in this low light. Alex here asleep in the woods meant Alex's house was hers to explore. She retraced her steps to the fire pit and over to Alex's back door.

She checked her phone: 3:03. A good Prepper would know what time sunrise began. Reason number...whatever. She'd make sure to be back in her sleeping bag by four at the latest.

Alex's non-tech community was a masterpiece of organization. He avoided smartphones, therefore he had to keep paper lists and records and she had less than an hour to find them.

Taking a cue from her successful search of Joanne's bookshelf, Giulia tried Alex's books first. Dust and pollen covered most of them. *Bulfinch's Mythology* and *The Golden Bough* were clean and heavily creased, but no handwritten notes fell out of either. Same for manuals on beekeeping and organic farming.

All right then, where else? She climbed the ladder to the loft. A narrow night table didn't even have a drawer. A low wooden frame kept the mattress off the floor. He might have built the extra-long frame himself to accommodate his height. She risked the flashlight, hooding it with her free hand.

More horns were carved into the sides of the frame. Alternating with them, the classic Greek key design like on his beehives. Horns twined with antlers. A row of key design, more horns and antlers, and so on around the bed.

No. Not quite around. Beneath the pillow, a vertical bar of the key design was a centimeter off-kilter. Giulia held her breath and pulled at the section of the frame. A shallow drawer slid into her hands.

Whatever she'd expected, this wasn't it. A couple of dozen black squares with white frames, three sides identical and the fourth wider. She touched one and her fingers remembered the feel from her childhood. Polaroids. Who still used old-fashioned instant cameras? Stupid question: As technology went, instant cameras were about as Luddite as it got.

She turned over the nearest photo and flipped it back so fast she created a breeze.

No. Personal morals must be set aside to find Joanne.

She turned over the photo again. The background was the same bower in the woods where she'd left Alex and his choice *du jour*. The consort in the photo, a brunette with a similar crown of daisies, lay spread-eagled on the deer skin blanket. Her closed eyes and slack mouth could have indicated deep sleep.

Giulia held the photograph at arm's length. The angle indicated the photographer had squatted or knelt between the brunette's legs to take the most explicit shot possible. She may have been deep enough under a version of the smoke and incense combination not to stir when the photographer arranged her in such an exposed position.

But there was the LSA cocktail in the teenagers' and Anne's systems.

It didn't make sense that Alex needed his women under euphoric and relaxing drugs to bed them. Everyone here looked up to Alex, took his advice as canon, deferred to him in all things. So why the explicit photos?

Simple answer: Alex was a pervert.

Nothing was simple.

She turned over photos one by one. Three blondes. Two brunettes. Cheryl. The cheesemaker.

Joanne.

She checked her phone: 3:42. No time to retrace the path to the clearing and look for Alex's hidden camera.

She turned over more photos as fast as her fingers could grasp their edges. Using Alex's blanket as a shroud, she activated her phone's flash and closed her eyes against the brief light. Shooting single pictures was taking too long. She held down the center button to take a burst. She moved the camera to the four corners of the drawer and took more bursts.

After returning the blanket to its former place on the bed, she turned the photos face down as close to their original positions as possible. A partly hidden one of a brunette with short, straight hair made her pause. She took another look at the thin face.

A curse almost formed on her lips. One of these days she

wanted to be wrong when she crafted a deduction from a jigsaw puzzle of clues.

She finished putting the pictures back the way they'd been when she discovered the drawer. With great care, she slid the drawer closed so the design didn't match in the exact same way.

She got one step down the ladder. She had to get out of here. Every second she expected to hear Alex opening the back door. Time to leave. Another step down.

She pressed her lips together. Another step.

Go big or go home.

She climbed back up the steps. Opened the drawer. Removed the photo of the thin-faced brunette. Slid it into her hiking boot. Adjusted the other photos so there was no visible gap. Returned the drawer to its same position. Climbed all the way down the ladder. Listened for noise other than the birds. Slipped out the back door and through the back gardens into Audrey's house. She positioned herself on top of her sleeping bag as though she were still conked out from last night's ceremony.

She didn't know herself anymore.

Forty-One

When the light behind the curtains turned pink, Giulia rolled up her sleeping bag. Still thirsty enough to chug an entire gallon of water without stopping, she dug out her toothbrush and headed to the kitchen sink.

Pepin barked good morning at her and she scratched his ears.

"I'll find you some breakfast, boy."

The dog must not have had faith in the stranger's knowledge of his house, because he bumped the stand-alone pantry with his head until the door popped open. Giulia poured homemade kibble into his bowl and refilled his water dish.

She did not think about the Polaroid in her boot. After downing six cups of water and and using homemade toothpaste which surprised her by not tasting of dirt and weeds, she turned herself a full three hundred sixty degrees to find the shower. Sink behind her, toilet stall a jog ahead and to her left, water purification gizmo next to her. Flower-shaped homemade hand soap on a shelf above the sink next to a pump jar of homemade dish soap.

Conclusion: The house did not possess a shower. Water conservation in the future meant body odor was okay but dirty dishes were not?

If she looked at the concept from a dispassionate angle, she supposed water for drinking and cooking trumped water for showering. Clean dishes stood in direct relation to water for cooking, always assuming anything in this cult was reasonably free of germs and bacteria. She wondered if everyone bathed in the Beaver River. Communal baths would be a sure way to conserve water and promote camaraderie in the new world. Then again, if the Downfall of Civilization as We Know It happened via nuclear bombs instead of an electromagnetic pulse, the river could become contaminated.

So would the entire community. Had none of these people ever watched reruns of good old classic terror tactics movies? *Testament, The Terminator, The Day After*, and that great *Twilight Zone* episode with Burgess Meredith, "Time Enough at Last?" All of them could be found on cable TV or the internet and the community members must use computers in their day jobs. If nuclear fallout destroyed the river, they should break open all the mead, because everyone would die in less than a week.

Wasn't she a little ray of sunshine this fine morning?

Giulia resigned herself to stinky armpits and packed up her knapsack. After another detour for more water, she walked onto the front porch. Not a sound from any of the houses, but every bird north of Pittsburgh was making enough noise to fill the human gap. The chickens in their enclosure took the cue from the other birds and added to the din.

The daisy-crowned hippie wandered out of the woods, clothed again. As she came nearer, Giulia heard her humming "Morning has Broken."

"Hi, Maria." She finished a verse as she climbed the two steps to Giulia's porch. "Isn't it a perfect day?" She kissed Giulia, wrapping her arms around her, and Giulia smelled scented oil and the sour aftermath of sex.

When they separated, Giulia said to gauge how much drug was still in the woman's system, "You're going to think I'm an airhead, but I can't remember your name."

A fluttery laugh. "A ritual night will do that to you. I'm Ariel."

"Sorry."

"No worries. The morning after my first ritual I forgot my own name. The twins weren't at that one, so Alex gave us the good stuff." She moved toward the door. "Can I come in for some water? I don't want to wake my husband."

Giulia filled the glass for her three times running. "I'll start breakfast if you'd like. Does everyone eat together for all the meals?"

"Sure. We're family. We cook breakfast in our own kitchens because not everyone wakes up at the same time." She sighed a sigh which radiated deep contentment. "We prop open our back doors when the weather's good. The aroma of frying bacon is better than any alarm clock."

Giulia found two cast-iron pans and her companion brought eggs and bacon out of the stone cellar. She wasn't surprised at Ariel's claim that the community shared all things in common since Alex the Horned Stud shared everyone's woman with himself.

Forget about STDs. The strength of the united community will erect a wall around the crops, the bacon on the hoof, the coffee plants, and the chosen naughty bits. Chlamydia and gonorrhea will never cross the Horned Barrier.

Ariel set up the kindling in the firebox and Giulia laid strips of bacon in both pans. "We'll only need the cooktop right above the firebox for breakfast. Bacon and eggs always cook fast. I'll get the bread."

Giulia monitored both pans since she didn't trust her helpful companion's synapses to keep firing.

Ariel's muffled humming resumed from the cabinet concealing her head. "Here we go. Right where it should be." She brought out half a loaf of brown bread with seeds in it and held it out to Giulia. "This is from our last baking. Poke it. Toast is all it's good for."

Giulia poked. "With a little butter and jam it won't be too bad."

"Mmm, jam. I'm absolutely starving. Sex always makes me hungry." Ariel sliced a piece of bread, impaled it on a toasting fork, and opened the stove door. "Stealing a little fire won't mess up your cooking hardly at all. Come on, bacon up there, hurry and get crispy." She turned over the bread. "I'm in my fertile cycle. The god must have chosen me because of it. My husband will be so proud."

"I see," Giulia said, thinking, "Are you sure about that?" and "The god?" They thought Alex was actually their god, not the god's priest? She'd have to remember to stroke Frank's ego when she escaped from here, because he'd been one hundred percent right about the Jim Jones infection. A cult was a cult was a cult.

"There. Toast." Ariel set the long fork diagonally across the sink. "Butter should be in the cupboard above your head. I'll go back down for jam."

Giulia found the butter in a covered bowl. "Blackberry or strawberry?" said the voice from the cellar.

"Blackberry, please."

"Good choice." The jar came up first, followed by the rest of her. Her sleeve pulled up to reveal a brand new sketched tattoo of horns and flowers. From this distance it could have been the product of a brown magic marker.

The logical conclusion squicked Giulia out: When Antlered Alex chose his consort *du jour*, he put his mark on her outside and in. Before sex or after? Did the chosen one wake up like an eager kid on Christmas morning to see the new tattoo she must make permanent?

Either way, it meant Alex had bedded every woman with a tattoo in his community. If the dead teenagers *The Scoop* exploited for ratings had run from here, they'd have the tattoos as well. Note to self: Ask Frank to check the teenagers' police reports. She'd try to bring breakfast conversation around to the tattoos. How did he mark the men?

With that question, Giulia exceeded the safety limits on her mental image quota. Sex with Frank was one thing. Imagining sex among strangers...no.

If her former Superior General could see her now.

Ariel's arm tattoo screamed "I'm new!" "I'm special!" "I'm chosen!" Ms. New-Special-Chosen scooped a generous dollop of butter onto her toast and covered the result with enough jam to make the finished product in danger of turning into a waterfall of blackberries.

"Audrey makes awesome jam," she said after swallowing a quarter of the toast in one bite. "Here. Try it."

Giulia took a much smaller bite and her stomach woke up like a bear's after six months of hibernation. She whimpered. Her companion giggled. "Told you."

Cheryl knocked on the back door. "The siren call of bacon has every man in the place either setting the table, making coffee, or drooling."

Ariel patted her daisies. "Did my sleepyhead husband report to Alex?"

"He did."

"I have to go see his tattoo design." She ran out the front door.

Cheryl took over the egg pan. "I know you're dying to ask, Maria. When the god inhabits Alex to choose and mark a consort, the god also inspires Alex with a complementary design to mark her partner with the next morning. Only three of the chosen have ever left the community. The honor can be overwhelming, I suppose, if you're not strong-minded." As though they were discussing nothing more startling than the crispness of the bacon, she said with a motherly smile, "How'd you sleep?"

Giulia said in the same nonchalant voice as Cheryl, "Like someone clubbed me over the head with one of these skillets."

"It does hit you like that the first few times. Your body will acclimate soon." She lifted the corner of an egg.

Giulia found a flat dish and transferred the bacon. No paper towels to drain it. Oh, well. She worded her next question with care. "The smoke from the incense was so pleasant and relaxing. I smelled pine, but are we allowed to know what else is in it?"

Cheryl transferred the eggs onto another plate. "Oh, sure. Last night's mix was patchouli, pine, cedar, and juniper oils. We tinker with it to match the seasons."

Giulia breathed a little easier. One worry off her neck. Now she had to find an opening to ask about Antlered Alex.

"Shouldn't we toast the bread? Ariel said it had crossed over to stale."

"No time, now that the eggs are done. Cold fried eggs are an offense to our hard-working chickens. I'll cut the bread. You've got jam and butter, I see. The starving masses will never notice bread versus toast the morning after a ritual."

Chanting male voices interrupted them.

"O nymphs of the breakfast table,
Bring us bacon to buoy our souls.
Bacon. Bacon. Bacon. Bacon."

Giulia laughed. Four faces squeezed against the screen door, all attempting Bambi Eyes. Cheryl took the bacon dish and waved it at them. Their tongues came out as one and panted.

"Go pour us some coffee, desperate creatures, and we will solace your palates with the food of the gods." Cheryl turned away with the bacon and the men scattered. "We'd better get out there before I eat these eggs myself."

Four more community members brought plates of eggs, bacon, and bread from their own houses to the tables. Mugs of hot colored water pretending to be coffee sat at every place.

Why Giulia Driscoll would never make it as a Doomsday Prepper, reason number six, superseding all other reasons: COFFEE.

She almost wished they'd given her a choice of whatever kind of herbal tea these people grew, but after last night not even the threat of death would make her touch any herbs they offered her.

Alex arrived—fully clothed, hooray—and downed a huge glass of goat's milk in one long swallow.

"Good morning," he said. "I see bacon in my future."

"Good morning, Alex," a ragged chorus answered.

Tim and Jim passed him the bacon and eggs. Cheryl had been spot-on about the morning after a ritual. Unlike the multiple dinner conversations last night, no one spoke this morning until all the plates had been emptied.

What fascinated Giulia almost as much as the whole "the god inhabits Alex" conversation was the completely normal way Alex's flock treated him after last night.

Olivier had nailed it, but she couldn't wait to tell him about this collective mental shut-off valve.

The cheesemaker and the goat milker stood first.

"I'm off to the cheese shed."

"I'm with the bees."

"Spinning for me," Cheryl said.

"Fletching arrows," the outdoorsman's wife said.

"We're working on the water purifiers," Tim and Jim said.

"We'll do the dishes," the accordion player and his wife said.

"Repairing the archery and shooting targets," the outdoorsman said.

Now that she knew what to look for, Giulia saw both their tattoos peeping out from their shirt collars.

"I'll kidnap Maria to mix feed for the animals," Alex said.

Giulia repressed a shudder. Not that word, Antler Boy. Not that word.

Forty-Two

Giulia kept a step behind Alex as they tramped to yet another shed, which led to yet another question: How had she not seen all these sheds before? Answer: Because all the sheds were hidden among the trees and had been painted in woodsy camouflage. She wondered which paint company had grabbed the opportunity to siphon money from Doomsday Preppers. Smart marketing.

The sheds followed an erratic pattern along the path from the circle of houses to the acres of crops. Even so, they could only be accessed by climbing over rocks or around bushes and trees. Sometimes this community didn't possess the brains of a bag of hammers. Those minor obstacles had the strength of a wet piece of toilet paper against an anticipated zombie apocalypse.

But logic wouldn't get in the way of paranoia here in Antlered Alex's domain where he led and his sheep followed. She tried to remember if he'd kept a step ahead of her on her first visit to his single-serving size farm.

It wouldn't come. Guys who took leadership for granted weren't on her red flag list for dating site connections. He hadn't come across as uber-patriarchal either.

Alex opened the third shed in the irregular row. Old-fashioned galvanized trash cans fitted with locking lids lined two of the three shed walls. A deep shelf holding buckets and scoops stretched the length of the back wall.

"We'll make four mixes," he said, opening the trash can

nearest him on the left. "For the chickens we want oats, wheat, corn, and peas. The peas are in the corner by you. One cup of them to start."

Giulia added the peas to one of the buckets and Alex poured wheat on top of them. They topped it off with oats and corn and she mixed it with her hands. As they started the goats' bucket she said, "What happened around the fire last night?"

He poured sunflower seeds in the bottom of the new bucket and Giulia added barley. She glanced up at him when he didn't answer right away. He appeared to be communing within himself. Giulia created a mental Cult Bingo card:

True Believer	God Speaks to Me	God Speaks through Me
The Old Ways	Family	Unity
Sex Magick is Power	Procreation = Survival	The World As We Know It

Her Convent Cult Bingo card wouldn't have had the sex parts. Every nun in training learned about the evils of the Particular Friendship early on.

Alex didn't speak until Giulia mixed the goat food and scooped corn for the sheep. "What did you think of it?"

Weasel. If he only knew what an accomplished liar she'd become from all her undercover work. Maria Martin decided not to play it too dumb. "I was startled, even after smoking with everyone. At first I didn't know who or what appeared in the smoke. When you came nearer I recognized you in your guise."

His benevolent face appeared again. She was really beginning to hate that face.

"You are perceptive. Cheryl was also raised as a Catholic and she was the only one to recognize me when the god possessed me. I wonder what qualities Catholics absorb to make them see beneath the veil." He added wilted dandelion greens to the pigs' bucket. "Perhaps it is the ingrained Catholic dogma of believing in what one cannot see. Corn cobs for the pigs, please. They're in the can behind you."

Giulia used her hands to load pieces of corn cob into a bigger bucket.

"Doomsday Preppers can fall off the edge of reason into a morass of useless paranoia." Alex mixed the corn cobs with the greens. "When I realized the world as we know it was headed full-tilt into destruction, I knew I had to create a community that would survive it. A little more wheat for the sheep, please."

One catchphrase uttered. Giulia had done her time at countless Sunday afternoon church Bingo sessions. Her mental Bingo dauber smooshed a big red circle over the first square.

"I bought this property years ago because I chose to live off grid when I wasn't at my day job. No one came here unless I invited them, so I used my annual vacation to meditate on what I needed to do." He studied the four buckets. "This is enough."

He picked up the two larger buckets. Giulia followed, again, with the two remaining ones. Alex latched the shed door.

"You understand the need for faith in something greater than ourselves. At the time, I had no such faith. I closed up my house and took a sleeping bag, a fishing pole, and a week's worth of mead out to the creek. This was August two years ago. After three days of silence and meditation, I learned two essential elements of life without creature comforts: The first was to find a recipe for natural mosquito repellent."

They reached the chicken enclosure and he let them out, grinning.

"You should have seen me. They targeted every square inch of my exposed skin. I see they're targeting you as well. We must have similar blood."

Ick. Giulia scattered feed in the sparse grass. The poultry dived on it. "I wouldn't want those beaks coming after me."

"They're not aggressive. On the other hand, it's a good thing your first milking went so well. Some of our family got hooved in the chest and arms their first time."

Family. Another Bingo square filled. They moved on to the pigs. Bacon on the hoof liked its food too.

"It would be evil of me to start an internet meme claiming bacon is vegan," she said.

Alex gave her a puzzled look.

"The pigs snarfed down those dandelion greens like they were Godiva chocolates. Pigs eat greens; greens are vegan; therefore, bacon is vegan. Aristotle."

Alex laughed. He had a good laugh. Giulia wondered how many of the community he lured in with it.

"The god never steers me wrong. You're one more proof of his wisdom."

As they headed for the goats, Giulia said, "You're not talking about the Judeo-Christian God, are you?"

"Not for a minute. Pour the feed into the troths before we let them out. The goats are aggressive when they're hungry." After the horned beasts attacked their breakfast instead of their humans, Alex said, "I knew of the gods of the major world religions in vogue today, and I wasn't impressed by the track records of their followers. When I went to the creek to cleanse myself inside and out, I wasn't sure what precisely I was preparing myself for."

Giulia remembered her six weeks of total silence retreat before taking final vows. Nothing special had happened to her then, except wanting a simple conversation about nothing in particular so bad she sneaked into the woods and began talking to the squirrels, like a demented Saint Francis.

"When the moon rose on the fourth night, I was empty and exhausted. A hollow vessel. As though he had been waiting for that precise moment, Cernunnos, the ancient god of the hunt, spoke to me."

Bingo square number three. If Alex kept this pace, she'd fill the card before he dragged her out to the archery range again.

"I see." Ray Liotta's ghostly voice from *Field of Dreams* popped into her head: "If you starve yourself, he will come." Not an exact quote, but the same principle if one was cynical enough to equate a dead baseball player giving orders to a guilt-ridden baseball fanatic with Alex's convoluted mentality and drug proclivities.

Giulia's tone of voice must not have met expectations, because Wild-Eyed Alex turned on her. "I am not speaking figuratively."

"I realize—"

"Nor am I being facetious. You should know something of the vision of the great mystics of Catholicism. Such privileged communication is the hallmark of the true believer."

Four squares down, five to go.

She bit the corner of her bottom lip in a gesture of repentance and coquettishness. "I wasn't making fun of you, honest I wasn't. I'm trying to process a lot of stuff right now." Wild-Eyed Alex might respond to either, thus she hedged her bet.

The thundering preacher light faded from his eyes. He shifted his empty bucket to his left hand and chucked her chin with his right. A leader who treated her like an empty-headed piece of fluff and who wanted to get into her pants. Ugh. What kind of women populated this community? Who thought paternalism with a touch of misogyny was sexy? At least when she became the Bride of Christ, God didn't use her for sex. She and Father Carlos were going to need a lot of extra time for her next confession.

"You're learning." Alex continued, "When I first heard the god's voice, I thought I'd been alone in the woods too long. After a few more words, the god convinced me of his reality. He told me he had seen my emptiness from my birth. My mother miscarried a twin in the womb. I had never told anyone about it, but Cernunnos knew. At that moment I realized the god wasn't all in my head."

Vindication for Giulia's twin theory. This case was too much like a roller coaster ride for her first-trimester nausea meter. She also wanted to wash her brain in Lysol the more Alex bared his rancid soul to her. Did his god tell him to take all those Polaroids, or were they Alex's offering to it?

The Hedge of Separation needed a sign above the ivy curtain: Abandon All Brains, Ye Who Enter Here.

"After I bowed before Cernunnos, he informed me withdrawing from this corrupt world wasn't enough. We must return to the old ways if we wished to survive."

Four squares left now. Joanne had swallowed this. She must be the empty-headed twin. No, she was the needy twin. The one who projected "beige" inside and out. But her neediness didn't extend to swallowing the Kool-Aid forever, since she escaped.

If she escaped.

What Giulia needed was a cadaver dog. No. First she needed to end this sleepover. Next, she needed to call Diane to ask if the police had searched for Joanne's body. Since Diane had been adamant about Joanne being alive, Giulia was pretty certain the police hadn't. Third, then: A cadaver dog.

Alex hadn't stopped talking. Oops. Now how would she fill her Bingo card?

"We have to get to the dandelions before the sheep do. The pigs need them more and there's plenty of grass for the sheep to supplement the grain mix we feed them."

Whew. Apparently Alex had held off on his revelations from beyond to instruct Giulia on the care and maintenance of the walking lamb chops. He handed Giulia the last empty bucket.

"Some would refer to my experience as a vision, but that is incorrect. Cernunnos did not appear to my physical eyes, nor did his voice sound in the ears of my flesh."

Giulia's face never broke character as she thought Alex had missed his best opportunity to use his camera. A photograph of an ancient god would've raked it in on eBay.

"By opening myself to all possibilities, I allowed Cernunnos to inhabit me. He inhabits me still. We are a twinned being, my flesh and his spirit. He has made me whole again as I should have been from before my birth. He speaks through me in the rituals when the sex magick allows his power to flow through my seed into that night's chosen vessel, as it was in the old days between himself and the moon goddess."

One, two, three squares filled all at once. Giulia nodded. She didn't trust her mouth not to reply as herself instead of Maria Martin.

Alex led her back to the feed shed without checking to see if she wanted to go somewhere else first, what a surprise.

"So you see, our community is united as one through faith, action, and procreation. The god's seed will create a new generation of believers to carry us into a new world. It won't be a paradise, because so much of the earth is poisoned, but we are the beginning. Future generations will look back on our preparations and take our values throughout the world."

What would Maria Martin say? Giulia's mouth opened and Maria came out: "I'm a little overwhelmed." She made Precious Moments eyes up at Alex. "But I'm also thrilled you're considering me for inclusion in your community. I'm not afraid of hard work, and I'm sure I can overcome my addiction to Primanti Brothers' giant sandwiches."

Alex got all paternal on her again. Giulia thanked her friends who kept raving about those sandwiches. She'd have to try one.

As Alex stroked Maria Martin's coquettish ego, Giulia Driscoll pictured the breaking news story on the local stations of all four major networks: "Doomsday Drug Dealers Arrested." Tim and Jim's faces would be pixilated out as the police raided the compound. A stone-faced cop would carry out from Alex's house a box of the photos with the god antlers and wig balanced on top. She and Frank would toast the arrest with ginger ale, because of little Zlatan.

Olivier would make serious bank out of these people when their lawyers demanded psych evals. She'd recommend him to

Jimmy as soon as they were in jail. Hello, Jessamine's college fund.

But for now, Maria Martin should continue to be eager to please. "Is anything special planned for this morning? I could use more time on the archery range."

"Excellent idea. We have time before lunch needs to be started."

Her phone vibrated. Thank you, God.

Frank's text couldn't have been better: MARIA, JENNIFER CALLED IN SICK AGAIN. WE'RE SHORT TWO PEOPLE. I NEED YOU IN HERE ASAP.

She showed it to Alex. His face darkened like the best evangelical TV preachers.

"Your boss calls all of you by first name and still orders you around?"

He should talk. "That's just his way. He's under a lot of pressure from the company owner to make the cleaning service turn a profit even after a bunch of us were let go for budget reasons." She texted a reply as Alex watched.

I'M LEAVING NOW. I CAN BE THERE IN ABOUT AN HOUR.

She put worry lines into her forehead. "I hate to cut my time here short, but I can't afford to lose this job. It pays more than my other one. I'm really sorry, Alex."

Her phone buzzed with Frank's reply: IF THAT'S THE BEST YOU CAN DO, I'LL HAVE TO PUT UP WITH IT.

"He doesn't appreciate you," Alex said.

"Oh, no, he does, really. I got a merit raise of fifteen cents an hour at my annual evaluation. Nobody else got a raise this year."

As they walked back to the central area, Alex said, "The community will discuss the possibility of you joining us. Your cooking and shooting skills are up to our standards. You are adaptable and seem to fit in with the others."

"Oh, Alex. That would be wonderful."

He kept talking as though she hadn't replied. "I will commune with Cernunnos at the full moon."

She didn't ask what communing involved. Most likely he

wouldn't have elaborated anyway. High priests, in her experience, wrapped the cloak of super-secret specialness tight about their shoulders.

Cheryl was at her spinning wheel and the redhead had dragged the mending basket and a chair next to her. The scene looked much more natural than yesterday's when the couples had occupied their porches like dolls posed in a doll house. Giulia scored one point to herself for this confirmation that yesterday's multi-person Ren Faire busyness had been staged for her arrival.

Giulia walked over to Cheryl. "The day job strikes again."

The women chorused, "Oh, no. You really have to leave so soon?"

Alex said, "Perhaps Maria can come out again on her next day off."

Maria Martin's bright smile hid Giulia Driscoll's desire to bow to his skill in putting her on the spot in front of witnesses. "Oh, yes, I'd love to. But won't Audrey be back? Where would I stay?"

"Do you have a tent?" Cheryl said. "Camping out here in the summer is fun."

Giulia smacked her forehead. "The most obvious solution is right in front of my nose."

"Occam's razor," Alex said.

Forty-Three

Giulia pulled into her own garage connected to her own not so tiny Cape Cod-style house a little after one. Frank's Camry was in the garage as well, its engine ticking as it cooled down. She opened the house door and went straight for the mailing supplies. The baggie with the pipe residue went into a padded envelope. She wrote a note explaining why she needed the results ten minutes ago and called DI's usual delivery service. Then she called her OB/GYN and demanded an appointment for tomorrow afternoon. Her lab contact would get the analysis to her by noon tomorrow; he'd performed miracles for her twice before.

Appointment made, she turned around to find her husband. Frank stood by the stairs pinching his nostrils together.

"What have you been smoking?"

"I don't know yet. The delivery guy should be here any minute to courier it to the lab." She sniffed her sleeve. "They also burned a mix of pine and patchouli and a few other things in the fire. Can you get me a trash bag? I want to save these clothes as evidence if needed."

"Evidence of what? Where are you going?" He detoured into the kitchen and tossed a folded white plastic bag up to her as she reached the second floor landing.

She caught it. "To use up all the water in the hot water heater on a shower. I'll tell you the rest in the bathroom if you have time now."

"I wouldn't miss this for anything short of catching you swearing on camera."

"Pigs will fly first."

"You're crushing my dreams, wife."

The doorbell rang.

"Please tell the courier it's a rush," she called from their bedroom. She stripped and stuffed her jeans, shirt, and socks into the bag. Her underwear went into the hamper. In the bathroom the water heated up as she undid her blonde braids.

Frank's footsteps came into the room as she started the second full scrubbing of her smoky, greasy head.

"Frank, my hair is shedding pollen and *tiny dead insects*. Let's not go camping for a while." She opened a corner of the shower curtain. "Stop laughing."

"Sorry."

"No, you're not."

"No, I'm not. Tell me more."

"Before the story of my Prepper sleepover, how can I request the use of a cadaver dog?"

"Tumblr would have a field day with some of our conversations. Mind if I open the window some more? My suit's wilting."

"Go ahead. Cadaver dog, please?"

Frank's voice receded. "You know Jimmy will do anything for you." The octagonal bathroom window squeaked and he spoke louder. "It would help if you could give him a reason which relates to an ongoing investigation."

"Two teenagers dead from OD'ing on homemade drugs."

"Oh, baby, you know how to make me sit up and beg."

Giulia stuck her dripping head around the shower curtain. "What did you say?"

Frank's cheeks could have been red from embarrassment, but the room was hot and steamy, so she let it go. "How much extra-strength anti-itch lotion do we have?"

As she used smooth, fragrant, mass-produced soap on the rest of her body, she could hear him banging around under the sink and in the hall closet.

"A quarter of a tube of something with a medicinal name."

"I will use that up in a heartbeat." She turned off the water. Frank's hand appeared, holding her bath towel. "Thanks." She dried herself with enough friction to make all the hair on her body stand on end and emptied the tube of lotion in less than a minute.

"It's a start. All my willpower is concentrated on not itching. Now I will tell you tales of goats and bacon and men in leather loincloths."

She began with the happy people staged in their cute houses performing their early Americana tasks. Frank laughed at her lack of prowess with a bow and arrow and did not share her panic over the herbs in the pipes. "You only got a mild case of the loops. Your thirst was probably a combination of whatever incense they burned plus the secondhand smoke." He made a thoughtful face. "I wouldn't rule out little Zlatan getting a taste of coffee with goat milk and sending your brain signals to drown the taste out of your system. Now give me the good stuff. What did you say about a guy in a loincloth?"

After setting the scene with pipes and incense and chanting, she described Alex when possessed by Cernunnos.

"Antlers? He wore actual deer antlers and a fringed piece of leather and nothing else?"

"Body oil. Something pungent with several scents I couldn't separate out, like the incense." Her fingernails reached for a series of bites on her neck, but she stopped herself. "By the way, you were right. The place turned out to be a cult like I've never seen before."

"I have a much lower opinion of people than you, my dear."

"It's about to reach a new nadir." She described Alex/Cernunnos' method of choosing a bed partner.

"No, please. Don't tell me the hippie chick's name is Ariel."

"Of course it is. Her husband's name is Orion." She sprayed anti-frizz goop into her hair. "This dye job needs to grow out right now."

Frank reached out from his seat on the toilet lid and pulled her into his lap. "I don't know. Maybe Zlatan likes blondes."

"Maybe Zlatan will learn from the start to look past superficial characteristics for people who are good at heart."

"Spoken like a true Franciscan. Or a true mom. Or both."

She kissed him on the nose. "Come into the bedroom with me. I need non-camping clothes."

Her hiking boots on the floor next to the bed faced her like the accusatory red shoes from the Hans Christian Andersen fairy tale. Her feet wouldn't come any closer to them. Frank bumped into her.

"Too tired to move?"

She didn't answer. He looked at her face, followed the trajectory of her gaze, and looked back at her. "I'm guessing it's something more than a spider?" He touched her arm. "*Muirnín? Sweetheart?*"

His touch startled her out of her mesmerized state. She skirted the boots and sat on the bed. He sat next to her, one arm around her. "What is it?"

"When I found Ariel and Alex asleep in the woods, I spied out his house."

"With just your phone flashlight? Not fun."

She shook her head. "No, with the light from the moon. Someone else could've been awake and chugging water. The flashlight would've been like the Bat Signal in a compound without electricity. His bed frame was carved with that Greek Key design; you've seen it. My second time going over it, I found one place where the carvings were out of alignment."

He squeezed her. "Nice."

She didn't respond to his affection. "The bed frame had a hidden drawer. In it were a couple dozen Polaroids."

"Who uses them anymore?

"Perverts and blackmailers."

"*Beidh mé damned.*"

Jarred out of her preoccupation, Giulia said, "Frank, please don't blaspheme."

He kissed her hair. "Sorry. Blame the surprise. Blackmail?"

"Possibly. All the photos were of drugged or sleeping naked women, flowers in their hair and with their legs spread to expose their most private parts. I figure Alex gave them an extra dose of something to make sure they didn't wake up while he posed them." She thought back to the herb garden in the front. "Morning glories and poppies. I saw lots of both flowers in a fenced-off garden."

"Morning glory seeds can be extracted to make LSA. Remember the tox reports I read to you? Poppy seeds would be my choice here. Opium would send these women into a dreamy paradise." He snapped his fingers. "If he's home-brewing opium, who's to say he's getting the same dosage in every batch? And who knows what other plants his chosen few use to get high? No wonder those kids OD'd."

"My client's missing twin had her own photo."

"Not good."

"I know. She's really why I want to borrow the cadaver dog."

"She's been missing for a few months, right? Plenty of time for the scent to rise."

Giulia broke her stare to glance at his face. "What?"

"Steve, the human half of the K-9 team, says the odor from rotting bodies takes a couple of weeks to reach the surface. Like the bubbles that pop on the water when you fart in a bathtub, he says. The dog can smell it when humans wouldn't have a clue."

On a normal day, Giulia would've smiled at that image and made a joke about how all men are really ten years old at heart.

Frank patted her hand. "Why are you still staring at your hiking boots?"

It all came out like the lid blowing off a popcorn maker and kernels exploding all over the room. "I pulled the blanket over my head and the drawer so I could turn on my flashlight to see the pictures. I turned every single one of them over. That's how I found Joanne's. I had to use my flash to take pictures of the pictures so I'd have evidence when I went to Jimmy so he could get an arrest warrant." She took a breath. "I stole one of the Polaroids."

She wasn't sure what reaction she expected from Frank. A lecture? His comforting arm releasing her? She wanted his arm around her more than anything right now. "I don't know who I am anymore."

He said in a slow, even voice, "Who was in the picture?"

"Anne."

"Anne your sister-in-law? *Cac naofa.* Your brother will...Right. I see."

"I tampered with evidence. I stole. What's wrong with me? I'm supposed to be on the side of justice. There's no way I can sneak back inside his house and return the picture. I don't know what to do." She started to get up. "Yes, I do. I have to give the photograph to Jimmy."

Frank sat her down again. He bent over and stuck one hand in each hiking boot. His right hand came up with the purloined photo. He turned it so the back was facing him and ripped the picture in half.

She snatched at the halves. "Frank, what are you doing?"

He turned away from her and held the two pieces at arms' length before ripping them in half again. Giulia kept grabbing at his arms as he ripped those into eight or ten pieces each. Giulia lost count. When he walked back into the bathroom she tailed him, protesting and trying to snatch the ragged bits of Polaroid. He shouldered her away, dropped the pieces in the sink, and emptied the bottle of hydrogen peroxide over them. The emulsion bubbled and warped; the bleach solution hissing as it destroyed the image of Giulia's sister-in-law drugged, naked, and post-coital from her liaison with Alex/Cernunnos.

"Why did you do that? Now I can't make it right." Without warning she burst into tears, exactly like a cliché. One moment she was trying to snatch the pieces of Anne's photo from Death by Peroxide. The next moment salt water gushed from her eyes and she was sobbing.

Frank sat her down on the edge of the tub. The cold porcelain on her bare butt where the towel didn't reach made her shiver. She kept sobbing, trying to get a coherent sentence past the tears dripping on her lips.

"*Muirnín*, listen." Frank stroked her hair. "You have multiple incriminating photos that will convict this guy. You have physical evidence of him supplying drugs to minors. We're going to nail his fringed ass to the wall and it'll be because of you."

"But, but," was all she managed.

"No 'buts.' And don't you dare say you don't recognize yourself or any other nonsense. You're the woman who puts justice and mercy above everything, and that's why you broke your own rules to try and save your brother's marriage." He handed her a tissue. "Although if you ask me, your sister-in-law doesn't know how good she has it without him, even stuck in rehab."

Giulia shredded the tissue. Frank set the box on her lap and she dragged several across her face. She ordered herself at least ten times to stop crying. The orders worked after a few minutes.

"I think your pregnancy hormones have kicked in with a vengeance." He kissed her gently on the lips and nudged her off his lap. "Go get dressed and talk to Father Carlos. I'm headed back to work. I'll let Jimmy know you're coming over sometime this afternoon."

Forty-Four

Giulia sat at the speckled Formica kitchen table of St. Thomas'
Rectory clutching a decaffeinated Pepsi. Father Carlos sat opposite
her drinking the caffeinated version.

"First of all, Giulia, you will listen to me and not spend the
next few weeks waking up in the middle of the night to mentally
flog yourself. Understood?"

She nodded.

"Good. We've discussed at great length the dichotomy between
telling a lie in the normal course of events and your necessary
undercover work in the cause of justice. The reason I absolve you
for what you must say and do undercover is precisely because we
both know you are serving the cause of justice."

Another nod.

"Good. Now one at a time: You have enough photographic
evidence to justify an arrest warrant, yes or no?"

"Yes."

"You have eyewitness evidence of minors being given alcohol
and drugs, yes or no?"

"Yes."

"You are about to rescue these minors and who knows how
many other women, yes or no?"

"Yes, but—"

He held up his hand. She shut up.

"Your sister-in-law has very little chance of reconciling with your brother or seeing her children, but if your brother knew about the photograph of her, 'very little' would become 'a snowball's chance in Hell,' yes or no?"

Giulia's mouth quirked. "Yes."

"Good. *Ego te absólvo a peccátis tuis in nómine Patris, et Fílii, et Spíritus Sancti.*"

"Amen," Giulia said automatically. "But—"

"Stop." Father Carlos, always smiling, always gentle, frowned at her. His expression startled her into silence.

"Right. Now go back to work. I hope your missing person is not buried in the woods." He stood. "What I mean is, I hope she's not buried anywhere and you find her alive within the week."

Giulia finished the Pepsi, then hiccupped.

Father Carlos smiled again. "The baby is telling you he knows you want caffeine but he appreciates your sacrifice."

She smiled back. "You're the baby whisperer now?"

He made a note on the refrigerator memo pad. "I'll talk to the Bishop. We could use the extra income. We're still paying off last winter's heating bill."

Giulia drove to Precinct Nine and their Bond Girl wannabe receptionist buzzed Frank. Less than a minute later, Giulia, Frank, Frank's partner Nash VanHorne, Jimmy Reilly their captain, and Jane Pierce, Giulia's former temp admin and Jimmy's permanent assistant, all crowded into Jimmy's office.

"You need more space," Giulia said as she moved a stack of file folders off the small round table in the corner.

"I won't hold my breath," Jimmy said. "Give me your power cord."

Her laptop booted. She connected her phone and uploaded the photos.

Nash pointed to the screen. "Aw, look at Frank vacuuming the house all Donna Reed in an apron."

"Screw you," Frank said without anger. "If you had any taste in music, you'd see I'm dressed as Freddie Mercury in Queen's 'I Want to Break Free' video."

"That was last Halloween," Jimmy said.

"My bad." Giulia scrolled through at least fifty holiday photos. "I haven't cleared off my pictures in ages. Here we go. I took these at three o'clock this morning with a blanket over everything to hide the flash."

Jane let loose with a string of unprintable words.

"Enlarge them, would you?" Jimmy said. "Hard to see from behind these two."

The immediate effect of Giulia increasing the size of the first shot: Everyone got much too up close and personal with three vaginas. All the men leaned away. Giulia scrolled through the next photos in the multi-picture bursts she'd taken until she found a series with more faces than lady bits.

"The washed-out brunette is my client's missing twin sister." She clicked some more.

"Stop," Jimmy said. "Do you have a better version of that skinny one on the left?"

More clicks. "How's this?"

"Frank, that's one of the kids from the park or the convenience store, right?"

Frank and Nash leaned closer. Giulia enlarged the picture and scrolled until the smiling, drugged face filled the screen.

"That's her."

"Giulia," Jimmy said, "please tell me you have a picture of the other teenager."

"I'll click slower." Another ten-picture burst and the camera focused on a different corner of the hidden drawer. Ten more and a third corner.

"There she is," Nash said. "See the vampire fangs tattoo on the side of her neck?"

Jimmy lifted Giulia half out of her chair and bear-hugged her. "Frank doesn't deserve you. I've been killing myself and Jane for days trying to figure out where those two fell from."

When Jimmy set her down, she said, "I have the exact address of this place and the name of the photographer."

"My wife is a queen among women, Reilly, and don't you forget it." Frank sat in his boss' chair. "What's his name?"

"Alexander Sila, S-i-l-a. Jimmy, could he look up two others for me, please? Louis L-a-r-a-b-e-e and Kurt with a K W-a-r-f-i-e-l-d."

While Frank typed, Jimmy made a phone call. A few minutes later, in walked a tall uniformed officer with blue-black hair, one single curl off-center on his forehead, and shoulder muscles so big they swamped his neck. The small office got as claustrophobic as though three more people had squeezed in with them.

"Steve Reeve, Giulia Driscoll."

"Ma'am." They shook hands. "Captain Reilly says Scout and I may be able to help you in connection with the teenage girls case."

Giulia explained who she was looking for. "Will Scout need a piece of her clothing? I can drive over to her apartment this afternoon."

"No ma'am. Humans have their own unique smell when they're alive, but when we're dead we all smell alike."

"That's interesting."

The mountainous Superman doppelganger smiled for a nanosecond. "It keeps things in perspective. When and where are we meeting?"

"Five o'clock tomorrow morning, here. Is it all right if I hitch a ride with you?"

"No problem, ma'am. See you tomorrow morning."

When he left, Nash said, "I am consumed by feelings of inadequacy."

"Reeve has that effect on people," Jimmy said.

"And my wife gets to spend an hour in the car with him tomorrow," Frank said.

"Forget him," Giulia said. "What kind of dog is Scout?"

"Golden retriever."

"Tomorrow will be a good day."

Frank cleared his throat. "Wife of mine, I am feeling even more inadequate, as our computer system is running like cold molasses and I am unable to dazzle you."

"Aww," from Jimmy and Nash.

Giulia winked at Jane. "Dazzle fades. I'd rather have your skills any day."

"Aww," from Jane, Nash, and Jimmy.

Forty-Five

"Morning, ma'am." Officer Reeve looked as crisp as though hour-long drives to tromp through woods were everyday five a.m. occurrences.

"Good morning. Thank you for coming out with me this early." Giulia swallowed a yawn.

"Let me introduce you to Scout." He gestured to the bright-eyed medium-yellow dog at his feet. The dog stood, always looking at his handler. "Scout, this lady is a friend."

Giulia held out her fist with the back of her hand up. Scout sniffed it, looked into her face, grinned at her, and wagged his tail. Giulia rubbed his ears.

She directed him to the compound the long way around, using the directions Alex gave her the first time she visited. Officer Reeve called her "ma'am" more times than she'd ever been called in her life. They parked near the creek. Giulia stayed by the SUV and watched Reeve and Scout take care of business. After a set of hand signals and words, the dog ran into the woods, exploring trees and mounds of dirt and bushes and the creek bank.

The sky grew brighter and brighter, the sun streaming through the trees and sparkling on the creek. Nineteen thousand four hundred seventy-three birds greeted it, but Scout wasn't distracted for a moment. Scout's fruitless searching lasted until seven a.m., when Reeve walked to a chestnut with massive roots and placed a stuffed cloth circle under several layers of leaves. Within five minutes, Scout zeroed in on the hidden object and lay down next to it. He didn't bark but looked over at Reeve like it was Reeve's turn in their game. Reeve unearthed the stuffed object and praised the dog. Treats were produced and consumed, and Scout returned to the SUV panting and happy.

The three of them climbed into the SUV and headed back to Cottonwood.

"This is all a big game to him, ma'am," Reeve said. "When he works hard but doesn't find evidence of a body, I plant a decoy with cadaver material embedded so he wins the game."

Giulia was considering the ramifications of Scout's failure. "I see."

"Ma'am, we have three possible conclusions from today's search."

Giulia snapped into focus. "Yes, I know. Either she's buried somewhere else, or she was buried too recently for Scout to find her, or she's not dead."

"Yes, ma'am."

"I think if the Doomsday Preppers killed her, they would've buried her close by. They've done their best to screen their compound from prying eyes in the sky and nosy trespassers on the ground." She tapped her fingers on the windowsill. "They could've cut her up and used her for compost, but they don't seem the type."

Reeve never flinched. "That's good."

They finished the ride in silence. Giulia checked her email even though it was too early for the lab results. She checked her texts even though Frank would wait until she reached home before giving her his arrest record search results.

At the police station, Giulia gave Scout a belly rub and received slobbery kisses in return. She handed her business card to Reeve. "Let me know if you need anything else from me to complete your report."

Frank was waiting for her at home with coffee and bagels ready at the kitchen table for both of them.

"You are a prince among husbands. And no, Scout did not find

Joanne's body." She clutched the coffee mug after her first swallow. "Oh, coffee, I'm sorry I cheated on you with a cheap knockoff of your awesomeness, but it was in the line of duty."

Frank spooned Giulia's homemade jam onto his pumpernickel bagel. "I should secretly make Vines of some of the things you say."

Giulia treated him to her teacher glare.

"Brr. Did the furnace just kick on? Joke. When you're done eating I have information for you."

Giulia savored the coffee. "I'm taking my time with breakfast, because I don't want to tempt the morning sickness imps to visit me. But you, sir, are a tease."

She cleaned the dishes and Frank brought his laptop to the table. "Since I don't know who's your suspect number one, I'll start with Warfield. He is so vanilla he wasn't worth my research time. One speeding ticket. No drugs, no DUIs, not even a parking violation."

"Good. I got a positive vibe from him, even though he's a tenor."

"Can't be. Tenors are the eternal Don Juans of the music world."

"Nonetheless."

"Moving on to Alexander Sila. The man likes his mind-altering substances. Tried to buy LSD from an undercover cop ten years ago. Got sixty days and a hefty fine. Busted for weed a year later. Got one hundred twenty days and a heftier fine. No third strike, so it seems he got a clue."

"I'm only surprised he wasn't arrested for drunk driving." She finished her coffee.

"Jail will do that for some people." He scrolled down the screen. "I take it back. No more dope convictions, but picked up three months after he got out when he busted into one of Penelec's power plants with—get this—a plumber's wrench."

"With a what?"

"Think of a monkey wrench like in old Saturday morning cartoons."

Giulia shook her head. "Why am I not surprised? A younger, more impulsive Mr. Anti-technology giving the advent of the New World a little assistance."

"He would have, if it weren't for the state of the art alarm system."

"Oh, dear."

"His wrench took out a bunch of computer terminals before security tackled him. He got seven years but played the model prisoner. Paroled after two and a half and pure as the driven snow ever since."

"Just a second." Giulia brought her iPad in from the living room and opened her case files. "I wonder how much his community members paid for the privilege of acceptance? He wants Maria Martin, but he only mentioned money to me once."

"Right." Frank typed. "Unless he pulled off a secret bank robbery, he had to get the cash for his truck somehow. Better-paying companies don't want to hire three-time losers."

"He could be using the library for internet access, although I didn't see the inside of his house. That is, the inside of his decoy house accessible from the road. All the houses in the compound are one hundred percent off grid."

Frank turned his laptop screen toward her. "Got it. He owns seventy acres along the Beaver River. Google Earth here shows a lot of trees and massive amounts of corn and wheat and a couple of other grains I can't identify. Look."

She enlarged the map and waited for it to redraw. "Beans and peas. Something low and green...broccoli, maybe. He told me he owned two acres. The community crops covered at least six." She tried to drink nonexistent coffee from her empty cup. "He's devious and clever and the worst kind of false prophet, the one who twists his religion for his own lust and power."

"Honey, you are the only person I know who uses the word 'lust' in a Dante's *Inferno* sense."

"Years of shoving classic literature down the throats of humanoid squirrels has served me well." She shrank the map and found the herb garden. "I saw morning glories and poppies in this chicken-wire enclosure here." Another spin of the laptop.

Frank grinned at her over the screen. "I do believe it's search warrant time."

Giulia's phone rang with the lab's ID. She stabbed the green button.

"Yes?"

"Ms. Driscoll, it's Jerry. I have your results. The compound contained forty-five percent chamomile, forty-five percent valerian, and ten percent lavender."

Giulia breathed. No opium. No LSA. In a calm voice which had nothing to do with her internal panic, she said, "Would you happen to know the effects of those herbs when inhaled by a woman in the first trimester?"

"Let me check on the valerian...right. Are we talking about smoking a whole pipeful of this mixture?"

Her breath stopped again. "No. No direct inhalation at all. Only secondhand, outdoors in a small group. After breathing in the smoke for approximately fifteen minutes, the person reported she felt a little loopy."

Jerry answered without hesitation. "Tell her she's fine. Chamomile is a calming herb. You've seen those teabags in the grocery store. Some weed smokers switch to it when they can't afford the illegal stuff. Valerian is a soporific and lavender is a sedative and muscle relaxer. The strength of all three was in the medium range. If your client felt the effects, it's likely because she never inhaled anything stronger than secondhand cigarette smoke."

Stress tears pricked Giulia's eyes. She swallowed to get to her normal voice. "Thank you for rushing this test. Please email the invoice and the results to the company address."

Frank's hands gripped the table edge. "What?"

Giulia blotted her eyes on her napkin. "It's okay. The baby is okay." She repeated the analysis and the effects of the herbs. "I've got a one o'clock appointment with my OB/GYN to see what she says, but little Zlatan is in the clear."

"We're going to break up this happy little sex and drugs cult and it will be the highlight of my week." He rubbed his hands over his face. "Where were we?"

Giulia had to think. "Suspects. We finished with the tenor and the Antler Stud."

He snorted. "The name of a cheap porn film if I ever heard one."

"I don't want to know how you came to that conclusion."

"Yes, dear. All right, Larabee. Five years back, his neighbors called 911 twice on him. Screams and sounds of furniture breaking. His girlfriend wouldn't press charges the first time, but the second time he shoved her through their screen door and started choking her on the sidewalk. Did six months for assault."

Giulia pulled her iPad closer. "Hold that thought." She opened another set of interview notes. "He told me he got six months as a juvenile for selling drugs, then enlisted in and quit the Marines."

"He's not a total liar. He did join the Marines after he got out on probation. Lasted all of fifty-three days."

"What else?"

"Is he charming?"

"Not particularly. If someone's into the caveman hunter type, he could be perceived as the one who'd come out on top of a Survival of the Fittest contest."

"Someone was. He got married a month after the Marine stint to a woman with an off-grid blog. They bought one of those miniature houses."

Frank's phone jingled with his text sound. He opened it and stood. "I have to run. I'll email you the rest of it." He closed his laptop and kissed her. "I'll call you if we need more ammunition for the search warrant."

Giulia drove to the office. Sidney locked the door as soon as she stepped over the threshold. "We demand the story."

Zane set his client chair in the middle of the room. "All the first thing in the morning work is finished and we blocked out an hour for when you came in."

"So dish," Sidney said. "Fried bugs for dinner?"

"Special filters for drinking your own urine?"

"Ew." Sidney made a gagging face at Zane.

Giulia countered Zane's urine filter suggestion. "Homegrown coffee with goat milk and honey."

Sidney stopped mid-laugh. "Home-grown coffee? Really? They didn't add any chemicals to it, right? How did they roast it? What about decaf?"

Zane gagged this time. "Goat milk is an offense against the human palate. You took one for the team, Ms. D."

"Sidney, the coffee was undrinkable even without the goat milk."

Sidney drooped. "You're the coffee expert. Drat. Okay, moment over. Take us through your two days living in a non-technical world."

What with all their questions, laughter, and appalled comments over Antlered Alex's duck-duck-goose ritual, Giulia didn't escape to her office for another forty-five minutes. Frank's email was the only one she paid attention to.

"Where we left off: A couple of months after Larabee and his wife moved to their little house, the neighbors stopped seeing the wife. The usual rationalizations came out: She changed jobs or everyone kept missing her by a minute or two. The neighbors on each side of the house thought they heard screaming fights between Larabee and the wife, but no one wanted to interfere. The wife's parents showed up and he told them she was on a weekend getaway with friends. Wouldn't let them in. The next day, the cops showed at Larabee's door because the mother swore she heard her daughter's voice yelling from somewhere in the house. They had a warrant, they searched the house, they found the wife locked in the basement. She refused to sleep with Larabee and he was keeping her there until she changed her mind. A slick lawyer weaseled his way into the jury's heads and he got only three years in jail with early parole because of good behavior."

Giulia banged the eraser end of a pencil on her desk. No

wonder people in the Middle Ages believed in all kinds of different demons tempting them to perform evil acts. So much simpler than believing your neighbor hatched evil plans out of his own head.

She dealt with her other emails. Invoices she forwarded to Zane, then divvied up three new client inquiries. The subpoena work went to Zane, the prenup to Sidney, the data discovery request she kept for herself. She paid the lab's rush fee out of her private PayPal account.

Her fingers stopped moving after she sent the payment. She turned to a new sheet on her legal pad:

Domestic assault → Lies → Major anger issues → "Me against the world" → More girlfriend issues → Moves to the sticks → Missing wife → More lies → Wife in basement.

Beneath it, another chart:

Hunts with Joanne → Goes out with Joanne → Claims...

What did he claim? She opened the notes on her iPad.

Claims the breakup was mutual → Joanne vanished April 3rd to Alex's cult → Joanne bails on the cult (when?) → Joanne's friends go public on Facebook accusing Larabee of kidnapping her → Larabee goes ballistic on Facebook and in person (twice).

That second visit, early in the morning when he kept her outside on his grass. She closed her eyes. Neighbors doing everything possible to see what was happening on Larabee's front lawn. An unwashed Larabee not letting her inside. A woman's voice from a hidden TV.

"Driscoll, your snarky assumption got in the way of your brain. That wasn't a TV show. He's got her in his cellar."

Giulia drew a tiny cellar below the arrow charts.

"Where? It's way too small."

The shelving units on all four walls of the storage cellars in the compound barely gave two adults room enough to stand. All of them had been excavated to the same pattern, it seemed. Perhaps the cellar dimensions of any Tiny House were also part of the blueprints. The cellars needed more than dirt. They needed stone-lined walls for food storage because no electricity meant no refrigerators or freezers. Like for the sourdough starter she'd brought as a cult-warming gift.

Which Cheryl had stored in a hidden recess lined with river stones to keep it cool in the summer. Giulia had stood back as Cheryl pulled a shelf out on a hinge to access her cooling niche.

She called Frank.

Forty-Six

At three o'clock, Giulia met Frank and Nash at the precinct and climbed into the back seat of Nash's gray Subaru Forester.

Within the first thirty seconds of the hour-long drive, Frank said, "What did the doctor say?"

Giulia angled her head toward Frank's partner.

"Frank can't keep his mouth shut, Giulia. You know that." He appeared to consider the implications of his statement. "I mean, he doesn't share bedroom secrets or anything, but he was worried about you and the baby so I got two earfuls all morning."

Giulia gave Frank a tight smile. "Darling, you make me feel so secure in the privacy of our relationship."

Nash slugged Frank's shoulder. "Flowers tonight, dude."

"Carnations would be a good choice," Giulia said. "The doctor read the printout and agreed with my lab contact's assessment. She sent me for a blood draw as a precaution and put a rush on it. The results came back right before I left to meet you. All baby-related levels of important blood elements are where they should be and my blood shows no traces of anything out of the ordinary."

Frank bent himself over the front seat, grasped her face, and kissed her.

"No fooling around on the job," Nash said.

Frank took a folded piece of paper from his jacket pocket. "Behold a warrant. This guy's arrest record plus the interview transcripts you sent with your statement of the woman's muffled shout from the house were exactly what the judge needed."

"I should've connected the dots sooner."

"You're not Jesus Christ the omniscient," Nash said.

Giulia chuckled. Nash's filter between brain and mouth malfunctioned at the worst times. Frank said, "Moron," and Nash turned five shades of red in rapid succession.

An hour later they parked on the connecting road to Meadow Lane.

"Cows, ugh," Nash said. "I grew up on a farm. If I never smell manure again, I'll die a happy man."

Giulia pointed out the windshield. "Getting stuck behind the accident on the expressway worked in our favor. Here comes Larabee's green Jeep."

Larabee drove past them down the long rural road. It turned left at a corner so far away the Jeep shrunk to the dimensions of a Matchbox car. Nash started the Subaru and they drove to the pasture fence at the end of Larabee's street.

"That's not a house," Frank said. "It wants to be a house when it grows up."

"Tiny Houses are cutting edge," Giulia said as they walked to the front door. "This one is about three hundred square feet. Note the weeds everywhere. They're all edible. Also note the side of the house to our right borders on the cow pasture. Cows don't pry into one's private affairs. The human neighbors will most likely keep tabs on us through the curtains."

"We have a warrant. They'll thank us for a week's worth of gossip." Frank checked the lock. "Deadbolt."

Giulia produced an extra-large paper clip from her pants pocket. "Step aside, officer of the law, and let the private investigator do her stuff." She snapped it in half and inserted one L-shaped end at a time into the lock.

"I taught her that trick," Frank said.

"Stop patting yourself on the back," Nash said. "It's on YouTube."

"Screw you."

"Not on your best day."

"Shush, boys, I'm concentrating."

Nash said in a quiet voice, "Old lady across the street staring at us from her porch just opened a cell phone."

"I'm on it."

Giulia heard with half an ear Frank's footsteps cross the street and return a few minutes later. At the same moment, the pins slid into place and the deadbolt slid back. "We're in."

"Our watchdog is back inside her door," Nash said. "Now she's looking at us through binoculars."

"Gossip fodder for a month," Giulia said.

They entered the house and locked themselves in. Giulia led the way to the trap door in the kitchen.

"How'd you know where it was?" Nash said.

"These houses are built from three or four standard blueprints, but they all have cellar access via the kitchen. It makes sense when you think about it."

Frank pulled up the trap and Giulia descended first. The cellar was definitely not designed to allow three adults to occupy the space all at once.

"I'll keep watch upstairs in case this guy comes back," Nash said.

Frank tested the shelf of canned goods on the left and Giulia started on the right one with bags of beans and packets of ramen. Neither shelf budged. They met at the middle shelf of paper supplies.

"This shelf is the lightest," Giulia said. "If he's left-handed, I should find a latch under the top...here it is." The switch clicked but nothing moved. "What did you do...wait a minute." She felt a second switch under the third shelf and pressed both of them at the same time. "Aha."

The dual clicks sounded like a muffled *bang* but the shelf swung free on silent hinges. She and Frank stared into a six by six foam-lined cave with quarter-inch PVC pipes set at regular intervals in one wall. A battery-powered desk lamp sat on the floor next to a futon mattress. A short stack of paperback books near the mattress, a tall stack on the other side of the lamp, and a lidded chamber pot were the only other objects in the room. The air stank of urine and feces.

A pale, thin woman balanced on the narrow section of clear floor in the yoga plank position. Her long brown braid fell over her left shoulder, its end pooling on the plywood. Wrinkled gray sweatpants and a matching t-shirt clung to her sweat-covered body. A faded brown tattoo of Texas Longhorn horns and wheat stalks decorated her left arm. The tableau lasted another few seconds until without a twitch from her biceps she jumped from plank straight into Giulia's arms.

"Please get me out of here, please, please." Her hoarse voice fell dead inside the crowded walls.

"Nash," Frank called up the ladder. "Coast clear?"

"Nothing but cows."

Giulia climbed out first, followed by Joanne, followed by Frank. Nash backed a step away from Joanne's effluvium, but recovered himself with an "Afternoon."

"Is it safe to leave? Are you sure?" Joanne said, crowding Giulia. "Can we move faster?"

"Talk later," Frank said. "Out now."

Nash drove his car over the edible lawn to the back door. Joanne and Giulia climbed in the back. Frank rode shotgun. Nash's Subaru ripped up more of the weeds in its trip to the street and freedom.

"Old lady's dialing her phone," Frank said.

"Wonder if she decided we're not the police after all?" Nash said, driving at the speed limit.

"Probably calling all the neighbors over to her house for an in-depth discussion of what she thinks we were up to."

"How did you find me?" Joanne's fingers clutched the seat. Her head kept swiveling to look out every window in the Subaru. "Did you hear me screaming? Who are you?"

"I'm with Driscoll Investigations. Your sister hired me to find you."

Joanne started to sob. Her lips cracked and bled; tears seeped into the bloody slits. "She-she can yell at me every day f-for the next six months and I'll t-take it and like it."

Giulia handed her a tissue which got soaked through in less than a minute. She passed across two more. Joanne sucked in several deep breaths and blotted her lips with the last one.

"Thank you. Did I thank you yet? I can't believe Di sent you after I lied to her like that. Did Nick make her do it?" She looked behind her and to each side. "Can't we drive faster? What time is it? Lou might come back and see me in here." She slid down in the seat.

"He's at work," Giulia said. "We didn't march in there without a plan." She put a hand over Joanne's.

"When did you hear me?" Joanne clutched the seat. "I tore his foam batting away last month, I think, and yelled through those air pipes when I could. I kept replacing the foam when he unlocked the door so he wouldn't notice. He keeps a TV hidden in the cellar and loves screaming monster movies. He kept them on all the time to force me to like them too. I timed my yells to match the movie screams."

"Last week, and I apologize for taking so long to figure it out," Giulia said. "He wouldn't let me inside. I thought it was because he was secretly watching TV and didn't want me to find out."

"Stupid vegetable patch muffled my voice then." She raised herself to see out the back window. "Can we please go faster?"

"We don't want to attract any attention," Giulia said. She held her phone close to Joanne's mouth, the voice memo function already recording. "Go."

Joanne blinked at it.

"From which point?"

"I have a mostly complete picture of what happened between the December breakup and when you and Alex connected. When did he invite you to join his community?"

"The middle of March."

"That tallies with Marjorie's information."

Joanne started punching herself in the temple. "God, Marjorie. I was so mean to her. What am I going to do?"

Giulia caught her hand and kept hold of it, which started Joanne crying again. "I'm a terrible person. I b-bought into Alex's sales pitch of being one of the p-privileged and chosen and I kicked everyone to the curb."

Giulia kept passing her tissues for one minute only by the car clock, then held out her hand for the last one. "Marjorie and her feline army are ready to welcome you back as long as you pay enough attention to the cats."

Joanne's lip split further when she responded with a small smile. "The cats will make sure I know the extent of my sin." She breathed in yoga style until the tears stopped. "I'm sorry. I've been schooling myself for weeks not to be a doormat anymore." She scowled at her hands. "I won't be able to hunt if these keep shaking."

"It's the reaction. It'll stop soon," Giulia said. "You're safe now."

Joanne stared out all the windows again. "I wish I was as sure as you are. Okay. Okay, On April third I left the apartment like I was going to work as usual, but Alex had me drive to this grade school in Pittsburgh. I ditched my car and started walking. He met me a couple of blocks later and drove me out to his—oh, wait, maybe I shouldn't tell you about that."

Giulia's facial expression was not as gentle as she would have liked it to be for a traumatized kidnapping victim. "He drove you out to his compound by Beaver Falls and began your indoctrination with hallucinogens and thought retraining."

"You've been there."

"Goat milk in the coffee," Giulia said to defuse the moment.

Joanne's face said it all. "It's disgusting, isn't it?" She looked out the car window, her fingernails threatening to rip holes in the cloth seat. "I'm really outside. I've been dreaming of freedom every time I fell asleep for...what's today?"

"July sixteenth."

Joanne's spine stiffened. "Two months. He's had me locked down there for two months. I haven't seen the sun or breathed fresh air or..." She pushed a fist against her mouth and inhaled. "Okay. I've got this." A brief smile flashed out. "I don't know what I want more: a shower, a toothbrush, or an extra-large pepperoni pizza."

"We'll get you all three. Alex drove you out to his Prepper compound. And?"

"Everyone was wonderful. They made me feel like I was an essential piece of their plan. We all worked together, ate together, played games together. It was everything I'd ever wanted."

"Why did you drop out of your old life without telling anyone?"

Joanne tugged at her braid. "Diane would've hit the ceiling. She didn't understand how everything and everyone were sucking the life out of me." Her lips cracked again at her ironic smile. "Desperation makes you stupid."

Giulia dug a Burt's Bees lip balm out of her messenger bag and gave it to Joanne.

"Thank you. Ow. Peppermint stings. Alex was forceful and organized and had a mission. Everything my last three guys didn't have."

"What about Kurt?"

The smile became genuine again. "He was funny. His ego was bigger than a third-world country, but he was great in bed."

Nash kept driving one mile under the speed limit. Frank kept scanning the roads.

"So anyway," Joanne said into Giulia's phone, "I bunked with one of the members while I got acclimated. You've been there, you said. Did you participate in a Horned God ritual?"

"Yes."

"How freaky was your LSA trip?"

"The twins were there," Giulia said.

"Oh, you got the family-friendly version. If the teenagers are there during the Horned God ritual, we smoke a mixture of herbs to relax us and make us open to the communal power of Alex and

Cernunnos. When the teenagers aren't there, everyone gets their own cup of morning glory tea. When he takes his chosen consort into his bower in the woods, they share a special brew with poppy seeds from a special drinking horn." She flexed her fingers. "It hit me like a freight train. I flew on a porno dream of horns and fire and, and, other body parts and didn't wake up until after sunset the next day."

"When did you find out about the homemade drugs?" Giulia kept her voice soothing.

Joanne's mouth twisted. "Right after I came out of it. Alex and Cheryl—the twins' mother, you met her, right?—apologized to me for like 24 hours straight. They're the amateur chemists in the group and I was the first one who didn't wake up early the next morning. I guess Alex's god didn't know what a lightweight I am when it comes to any kind of drug."

Giulia phrased her next question with care. "Are you considering bringing sexual assault charges against Alex?"

Joanne stared. "Why?"

Giulia stared back. Right then her phone reached its recording limit. She tossed it in her bag and flipped open her tablet. Fingers poised to type, she looked up at Joanne, who shook her head.

"I get it. No, I'm not. Our sex was totally consensual. I knew we were drinking hallucinogens and I figured the extra drink we shared was more of the same. I was fine with it all. I was thrilled to be chosen."

Giulia typed without comment. The traffic increased and Joanne slid farther down in the seat. Her fingers alternated between clutching themselves and the seat. Her fear sweat overpowered the air in the car. Frank cracked his window.

Joanne said in a meek voice. "I'm sorry. I know I reek. Louis wouldn't give me any soap and only brought me water enough to drink." Her fingers gripped themselves tight enough to turn all the knuckles white.

Frank and Van Horne said the right things. Giulia said, "Why did you leave Alex's compound?"

Joanne tried to slump but her knees were almost on the floor of the car already. Instead she sat halfway up and stared at her hands.

"It was great the first month or so there. We worked hard, but I'm not afraid of hard work. I taught myself to cook and keep busy without technology. We smoked and drank Alex's concoctions and everything was happy and mellow." More hand staring. "One morning I couldn't remember the steps of one of my go-to recipes. I'm not exaggerating when I tell you that I used to know three hundred recipes by heart. It's what I do...what I did. It scared me. I never did drugs before I joined Alex's community. I thought, how many brain cells have I killed in four weeks? So I stopped inhaling. Then I stopped drinking the tea. That took some sleight of hand. Within two weeks it was like I de-fogged my brain."

Giulia took it all down. "And?"

"At the two-week mark a cat wandered into the compound and the dogs tore it to shreds."

Giulia shuddered. The memory of adorable Pepin the moose flopping at her feet included the size of Pepin's teeth.

"Right, you've met the dogs. They're not pets. They're guard dogs." Joanne placed her hands flat on the lap. "Alex made me get rid of my cats as proof I was one of them. He told me to bring their meat for my first supper here, but I gave them to a farm that needed mousers and shot two small coyotes instead."

Frank muttered something. Giulia refrained from kicking the back of his seat.

Joanne said, "I thought of my cats and the drugs and how we all were these artificially happy little Alex-robots and a voice in my head kept saying over and over, what the hell was I doing?" She shrugged. "I was sharing my tent with these two teenage runaways. They were heavy into Alex's concoctions, but they wouldn't listen to me when I talked about moderation. Guess Alex recruits for pig-headedness too. I sat up three nights in a row doing the whole soul-searching thing and when everyone was zonked after the next Horned God ritual, I sneaked out."

A vivid flashback of the weeks before she left the convent seared Giulia's brain. She shook it off. "You left everything?"

"I didn't have much, but yeah. I wasn't going to carry my giant water purifier or my stock of dried beans and granola. I took my bug-out bag and hit the road." She slumped again. That was a miserable trip. It took me four days to walk to Louis' place."

"Why him and not Diane or Kurt or Eddie?"

Joanne's lip trembled but she got hold of herself. "Louis once tried to join Alex's community, but Louis doesn't play well in groups. I figured he'd understand and give me a beer and a sympathetic shoulder." She glared at the back of Van Horne's head like he was a surrogate for her hate. "Is that the pinnacle of stupid, or what? When I showed up at Louis's door, I cried about how Alex had made me feel special and equal and how I planned to stay in his community forever and how depressed I was because I couldn't hack it."

"And he locked you in his cellar?"

"Bingo. He slipped me a roofie and I woke up in that padded cave." Joanne sat back against the seat after she completed her story, but she didn't relax. She stared at people in passing cars and on street corners as though Larabee would appear from behind them and snatch her out of the car and back into his cellar prison.

At last Frank said, "Five minutes to the precinct."

Joanne looked down at herself. "They're going to think I've been dumpster diving. I'm a professional." A sad half-smile. "I used to be a professional."

Giulia squeezed her hand. "Don't worry about them. We have your back."

When Joanne climbed out of the car she stood still for a moment and raised her face to the sky.

Giulia nudged her. "We should get inside."

The receptionist, impeccable in peach silk, wrinkled her nose as they passed. Frank led Giulia and Joanne into one of the waiting rooms and went to find Jimmy. Nash detoured into the crowded detectives' office.

"I'll send someone out for new clothes," Giulia said. "What size are you?"

"I have no idea. I was a fourteen when I left Alex's community." Acid infused Joanne's voice. "Louis said he wanted me to slim down before we resumed our relationship. He fed me a cheese omelet every morning and venison with a hunk of lettuce every night. I wasn't getting skinny; I was building muscle so I could kick his ass. And if I could have found a knife, I would have cut his dick off and shoved it down his throat."

The door opened on her last sentence. "Giulia, you never fail me," Jimmy said.

Giulia performed introductions. "Jane, you're better at this than I am. What size would you guess Joanne wears?"

Jane didn't react to the stench at all. "Hi. I used to work for Giulia. Okay if I put my hands on your hips and shoulders and legs?"

Joanne stretched out her arms and stood in place. Giulia saw her flinch, but Jane was all business and Joanne kept her skittishness under control.

Jane stepped back. "Ten and small." She looked at Jimmy, who was talking with Giulia in a low voice. "Can she use our employee shower?"

"Certainly. Ms. Philbey, my assistant will take you back there and fix you up with everything you need."

Joanne showed the first hint of her taut body relaxing. "A shower. Oh my God."

Giulia picked up her messenger bag. "I'll bring back clothes. Jane, do you have toothbrushes and paste back there?"

"We've got it all."

Giulia called Diane from the Nunmobile. Diane shrieked, apologized, and repeated the news at the top of her voice. Several different voices cheered at the other end.

"You are the best private eye in the state. Where is she? Is she okay?"

Giulia explained the next steps in the process. Diane promised not to descend on them until Giulia called with permission. Giulia hoped she meant it.

She returned to the precinct twenty minutes later with a bright blue cotton shirt, a pair of white capris, a few choices of underthings, and flip-flops. The receptionist gave her directions to the employee area, and she found Joanne wrapped in one towel and drying her hair with another.

Giulia handed her the bag. "I called Diane. She'll pick you up when we're through here. One of the Dollar Stores was the only place nearby I could find. I'm sorry."

Joanne snatched it, her trembling down to a minimum now. "Clean clothes. You are a godsend." She vanished into a toilet stall and returned five minutes later. "I feel human for the first time in two months. Okay, Private Eye, it's time to make a statement, right? Let's go."

Forty-Seven

Joanne's repeated story took most of an hour. Giulia supplemented the gaps. When Giulia spread out the photos of the drawer of Polaroids, Joanne stared at them without speaking for a long minute.

"He took pictures of us afterward?" Her voice trembled again, but not with imminent tears. "He kept them under his bed?" Foul language worthy of her twin sister spewed from Joanne's mouth. "Give me a minute, please."

She shoved back her chair and walked out into the detectives' room. No one paid attention to her. After two circuits of the room, she returned to Jimmy's office.

"I apologize. What do you need me to do?"

Jimmy said, "Can you identify any of the women in these pictures?"

With a set jaw and a firm hand she scanned the faces and gave them names of several of the women. "Sherry's under eighteen, I remember. So are Tessa and Ashlyn."

Jimmy brought out photos of the girls from the park and the convenience store. Joanne lost all color in her already washed-out face. "Ashlyn and Tessa. I thought they were sneaking extras from Alex's opium and morning glory storage. Damn them for being young and stupid. Damn Alex."

She signed her statement and Frank went with Nash for arrest warrants for Larabee and Alex. The receptionist appeared with a large pepperoni pizza and a six-pack of Coke. Joanne's face at the first bite was comical.

"It's after six thirty," Giulia said when the food was gone. "Frank and Nash should have caught Louis at work by now."

"The cops won't hold him." Joanne tensed up again. "He's devious and paranoid and an experienced hunter. He'll disappear the minute he sees them coming. He used to boast he could spot a cop even if the cop was wearing swim trunks on a beach."

"I don't like to brag, but my husband is half the arresting team."

Joanne shook her head. "Sorry, but everyone underestimates Louis. I sure did." She shuddered, the wave running from hair to feet.

Frank's specific ring tone came from inside Giulia's messenger bag. Giulia put the call on speaker.

Anger and disgust fought for dominance in Frank's voice. "Bastard got away."

Giulia considered cursing for a millisecond.

"Either someone in the warehouse saw us and warned him or he has a sixth sense for cops."

Joanne said in a tight voice, "You're not the first. Louis likes to brag about how he's smarter than any cop or drill sergeant."

From the phone: "Is Jimmy still there?"

"Right here," Frank's boss said.

"We're heading to his house next."

"No," Joanne said, the shaking back in her voice. "He'll think I went back to Alex's compound."

"Why?" from the phone and Giulia.

"When he first locked me up I begged him to let me go. I promised I'd go back to Alex's and never tell anyone what happened. He knew I'd wiped my old life clean and I tried to convince him no one would come looking for me." She turned a helpless gaze on Giulia. "He'll come for what he thinks belongs to him."

Frank said, "Jimmy, what do you think?"

Jimmy said, "Make sure you catch 'em both at the same place."

"On our way." Frank ended the call.

Giulia took Joanne by the arm. "We're heading out."

"We are?" Joanne stood. "All right. Thank you for the food and the shower." She shook Jimmy's hand. "Throw away the key when you lock them up, will you?"

In the parking lot, Joanne stood on the asphalt and inhaled a huge breath. "Fresh air and exhaust fumes. It's wonderful. Listen to those car horns. Look at that sky. I'm going to re-start my cake business with a line of four seasons themed baked goods." She glanced at Giulia. "Are you impressed at how normal I sound? Don't believe it."

Giulia opened the Nunmobile's passenger door. "Let me drive you to Diane's house."

Joanne buckled herself in. "Your cops know the community will barricade themselves in and shoot to kill, right?"

Giulia tapped the keys on the steering wheel. "I should've thought. We can't have that happen."

Joanne's yoga-sculpted muscles flexed. "I don't want Alex to die as a martyr to the anti-technology revolution. I want him to rot in jail."

"So do I." Giulia inserted the key into the ignition but didn't start the car. "We need a distraction for when the police arrive."

"Why do you look like that? I think it's a good idea."

"You know that feeling you get in your stomach when you drop from the highest point of a roller coaster?"

"Ugh, yeah. I hate roller coasters. Diane dragged me onto a ton of them when we were kids."

"The perfect distraction is giving me that feeling." She took out her cell phone. Hesitated another few seconds. "Use the tools at hand." She made a face. "Now I sound like a cheesy motivational poster."

The number was last on her extensive "recents" list. She punched it.

"You've reached *The Scoop*. We want to know all the details!

Leave us a message with your story and our investigative team will turn over every rock."

Giulia rolled her eyes. "Ken Kanning, it's Giulia Driscoll. Pick up."

Forty-Eight

Kanning must have been eating a late supper, because his first word sounded like "Frs-kll?" A cough. A gulping noise. "Did hell freeze over?"

"Good evening. Would you care to act professional while discussing a possible news story or shall I hang up?"

"What? Hell, yes." Another cough and gulp. "I mean, Hello, Ms. Driscoll. Thank you for calling *The Scoop*."

Joanne hissed at Giulia. "What are you doing?"

Giulia made push-back motions at her. "Mr. Kanning, I'm calling in regard to your abortive attempts to infiltrate a Doomsday Prepper compound up by Beaver Falls."

Kanning indulged in language Sister Mary Regina Coelis would never have allowed from any of her students.

"Mr. Kanning, I am quite willing to call the Keystone Action team from one of the network affiliates. I believe their ratings topped yours in the midsummer sweeps."

A sound like Kanning was choking on a fish bone preceded a moment of silence.

"Ms. Driscoll, I'm pleased you keep up with *The Scoop*. We're still trying to gain access to that particular den of thugs."

"I thought as much." Go big or go home, she reminded herself. "I'm driving up there as soon as we complete this phone call. Do you recall the teenage girls who were found dead in the park and behind a convenience store a few weeks ago?"

He was salivating. She heard it in his quickened breathing. She scowled at Joanne, who alternated between extravagant facial expressions at Giulia and scanning the parking lot for—probably—Louis coming after them with a rifle.

"Yes," was all Kanning said.

The man could learn. "The drugs they overdosed on came from the Prepper compound. I can get you in there."

"Holy shit, I'll sleep with you if you can do that. Hell, we'll both sleep with you."

Or not. Giulia hung up.

"It's a waste of energy," she said to Joanne, "but I hate that man with a passion."

"Why are you calling that pair of leeches? They're as low as the scum in a garbage disposal." Joanne kept checking the parking lot.

Giulia's phone rang.

"Can you think of anyone else who'd drop everything to meet me at Alex's compound and is guaranteed to create instant pandemonium?"

She answered the call.

"Ms. Driscoll, please accept my apology for my unprofessional outburst." Kanning turned up the charm. "*The Scoop* would be indebted to you for your assistance in cracking the wall of secrecy around that particular enclosure."

"In this one instance we can be of use to each other," Giulia said. "Meet us in the parking lot in front of the tennis courts at Bradys Run park. I'm leaving now."

She ended that call and dialed Frank. "I'm driving Joanne to her sister's and then I'm meeting Ken Kanning at Bradys Run."

"You're what?" Frank's voice cracked.

"I'm using *The Scoop* as misdirection for when you and Nash get to the Prepper compound. I'll call you back when we have a detailed plan."

Giulia ended that conversation and held her phone out to Joanne. "It's less than ten minutes to your sister's. Want to give her a call?"

Joanne took the phone but didn't dial. "Why didn't you say 'we' were going to Alex's?"

"Because you've been through a horrible experience and I'm not about to drag you into potential danger." She started the car.

"Stop." Joanne's fingers kneaded themselves again. "I don't need protecting. Don't look at me like that. I can help." More kneading. "I'm not scared of Alex because he'll have a bunch of his flock there for dinner, he always does. He'll be all benevolent and forgiving in front of them. Besides, don't they think you're coming back?"

"They do, which is why I'm not concerned about their reaction when they see me."

"Louis will recognize you when he shows. You don't want to make him mad. He's unpredictable." A brittle laugh. "That's the understatement of the year. He'll barge in there with guns and he won't believe them when they say I'm not there." She bent over herself and began rocking back and forth in the seat. "Damn, damn, damn, I don't want to do this."

Giulia put a gentle hand on her back, but Joanne flinched anyway. A moment later she sat up.

"I don't want any of them to get hurt because of me. If Louis sees me, he'll waste time humiliating me." Her hands grasped Giulia's. "Your cops will be there to take him out, right? It won't last long, right?"

"Yes and yes. They know what they're doing."

Joanne's hands squeezed Giulia's. "All right then. I'm going with you." Her firm voice slipped. "Could we please start moving before I chicken out?"

The Scoop's white creeper van was waiting for them at the rendezvous point. Giulia had never truly understood the old Biblical phrase "girding one's loins" until now.

"Let me talk to them," she said to Joanne.

Joanne had regained control of herself on the ride. "You're the professional, but if he shoves his microphone in my face I won't guarantee the outcome."

Giulia opened her door. This new Joanne was going to startle some of her old friends.

Kanning jumped over the running board onto the asphalt, hand outstretched. "Ms. Driscoll, thank you again for contacting *The Scoop*. I don't remember if you've been formally introduced to my cameraman and associate producer."

The bald cameraman with his bird's-nest beard came out to meet them. Giulia had never seen him without the gigantic multi-part TV camera attached to his shoulder, that was certain.

"Pit Bull, meet Giulia Driscoll, Private Investigator. Ms. Driscoll, Pit Bull."

The cameraman's massive hand shook Giulia's in a firm business manner. The Eye of Sauron tattoo on the back of his hand with "Eye See You" above it undermined the businesslike effect.

Giulia checked the weather app on her phone. "Gentlemen, we're on a schedule. Sunset is at eight twenty-five, but the compound is covered with trees which will block out the light sooner. I will lead you to a secluded place to park at the far end of the compound. My passenger and I will go around to the owner's driveway and use the hidden entrance to the central compound area."

Pit Bull made a move for the van.

"Sir, please do not videotape me."

Kanning gestured him back.

"Thank you. My passenger has been held captive by an ex-boyfriend, Louis Larabee. He eluded the police at his place of business and we have reason to believe he will try to recapture her at the compound."

Kanning's fingers twitched. For the sake of cooperation, Giulia relented. "Mr. Kanning, please feel free to make notes."

"Yes," he hissed under his breath. He took out an Android phone. His thumbs moved over the keypad at supersonic speed.

Giulia allowed him two minutes. "You're going to be our

misdirection. The police are also on the way to the compound. Larabee is a skilled hunter and he's angry and desperate. The members of the compound know me and my passenger."

"They're all great shots," Pit Bull said.

"You think they'll circle the wagons for you," Kanning said. "You want to stop a good old-fashioned shootout."

"Correct. The arrival of the police might make the compound members think they're being raided." She held up a hand. "They are, but only a fool advertises it. They're supplying home-grown hallucinogens and alcohol to minors. The runaway teenagers found in Cottonwood died because of them."

Kanning said over his shoulder, "We have achieved paradise, Bull."

Giulia stifled her honest comment on Kanning's attitude. "When the compound members see the police, they're going to try to destroy evidence. You will be there filming everything and cutting off people's paths as you try to acquire sound bites. This will give the police the time they need to capture Larabee and the compound's leader, along with whoever makes a dash for their cellars or for freedom."

Pit Bull said, "You sure can give orders."

Giulia stared him down. "We're leaving. Follow my car."

Forty-Nine

Giulia pushed through the concealed entrance in the hedge and stepped into the central clearing, Joanne at her back. They'd caught the tail end of supper. Ariel and her husband sipped mead. The accordion player and his wife faced each other on two chairs singing the chorus of "The Lion Sleeps Tonight." The cheesemaker buttered bread and handed it to her husband. Horizontal sunset rays striped the table.

Tim looked over when the ivy rustled. He waved at them with the piece of bacon in his hand. "Hey, Maria. Who you got with you?"

Jim's head popped up from behind Tim's back, his fingers still on his sneaker laces. "It's Phoebe. Whoa, you look hot."

The music stopped. The mead glasses hit the table. The goat-milker coughed on a bite of bread. Everyone crowded around Giulia and Joanne.

"We missed you."

"Alex said you weren't coming back."

"Give me your workout regimen, please."

"Are you hungry?"

Joanne answered the last question. "Starving."

The twins became perfect gentlemen. They led Giulia and Joanne to their vacated chairs and shoved their own dirty plates out of the way—well, almost perfect. Tim ran into their house and returned with clean plates, cups, and utensils. Jim poured mead. Ariel stabbed slices of meat and cheese. Orion buttered bread.

Joanne took a bite of meat and closed her eyes. "Mutton. I love mutton."

Giulia hid her smile at Joanne's delight in eating something other than venison.

"Don't diss the bread," Jim said. "It's my first try."

"Now that you're back you'll make cake for us again, right, please?" Tim said.

"What happened to you?" the accordion player's wife said. "You look stressed."

Pepin and another dog barked from inside the octagonal house. Giulia had forgotten the dogs. "What's up with Pepin?"

Jim said, "He's having a night o' love with Rana in Orion's house. Alex says we should breed them."

Tim gestured over his shoulder. "Lassie and Boris are in our house."

Giulia breathed again.

In between alternate bites of cheese, meat, and bread, Joanne told the story of her past two months. She didn't mention weaning herself off the drugs. Instead, she played up her old mindset of being unworthy of Alex's attention and the responsibility of leading the apocalypse survivors into the future. In this version, she escaped Larabee's hidden room by bashing him over the head with the lamp because her muscles were finally strong enough to overpower him.

"We should never have offered him a place in our family," Ariel said.

"Alex never made a judgment mistake like that before," the cheesemaker said.

"Shh," the accordion player said.

Alex's deep voice said, "Phoebe."

Giulia hadn't seen him arrive, again. If he was in "the god is possessing me" mode, *The Scoop* would be sending her flowers and chocolate tomorrow.

Joanne channeled her inner Method Actor, exactly like Giulia had coached her to do during the drive. She ran to Alex and threw her arms around him. "Alex, I should never have left here. I was so wrong. I've been punished. Please take me back into the community."

Alex unpeeled her and set her at arms' length. "Cernunnos sent me a vision of captivity and flight. I understand now. He was speaking of you."

Tim and Jim started talking together. Ariel and her husband joined in. Alex held up his left hand. "Stop. Phoebe, how is it that you and Maria are together here?"

Giulia stood, shamming respect. "My cleaning service job sent me to a satellite location because they were short-handed again. Phoebe flagged me down on my way home."

Joanne stepped away from Alex and hugged Giulia. "She took me to her apartment so I could shower for the first time in two months. She even bought me clothes. She's my new bestie."

Giulia-as-Maria returned the squeeze. "You're so brave. Isn't it cool how we belong to the same community? It's like we were meant to find each other."

A rapid glissando turned everyone's head. The accordion player keyed the opening bars to "In Heaven There is No Beer." The hippies placed one arm on each other's waists, the other hand high on their partner's shoulders, and began to polka. Tim grabbed Joanne and Jim took Giulia. The cheesemaker and her husband joined in a moment later. Last, Alex offered a hand to the accordion player's wife.

They polkaed around the table, between the front vegetable gardens, up onto porches and down to the fire pit. The song switched to the "Beer Barrel Polka" and everyone changed partners.

"There should be a polka about mead," Tim said as he swapped partners with the goat-milker.

Alex took Giulia from Jim. "Your resourcefulness and generosity please us. We want you to move here as soon as possible."

Giulia made happy-sappy conversation while thinking, "How does he maintain perfect breath control after two polkas?" and "I can't wait to testify against you in court."

BASH!

Louis Larabee charged through the hidden entrance. Shredded ivy vines hung from his left ear and both shoulders. His left hand held a Glock. Tim and Ariel stutter-stepped in front of him. Tim pushed Ariel toward her husband. Larabee grabbed Tim and shoved the Glock under his chin.

Giulia yanked her phone out of her back pocket and hit Send on the one-word text she'd pre-written to Ken Kanning: NOW.

Fifty

The cheesemaker screamed. The music jangled into silence. Jim pushed Joanne under the table and stood in front of her, a gallant gesture despite his birch tree build. The remaining community members froze in their last dance positions.

"Look at the loser freaks." Larabee's voice showed minimal signs of stress and the gun didn't tremble at all. "You can't hide from a real hunter, Josie. I knew you'd come crawling back here. Show yourself."

Giulia sent psychic hurry-up vibes to *The Scoop* and her husband. They should've been here before Larabee.

"Let go of my brother, Louis," Jim said.

"Fat chance, incestuous faggot."

Jim's stunned expression was comical.

"You know what they say about homophobes." Tim's jaunty reply cut off at the last word as Louis jabbed the gun barrel harder into his throat.

"I want what's mine, freaks." Louis detached the gun from Tim's throat to wave it at the group. "Unless you want to go all Donner Party on this pissant for breakfast tomorrow." The gun returned to its previous position.

Giulia stepped toward Louis and Tim. "I'm sure we can talk about this."

Louis did a textbook double-take. "You?"

Joanne crawled into view and stood. "Louis, don't do this."

"There you are, you disobedient pig. Get your fat ass over here."

The hippie moved to Giulia's left. Giulia flipped a mental coin on whether he was saving his own skin or about to add his own attempt to talk Larabee down.

Where was her cavalry?

Larabee tightened his grip on Tim and planted his back against the hedge. "Don't try to distract me, asshole. Everybody stay nice and still and think about living until your next polka."

Bang. The hippie cried out and fell to the dirt. Blood spurted through his fingers as he clutched his right foot.

"Honey bun?" Ariel got two strides closer to him before another bullet sprayed up dirt in her face.

"I said stand still, you stoner twits."

The gun was at Tim's neck again. He grimaced when the hot muzzle contacted his skin.

Joanne said from her current position, "Louis, this is between you and me. Don't take it out on them."

"You shouldn't have run back to them like the spineless lard-ass you are at heart."

Giulia increased her psychic Ken Kanning vibes. Her position next to Alex was in Larabee's direct line of sight. She needed Kanning and Pit Bull to give her an opening.

"Louis, let Tim go and I'll come back with you."

Larabee's laughter spooked Giulia.

"You'll say whatever you think I want to hear to rescue this little piece of shit."

Joanne clutched her hands in a praying position. "No, Louis, I swear. They don't want me anymore. They said I wasn't worthy because I ran away."

"You like running, don't you?"

She took another step closer. "You knew I needed someone to be strict with me. You need to help me learn my lesson again."

Another skin-crawling laugh. "Don't worry. I will."

BASH!

"We found it, Scoopers! A Doomsday cult plying innocent teenagers with drugs and booze to force them—aagh!"

Ken Kanning collapsed to the ground at the no-longer-hidden hedge entrance. Pit Bull's camera followed Kanning down, the lens whirring in close on the blood running from Kanning's right arm into the dirt.

"Who the hell are these idiots?" Larabee's gun was again at Tim's neck.

"I wish we had a live feed," the face of *The Scoop* muttered as he struggled upright. The late sunlight faded to twilight by the time he got himself vertical. "Light," he said in a quiet voice and the camera's spotlight illuminated a swath of the central area.

Kanning switched the microphone to his left hand and jerked his head at the hedge. The camera swooped up and put Larabee in the spotlight.

Kanning's voice filled the clearing. "This may be the first time I've been shot in the line of duty, but *The Scoop* never runs away from a story. Directly in front of me a desperate man holds a fragile boy hostage. Is it the drugs? Is it the poisonous moonshine they brew in their hidden cellars?"

"Hey," Tim said. "I'm not fragile."

"Shut up, you with the mike," Larabee said.

Cheryl stumbled through the mess in the new, larger entrance. "What's going on? Jim? Tim?"

"Will he shoot this innocent young man? Does no one in this group of supposed brave pioneers have the guts to save one of their own?"

Cheryl screamed her son's name.

"Shut up," Larabee shouted.

Alex's booming preacher voice cut through the din. "How dare you attack my sacred circle, blasphemer?" His hands beat a syncopated rhythm on the table. *Thump, thump-thump, thump. Thump, thump-thump, thump.*

Cheryl stopped screaming. Ariel stopped crooning over her husband. Her husband stopped putting pressure on his bloody foot.

"Scoopers, we're not quite sure what's happening." Kanning paused while Pit Bull, still holding the camera steady, bent his head and whispered to his boss.

Thump, thump-thump, thump. The size of Alex's hands or the wood of the table or both made the sounds resonate at the lower threshold of Giulia's hearing. *Thump, thump-thump, thump.*

"Apparently the cult's leader is channeling their private god. I promise our Scoopers we'll find out which god and what psychic control he and it have over these hostages."

Larabee pointed the Glock at Alex. At Giulia. At Joanne. At Kanning. Then back to Tim's throat. Kanning's eyes slewed toward Alex. The camera took the hint and poured its light along the table, framing Alex and his drumming hands.

The hippie stood. The accordion player set his instrument on the ground.

Over the unchanging drumbeat, Alex cemented Giulia's chances at a delivery from one of Cottonwood's florists tomorrow.

"My people are the hunters," Alex said in his "possessed by the god" voice. "My people share my strength. I protect my people. I give strength to my people."

Larabee's deer in the headlights expression shifted from Alex to the houses behind him. Tim grunted as Larabee's muscular arm tightened around his chest and the gun moved from his throat to his temple.

Two uniformed police officers ran into the clearing behind Alex. Their flashlights increased the twilight plus spotlight chiaroscuro effect.

Alex kept drumming. "Show them my people's strength. Show them my people's strength."

"At last the city's finest make an entrance, Scoopers. How many more guns will threaten our lives tonight?"

Larabee glared at the uniforms flanking Alex. "Don't come any closer or I'll blow this pretty-boy's head off."

Frank and Nash skirted the beehives, Larabee's view of them blocked by the cheesemaker and her husband.

Thump, thump-thump, thump.

The uniformed officer on Alex's right said, "Shut up with that noise."

"Where is a true hero?" Kanning swept the crowd with his injured arm, spattering blood on the dirt. He grimaced at the camera. "Only a coward hides behind a gun and a helpless boy."

"Shut up," Larabee said, his voice rising on the second word. "Everybody shut up!"

"Drop the gun and step away from the boy," Frank said.

Larabee twisted himself and Tim to face Frank. He gave Frank a physically impossible order.

"I'll count to three."

Another impossible order.

Thump, thump-thump, thump.

"Stop that damn drumming," Larabee said.

"One."

"Louis, please let Tim go." Joanne walked forward.

"Two."

"I don't want you to get hurt, Louis."

"Three."

The drumming stopped.

Joanne leaped the intervening distance with her yoga-trained muscles. Tim butted the back of his head into Larabee's nose. Joanne knocked the gun away from Tim's face. It fell to the ground but didn't go off. Every community member swarmed Larabee at the same time Frank and Nash dived on him. Kanning narrated the chaos. Tim ran to the safety of the nearest front porch at Olympic-worthy speed.

Joanne said, "Everybody get off him."

Fifty-One

Pit Bull widened the spotlight beam.

Joanne stood over the pile of hypnotized bodies, the Glock aimed at the last place Larabee had been visible.

"All of you, get off him."

No one moved.

Joanne fired one shot into the hedge. Twig and leaf shrapnel exploded onto the community members. They fell away, blood dripping from their faces and scalps. Frank had wormed under the amateurs and twisted Larabee's arms behind his back. Nash snapped handcuffs on Larabee's wrists.

"Back away, detectives," Joanne said. "I'm an excellent shot, but I don't want these bullets to go through him into you."

"Josie, what are you talking about?" Larabee struggled against his captors.

"You drugged me, you locked me up, you beat me, you starved me, and my promised reward was a life with you. And I was supposed to be grateful."

"Joanne." Giulia hadn't talked down a violent student in five years, but the memory was sharp as glass. "He isn't worth the jail time."

"The hell he isn't." Joanne never looked away from Larabee.

"You just got your freedom back. Don't throw it away on this piece of trash." She walked toward Joanne with measured steps.

"I'm going to shoot his dick off and then I'm going to shoot his left hand off." Joanne's spotlight-enhanced shadow on the hedge loomed over the three men on the ground. "You want to know why? Because he beat me with his left hand. Every time I fought back. Every time I refused to eat. When I begged him for a new chamber pot and he wanted me to feel his power he beat me and then he left the overflowing one in there for days and days." Her voice rose. "Move, gentlemen."

Giulia swept Joanne's legs out from under her. The gun arced into the shadows and landed with a hideous jangle of notes onto the accordion. Joanne wrestled Giulia for a few moments, but Giulia wrenched Joanne's right wrist back far enough for Joanne to cry out in pain. Giulia twisted the other wrist and Joanne collapsed with a curse and a sob.

All the community members started talking again. Giulia handed Joanne to Nash and grabbed the sleeves of Kanning and Pit Bull.

"Find Alex. The guy who was drumming on the table."

Pit Bull ran the spotlight around the clearing.

"He's going into his house."

"Frank, follow us," she shouted over the clamor.

She ran ahead, Kanning and Pit Bull a few steps behind. She trusted Frank to keep with them. The front door of Alex's house clapped against the frame and bounced open. Giulia pounded up the two steps and into the living room. "Up there. Up in the loft." The spotlight caught Alex crouched next to his bed at the exact spot of the hidden drawer. His head turned and the light glinted off his wild eyes. Frank climbed the ladder two rungs at a time and tackled him. Alex landed a punch to Frank's cheekbone. Frank countered with a blow to Alex's jaw. Alex tried to twist out from under Frank and they rolled off the narrow loft. They performed one more twist in the air and Alex landed on his back with Frank on top of him.

Frank spoke over Kanning's head to Giulia. "Would you please find out what he didn't want the police to see?"

As Kanning jabbered into his microphone Giulia climbed the ladder and gathered the scattered Polaroids into the shallow drawer. She balanced the drawer in her left hand and gripped the ladder with her right as she descended. While the spotlight stayed on Alex and Frank, she walked out to the porch and called to one of the uniformed officers, "May I borrow you and your flashlight?"

Back inside, she shone the light on the contents of the drawer while blocking it from Pit Bull's camera. "They appear to be photographs of naked women under the influence of drugs." She said to the officer, "May I ask you to hold Alex?"

When she had Frank to herself, in a manner of speaking, she shone her phone's light on a certain photograph. "See that picture in the corner?" She raised her voice over Kanning's. "Doesn't it look like one of those poor teenage girls found dead in Cottonwood?"

All those weekends in the orchestra pit at the community theater had imbued Frank with acting skills. "Why yes, it does look like one of them. The one with the vampire fangs tattoo. She was only sixteen."

Alex cursed and roared as he struggled with the uniformed officer. Frank left Giulia and helped drag Alex outside. Giulia kept the drawer against her hip and away from *The Scoop's* camera. Kanning chewed more scenery than five community theater actors. Pit Bull tried to get a shot of the drawer but Giulia blocked him from every angle.

When Giulia reached the porch, the central area was lit through the tattered hedge with headlights from four police cars and an ambulance. Tim was giving a statement as an EMT treated the muzzle burns on his neck. Cheryl admitted to a police officer how she allowed the twins to drink mead and smoke drugs with the adults. The cheesemaker and her husband, subdued and pale, showed a different officer the stores of poppy and morning glory seeds. Ariel and her husband were being loaded into one of the police cars. The accordion player sat on the ground next to his damaged instrument. "Gee, dad, it was a Wurlitzer," he muttered. His wife put her arms around him.

Kanning dashed from one cluster to another as the community members talked in changed voices of a vision of Cernunnos telling them to attack and how Cernunnos had been a god of peace and pleasure until this night. When an EMT saw the blood on Kanning's sleeve, Kanning became the star of his own show as he described his brush with death for the sake of giving his Scoopers the Story As It Happened.

Giulia handed Frank the drawer of photos and he disappeared in the chaos. Nash had already made off with Larabee.

Joanne sat at the table with her head in her hands. Giulia sat next to her.

"Thanks for stopping me." Joanne said without looking up.

"You're going have to appear in court for threatening him with the gun."

"I know." A hand detached from her face and waved in the general direction of the beehives. "VanHorne told me. He said you should drive me to the police station."

"Would you rather have gone to jail for shooting his junk off?"

A long pause. "No. He's stolen enough of my life."

The remaining police officers led the rest of the community to various cars. Now that the noise had lessened, Giulia heard the dogs losing their minds inside the locked houses. She told one of the uniformed officers about them and he called animal control. More cars arrived with evidence and forensic experts.

Giulia jogged Joanne's elbow.

"Let's go. I'll call Diane. She's probably haunting the precinct by now."

Joanne stood. "I've ruined my life."

"Not at all. You forgot about Kurt Warfield."

"Are you serious?"

"He is. He told me to ask you to call him when I found you."

Joanne looked around at the wreck of Alex's community. "Kurt's ego doesn't seem so awful now. Besides, he likes cats."

They walked through the breach in the hedge to the Nunmobile.

"I'll tell you stories of my convent years on the drive back."

"Whoa. Really?"

"If you lie about being a nun, you go right to Hell on the express escalator." Giulia started the car.

"Like in those old *Tom and Jerry* cartoons. I remember them. I think some binge TV is in my future."

"And a cat?"

"And two cats."

Fifty-Two

Two days later, a spectacular bouquet of lilies and roses adorned Giulia's desk. The card from *The Scoop* had read "This could be the beginning of a beautiful friendship." She used the card to test the office's new document shredder.

Giulia finished a phone call with Father Carlos, who'd offered to be intermediary between Giulia's brother and sister-in-law.

"My friends who run the shelter where Anne is staying have let me know she's back to normal and ready to talk to you."

"Good. Has she talked to you yet?"

"At great length. She inflated my ego by confirming my suspicion about the drugs."

A doorbell rang at the other end of the call. "She stole a supply."

"Her and those poor teenagers who died in Cottonwood. Apparently LSA is as addictive as LSD."

Father Carlos said, "I promise not to be a thundering voice of recrimination."

Giulia laughed. "As if you would."

"I'm bringing her parish priest with me to meet with your brother today."

"Salvatore agreed to talk to you? You're a magician."

With a tinge of humor, he said, "I prefer The Wizard in Black."

"You're also a saint, O Wizard, for entering the equivalent of an American football game while dressed for soccer."

She hung up and stared with distaste at the box of assorted herbal tea. When Zane knocked, she opened her door with relief.

"Delivery."

A box from Diane Philbey sat on the table under the window.

Sidney said, "That looks like a bakery box."

"I haven't eaten lunch," Zane said. "This will not be good for my abs."

When Giulia lifted the lid, they first saw a standard number ten envelope. The letter attached to the check inside said, "Already left a glowing Yelp review. Joanne says she hopes she's not out of practice."

Giulia folded back a layer of parchment paper and both her employees said "Ooh," like they were watching fireworks. The circular cake had a miniature Nunmobile on top crowned with a tin foil hat.

Zane went into the file cabinet in Giulia's office and came out with paper plates, plastic forks, and a wicked serrated cake knife. "Ms. D., it's eleven o'clock. Time for tea."

Giulia grimaced. "I'll pass on the tea, but we are definitely cutting into this cake."

The first slice revealed lemon cake with raspberries and cream filling.

"Nobody faint," Sidney said. "I would like a piece too."

They stared at her.

"A really thin piece."

"Only if I can take a picture," Giulia said.

"Wait a minute. What's the matter with me?" Before Sidney broke her own rule of eating nothing except all-natural, organic food, she unbuckled her combination messenger and diaper bag.

"I bought this three days ago and keep forgetting it because you were hanging with the weirdos." She handed Giulia a flat box wrapped in pink and blue baby shower paper. "I'm early, but I wanted to make sure the store didn't run out."

Giulia tore off the wrapping. "My own placenta art kit. Sidney, you are the best." A multicolored print of a treelike image with a squiggly trunk adorned the shiny silver box. "I can't wait to show Frank. Zane, see? We told you they were real." She held it out to him.

Zane backed away, his plate of cake trembling in his hand. When the backs of his knees hit his desk, he crawled under it.

"Ms. D., you know how I said I love my job?"

Giulia and Sidney said, "But not today."

Alice Loweecey

Baker of brownies and tormenter of characters, Alice Loweecey recently celebrated her thirtieth year outside the convent. She grew up watching Hammer horror films and Scooby-Doo mysteries, which explains a whole lot. When she's not creating trouble for Giulia Driscoll, she can be found growing her own vegetables (in summer) and cooking with them (the rest of the year).

The Giulia Driscoll Mystery Series
By Alice Loweecey

NUN TOO SOON (#1)
SECOND TO NUN (#2)
NUN BUT THE BRAVE (#3)
THE CLOCK STRIKES NUN (#4)
(May 2017)

Available at booksellers nationwide and online

Visit www.henerypress.com for details

Henery Press Mystery Books

And finally, before you go...
Here are a few other mysteries
you might enjoy:

MURDER IN G MAJOR

Alexia Gordon

A Gethsemane Brown Mystery (#1)

With few other options, African-American classical musician
Gethsemane Brown accepts a less-than-ideal position turning a
group of rowdy schoolboys into an award-winning orchestra.
Stranded without luggage or money in the Irish countryside, she
figures any job is better than none. The perk? Housesitting a lovely
cliffside cottage. The catch? The ghost of the cottage's murdered
owner haunts the place. Falsely accused of killing his wife (and
himself), he begs Gethsemane to clear his name so he can rest in
peace.

Gethsemane's reluctant investigation provokes a dormant killer
and she soon finds herself in grave danger. As Gethsemane races to
prevent a deadly encore, will she uncover the truth or star in her
own farewell performance?

Available at booksellers nationwide and online

Visit www.henerypress.com for details

GHOSTWRITER ANONYMOUS

Noreen Wald

A Jake O'Hara Mystery (#1)

With her books sporting other people's names, ghostwriter Jake O'Hara works behind the scenes. But she never expected a séance at a New York apartment to be part of her job. Jake had signed on as a ghostwriter, secretly writing for a grande dame of mystery fiction whose talent died before she did. The author's East Side residence was impressive. But her entourage—from a Mrs. Danvers-like housekeeper to a lurking hypnotherapist—was creepy.

Still, it was all in a day's work, until a killer started going after ghostwriters, and Jake suspected she was chillingly close to the culprit. Attending a séance and asking the dead for spiritual help was one option. Some brilliant sleuthing was another-before Jake's next deadline turns out to be her own funeral.

Available at booksellers nationwide and online

Visit www.henerypress.com for details

ARTIFACT

Gigi Pandian

A Jaya Jones Treasure Hunt Mystery (#1)

Historian Jaya Jones discovers the secrets of a lost Indian treasure may be hidden in a Scottish legend from the days of the British Raj. But she's not the only one on the trail...

From San Francisco to London to the Highlands of Scotland, Jaya must evade a shadowy stalker as she follows hints from the hastily scrawled note of her dead lover to a remote archaeological dig. Helping her decipher the cryptic clues are her magician best friend, a devastatingly handsome art historian with something to hide, and a charming archaeologist running for his life.

Available at booksellers nationwide and online

Visit www.henerypress.com for details

FINDING SKY

Susan O'Brien

A Nicki Valentine Mystery

Suburban widow and PI in training Nicki Valentine can barely keep track of her two kids, never mind anyone else. But when her best friend's adoption plan is jeopardized by the young birth mother's disappearance, Nicki is persuaded to help. Nearly everyone else believes the teenager ran away, but Nicki trusts her BFF's judgment, and the feeling is mutual.

The case leads where few moms go (teen parties, gang shootings) and places they can't avoid (preschool parties, OB-GYNs' offices). Nicki has everything to lose and much to gain — including the attention of her unnervingly hot P.I. instructor. Thankfully, Nicki is armed with her pesky conscience, occasional babysitters, a fully stocked minivan, and nature's best defense system: women's intuition.

Available at booksellers nationwide and online

Visit www.henerypress.com for details

FIXIN' TO DIE

Tonya Kappes

A Kenni Lowry Mystery (#1)

Kenni Lowry likes to think the zero crime rate in Cottonwood, Kentucky is due to her being sheriff, but she quickly discovers the ghost of her grandfather, the town's previous sheriff, has been scaring off any would-be criminals since she was elected. When the town's most beloved doctor is found murdered on the very same day as a jewelry store robbery, and a mysterious symbol ties the crime scenes together, Kenni must satisfy her hankerin' for justice by nabbing the culprits.

With the help of her Poppa, a lone deputy, and an annoyingly cute, too-big-for-his-britches State Reserve officer, Kenni must solve both cases and prove to the whole town, and herself, that she's worth her salt before time runs out.

Available at booksellers nationwide and online

Visit www.henerypress.com for details